"WHAT DO YOU WANT FROM ME, BURKE?"

Jill's voice was a tortured whisper, her body hot, her body cold, her body in need of his.

"What do you want from me?" he countered.

"You're evading the question," she accused, turning her back to him. Her hair flowed like a silken waterfall to her tiny waist. Burke had the strong urge to drown himself in it. "Besides," she added, taking another mouthful of champagne, "you know what I want."

"What?" The word was blunt, bold, yet braided with brittle threads of vulnerability.

Jill glanced over her shoulder, her eyes meeting his.

"Say it," Burke demanded.

"All right," Jill answered. "I want you to take this glass out of my hands, tangle your fingers in my hair, kiss me silly and senseless, carry me to the bedroom and teach me what it is to truly love."

ABOUT THE AUTHOR

Award-winning writer Sandra Canfield is also
known to romance fiction fans as Karen Keast. As
well, she is half of the Sandi Shane team. She lives
in Louisiana with her husband Charles, who is her
number one fan and a sounding board for the
ideas in each of her books. *Voice on the Wind* is
her second Superromance. Her third will be
published in October.

Books by Sandra Canfield

HARLEQUIN SUPERROMANCE
213—CHERISH THIS MOMENT

Don't miss any of our special offers. Write to us at the
following address for information on our newest releases.

Harlequin Reader Service
901 Fuhrmann Blvd., P.O. Box 1397, Buffalo, NY 14240
Canadian address: P.O. Box 603,
Fort Erie, Ont. L2A 5X3

Sandra Canfield

VOICES ON THE WIND

Harlequin Books

TORONTO • NEW YORK • LONDON
AMSTERDAM • PARIS • SYDNEY • HAMBURG
STOCKHOLM • ATHENS • TOKYO • MILAN

Published March 1987

First printing January 1987

ISBN 0-373-70252-3

To Penny—
for giving me a chance to have a sister.

CHAPTER ONE

JILL MCCLAIN FIRST HEARD THE NEWS as she passed by the office alcove housing the soft-drink machine.

"Hey Jill, know what?" the receptionist asked, pounding the Coke machine with her fist and ritually reinserting the change the metal beast coughed up. "Burke's coming back."

"Did you hear about Burke?" Charles Evans, the newest person to join the law firm of Rawlins, Rawlins, Nugent and Carson, asked before Jill had a chance to reply to the first inquiry. Both he and Jill passed like course-charted ships, he in the direction of his office, Jill toward the senior Rawlins's office.

"Yeah, Cindy just..." she called over her shoulder only to be interrupted once again.

"Guess what?" Ellen, the bright-eyed, buxom law clerk, said breathlessly.

"Burke's coming back," Jill answered, a devilish grin on her lips and no hesitation in her clipped steps.

"Ahh, someone's already told you," the woman groaned, pouting prettily as she balanced a stack of old law books and current briefs.

High heels clicking to a halt, Jill paused only long enough to push open the frosted-glass door inscribed with the name Andrew Rawlins. She immediately encountered the woman who'd been the senior partner's secretary for what everyone affectionately said had been a thousand years. Ida Tumbrello would always reply that actually she'd been there only a little over nine hundred years, but that it had been long enough for her to remember Rawlins, Rawlins, Nugent and Carson, when it was nothing more than Rawlins and raw.

"Mr. R. sent for me," Jill announced when Ida's heart-shaped face glanced up from the typewriter.

The secretary smiled. "He said to send you right in." Her smiled widened, sending wrinkleless cheeks upward and causing lights to jump into ageless eyes. "Did you hear that Burke's coming back?"

Jill returned the smile in full measure and added a dollop of teasing. "There is a mild rumor to that effect. In fact, I heard the news four times in three yards." Then, in keeping with the gravity of the announcement, Jill asked softly, "When?"

"He's already in Boston and plans to be in the office in the morning." For the briefest of moments, the older woman looked as if she might cry. Ida's fawn-brown eyes glistened, and a suspicious pink rosed the end of her fair-skinned nose. "Needless to say, Andrew is beside himself. He said it's like a thousand Christmases rolled into one." The statement needed no comment, and both women savored the sweetness of it. Finally, the secretary sniffed and inclined her gray-haired head toward the door behind her. "Better get in there before the old coot has my hide for detaining you."

"Right," Jill said, "and mine for letting you detain me." She tapped once on the door, turned the knob and entered the plush, red-carpeted office of Andrew Rawlins. "You wanted to see me, sir?"

The tall, thin man who stood staring out the wide wall of glass turned, presenting Jill with a face and figure that she never failed to mentally categorize as distinguished.

A healthy and full cap of snow-white hair framed a lean, angular face, while silver-green eyes shone brightly and wisely. Jill always fancifully imagined that her boss had been told at least part of the secret of life. A white mustache, neatly manicured, lay atop sensitive and pleasing lips. Those lips were presently smiling with a sincerity that had been absent for the past eighteen months. It was a sincerity that came straight from the man's heart.

"Are you aware of how pretty Boston can be in the spring?" Andrew Rawlins asked.

Jill's lips curved upward at the unexpected question. "You're right, sir. Boston is spectacular in the spring. But with all due respect to the city, I suspect anyplace on earth would seem pretty to you right now."

His eyes made no pretense of hiding a diamond-bright sparkle. "Then you've heard?"

"I don't think there's anyone left in the northern hemisphere who hasn't." As she had moments before with the secretary, she sobered. "I'm very pleased, sir. For him and for you."

"Thank you."

"How is he?"

An image of Burke Rawlins as she'd last seen him flashed through Jill's mind. He'd been dressed in somber black, standing beside his wife's newly turned grave. There had been a blandness to his features, a stark deadness in his eyes, that had said without a doubt that Nicole Rawlins was taking a part of him into eternity with her. Maybe the best part of him.

"He's..." Andrew Rawlins sought out the phrase to best describe his son. "He's all right. It's been a rough year and a half, but I think he's finally learned that there is some truth to that old cliché about life going on." The man before her sighed, and Jill suspected he was thinking of his own wife's death more than ten years before. "It's something we all learn," he added, confirming Jill's suspicion.

"It'll be good to work with Burke again," she said, bringing the conversation from the past and back to the present. She couldn't help but wonder if all the rumors she'd heard over the last eighteen months were true. Like the rumor that Burke refused to get behind the wheel of a car. Like the rumor that he'd fled Boston and become a beach bum down on Cape Cod. Like the rumor that he'd grown a beard and long hair, and that he could now race like the wind with legs athletically at their best from long hours of running along the Atlantic shoreline.

"And that's the very reason I've sent for you," Andrew Rawlins said. "How do you feel about you and Burke working together on the *Stroker* case?"

Jill McClain was known for three things: her petite size—Burke Rawlins had once called her "an elf in search of a fairy tale"—her aggressive zeal for her law career and her bold-faced honesty. It was the latter quality that formed her next words. "You know very well that every lawyer in this office, probably every lawyer in the city, would kill for that case. Me included. And I'd love to work on it with Burke."

"Good. Very good." The man turned toward a wall-unit liquor cabinet of gold-and-black-swirled mirror glass. The late-afternoon sun glinted faintly in its marbled depths, casting a warmth about the elegant office. "Let's have a drink to finalize it then. What can I get for you? Chablis, gin and tonic, amaretto and soda..."

"Chablis will be fine," Jill interrupted, trying to hold in civilized check the whirlwind emotions swarming over her body.

The Stroker *case!* How many nights had she fallen asleep dreaming about arguing in court what was fast becoming Boston's most famous case? Precedents were going to be set that would be quoted for a long time to come, and any lawyer doing a good job had a prominent career signed, sealed and delivered at case's end—regardless of the verdict. But more than that, the case fascinated her, fascinated all sixty inches of her, from the top of her strawberry-blond-haired head right down to her rose-polished toenails. She didn't really know why; it just did. But then, the case had captured the attention of a lot of people, particularly people in the media. The case had all the ingredients guaranteed to sell papers—an elite Bostonian family whose members were fighting one another for control of its riches, plus the added and irresistible complication of an illegitimate child stepping out of the shadows for her share of the wealth. *The* Stroker *case!* Jill thought, resisting the urge to jump up and down and shout. Just wait until she told her sister...

"...your sister's getting married."

Jill dragged her attention back to duty and tried to piece together what her boss had just said.

"I hear it's sometime this spring."

"Yes, sir," she replied, hoping she hadn't missed anything important. "My sister's getting married in May."

"You two are close, aren't you?" Andrew Rawlins asked, as he handed Jill a tulip-shaped Waterford wineglass.

His comment didn't surprise her. He took the time to know about everyone who worked for him. "Yes, we are," she answered, reaching for the Chablis and wondering if his investigation had revealed just how close she and Mary were. "It's just the two of us. Has been for a long time."

"I'll expect an invitation to the wedding."

"I'll see that you get it."

"May I propose a toast?" the man asked, raising his glass of Canadian whiskey. "To sons and sisters and the *Stroker* case."

"I'll drink to that," Jill McClain said, bringing the glass to her rose-glossed lips.

ON THE OTHER SIDE OF TOWN, in a furnished apartment he'd signed a lease on, sight unseen, Burke Rawlins lifted a glass to his lips and took a long, slow swallow of bourbon and water. The amber liquid slid down his throat comfortably. He felt as if he were greeting an old, familiar friend, but then his life for much of the first six months of the past year and a half could be summed up in one word: bourbon. Bourbon on the rocks, bourbon off the rocks, bourbon shallow and deep. Bourbon morning, noon and night—sometimes all night. But the interesting, and frustrating, thing, Burke had come to realize, was that no matter how much bourbon he consumed, it was never enough. No matter how dense the stupor, he could still remember. He could still remember the accident. He could still remember Nicole limp and lifeless in his arms. He could still remember how the earth-grave had swallowed her up, mounding itself over her in a way that suggested suffocation. He could still remember fighting the urge to fall to his knees and claw the thickly clotted brown dirt off her, as if it were the burial killing her and not the accident that already had. And most of all, no matter how much he drank, he could still remember the guilt—that overwhelming feeling that if justice were truly served, as he'd been taught to hope in the end that it was, he would be dead instead of her. Or, at the very least, dead along with her.

Once he'd realized that no amount of bourbon would give him the peace he sought, Burke had dried himself out and looked for some other way to cope. He'd turned to running and could now truthfully say that he'd left more footprints on the beach of Cape Cod than any other human being. For long hours every day, and sometimes on sleepless nights, he'd run, just run, until his mind would empty of everything, until the only thing in his head was the sound of his feet pounding the earth and the salt sea pounding the shore.

He brought the glass once more to his lips. This drink was the first he'd had since swearing off, and it was the only one he'd allow himself. But, God, he had to have this one! He couldn't face coming back without at least one friend. And how in hell could he run at breakneck speed down the congested streets of Boston?

As if to prove his point, he edged back the sliding-glass door leading to the balcony and stepped out into the brisk March air. A breeze rushed toward him, tumbling a lock of brown hair across his forehead and swaying the nest of darker-brown hair that peeped from the vee of his knit shirt. Five stories below, people milled about absorbed in late-afternoon activities. A woman pushed a stroller with a crying baby in it, a man carried a sack full of groceries into the apartment building across the street and a group of kids, laughing in the probable planning of mischief, ambled by. An occasional car horn honked. A siren wailed way off in the distance—a dismal sound that Burke tried hard not to think about because it, too, was something he was all too familiar with. That and the hollow sounds of hospital halls...and the even hollower sounds of grief.

I'm sorry, Mr. Rawlins, your wife was dead on arrival... dead on arrival... dead on arrival...

Now, as then, Burke had an overwhelming need to deny that death, to simply say, "Hey, there must be some mistake here. Nicole and I were just on our way home. If you'll let her off that table, we can make it back before the rain gets heavy." Yet, in his heart, despite the shadows of shock, he had known she was dead the moment the car hit them. Without a doubt, he'd known it the moment he'd dragged her into his arms. But he'd prayed all the way to the hospital for a miracle, a miracle that he'd railed against God for withholding.

Somehow, for a reason that made no sense at all to him, her death was harder to take because he himself had walked away totally unscathed. He was almost—no, dammit, he thought, raking fingers through his wind-tossed hair, he was more than almost—he was downright angry with her for not walking away uninjured, too. This anger was just one more thing to feel guilty about.

Then, of course, there was the "if" guilt. If his reflexes had been just a shade quicker, could he have avoided the collision? If he'd been paying just the slightest bit more attention, would Nicole be beside him now? If he hadn't been laughing and teasing her, telling her what he was going to do to her when he got her home, would he have gotten her home?

Burke shoved the devil-owned "if" from his mind, knowing that the power of the hateful word lay in the fact that it always posed a question that could never be resolved. He heaved a deep breath and emptied the glass to the tune of clattering ice cubes. It was now time to resolve this tragedy in some way if he was to go on living. A man could hurt only so much. Beyond that point, the body went numb and closed down all pain receptors.

Which was where he presently was emotionally. He felt nothing—except some basic human instinct to survive. To do that he had to get back to work. Tomorrow he'd be back at his desk, briefs and documents before him. Tomorrow the beard would be gone, like the long hair he'd shorn days ago. Tomorrow he'd be dressed in a suit and tie and a clumsy awkwardness. Tomorrow he'd try to find the rhythm of life again. But right now, he thought, once more entering the small apartment, he had to get rid of this beard and get settled in.

Twenty minutes later, he stood before the bathroom mirror and made one final sweep of the sharp razor. It left a smooth-cheeked stranger staring back at him. It also left him feeling peculiarly vulnerable, as naked emotionally as he now appeared physically. Suddenly, and with a force that surprised and frightened, a sense of panic hit him. Maybe he shouldn't have come back just yet. Maybe he needed more time. Maybe...

The walls of the apartment closed in, tight, tighter, and it suddenly became imperative that he get out. Out where he could breathe, out where he could feel the freedom of the wind, out where he could feel the mind-oblivion that came from exhausting fatigue. Ramming down the zipper of his jeans, he shed them and yanked the knit shirt over his head. His recently cut hair fell in forgotten disarray. A worn gray sweat suit and running shoes later, he bolted out of the apartment, took the stairs in favor of the elevator and hit the front door of the apartment complex at a run. Nearly colliding with someone entering the building, Burke apologized without ever looking up or back.

He just ran.

He ran, dodging in and out of startled passersby. He ran by shops closed and closing. He ran against red lights and with green. He ran until the wind chaffed at his newly shaved and tender face. On and on he chased himself until his lungs stung with the need to burst, until his breath was a prickling, reedy gasp in his pressured chest, until his legs ached with their lead weight. And when he thought that to run one more step would be instant death, he ran on . . . and on . . . and on. Because the demon behind him would not let him stop.

THE SOUND OF RUNNING WATER filled the bathroom as Jill washed away the day's makeup. Shutting off the faucet, she patted her oval, freckle-dusted face dry, then spent seconds removing her contact lenses and storing them in their case—a floral-designed, Limoges porcelain confection that Mary had given her for her thirty-fourth birthday two months before. Jill blinked, then blinked again. That felt better, she thought, standing on tiptoe and studying her red-veined eyes in the mirror. Even without the contacts, which were tinted a pale blue, her eyes were an aquamarine, a shade somewhere between high sky and deep sea. Right now, however, those aquamarine eyes were tired from reading too many law books and from too many hours of wearing the sometimes irritating contacts. Reaching for a pair of glasses, she slid them on, through strawberry-blond curls that wisped about her ears and fell in riotous play down her back. She grabbed a robe from its hook and eased the butterfly-yellow satin over her shoulders. She turned off the bathroom light and headed her bare, size-four feet for the kitchen.

There, she tossed a got-everything-on-it-except-the-kitchen-sink pizza into the oven, poured herself a fizzing cola and dragged the receiver from the wall phone. She dialed her sister's number. As she did so, a fresh burst of excitement flooded her. *The* Stroker *case! Just wait until Mary hears!*

The phone began to ring. It rang and rang and rang. Jill frowned and checked the kitchen clock. Ten till seven. She'd stayed at the office later than she'd realized. Again. Mary and Rob had probably already gone out for the evening. Was this the night they had tickets to the theater? The number rang once more. Jill sighed and hooked the instrument back on the wall.

She checked the pizza through the oven door, saw that the cheese was beginning to bubble, and leaned back against the edge of the cabinet. She was hungry. And tired. She started to bring the glass to her lips but stopped midway. Tired, and something else. She was...something else. A niggling something she'd felt often of late, but it was a something she couldn't quite identify. She intuitively knew, however, that it had to do with her sister's upcoming marriage. No, more truthfully, it had to do with the relationship Mary McClain had with Rob Sheffield.

Not that she coveted the happiness her sister had. She didn't. Not for a moment. Heaven only knew, it was more than time that her elder sister found someone to share her life with. In fact, Jill had begun to think that she never would. And for one very good reason: Mary didn't seem to be looking. Sixteen years older than Jill, she had always seemed content to play the role of older sister and old-maid schoolteacher, and when their parents, Margaret and Edward McClain, had died in a plane crash the summer Jill was fifteen, it had just seemed natural that Mary became more mother than sister. It was a role she took to as if she'd been made for it. But it was a role that narrowed her already narrow personal life even more. Not that she seemed to mind, but Jill minded for her. No, she was thrilled that Rob Sheffield had come along. It was just . . .

Just what?

The oven timer pinged, saving Jill from searching for an answer she wasn't sure she could have found anyway.

Ten thousand calories later—Jill consoled herself that at least her cola was diet—she tidied up the kitchen, showered and slipped into bed with a law book almost half her weight. She read until a quarter to twelve, at which time she shut off the light and slid beneath the cool layers of fresh sheets. She wriggled. She stretched. She stretched again over mile after mile of percale. Her feet, her hands, her body touching nothing, she suddenly frowned. Was it possible that she'd just discovered the answer to the question "Just what is the matter with me?" Might the answer be found in all the spacious room she had in her king-size bed? In all the room she had in her life?

Despite a successful career she loved, some part of her, some woman's part, still felt empty. Was it possible that she needed, wanted, to have someone to share her life with—the good, the bad and all that came in between? She'd spent all of her time and energy pursuing a career, to the exclusion of love. Oh, she'd had relationships. Even meaningful relationships. But no relationship had ever matured into a "forever" commitment. It hadn't mattered then. It was only now, as she was getting older—she *was* thirty-four, she reminded herself—that it mattered. She sighed. She wanted someone who would look at her the way Rob looked at Mary. She wanted someone who would love her to distraction the way . . .

She stopped, surprised by the name that came to mind. She wanted someone who would love her to distraction the way Burke Rawlins had loved his wife.

Burke Rawlins.

She wondered if he'd changed all that much. She hoped not. She and Burke had worked hard and well together the three years she'd been at Rawlins, Rawlins, Nugent and Carson, and furthermore, they'd managed to like and respect each other in the process. They'd been able to make each other laugh at that uncomfortable moment when one always took oneself, and life, too seriously. What if he no longer smiled, laughed, teased? Jill couldn't imagine such a tragedy. But then, she couldn't imagine the hell he must have been through. Which brought her full circle in her thinking. Would any man ever care enough about her to walk through the same hell?

She turned to her side, cozied her cheek into the pillow and forced herself to at least give sleep a chance. Right before it washed its soothing waves over her, though, two thoughts flitted through her mind. The next to the last was in the form of a statement: She had been assigned to the *Stroker* case! The last was a question: Where were all the men like Burke Rawlins hiding?

"He's BACK," Cindy commented.

"Have you seen Burke?" Charles Evans asked.

"He looks good enough to eat," buxom Ellen whispered conspiratorially.

Balancing the contents of two Styrofoam cups, Jill smiled at the last remark and walked down the hall. She paused before the door that had been closed for the past year and a half. It presently stood ajar.

"Knock, knock," she called out in deference to the steaming coffee she carried. When she heard no reply, she eased through the slit and into the room. "Burke?" she said softly.

The man staring out the window didn't turn, didn't flinch a muscle. In fact, he wasn't even aware of her presence. Jill's first reaction was that she should respect his privacy and slip unnoticed out the door, but she didn't because of a stronger, second reaction. That reaction had everything to do with the captivating way the morning sun was streaming through the window and solar-skipping in yellow-brown hair until it looked as if it had been sprinkled with glitter. The same bold sun fell across the wide shoulders straining against the navy suit jacket that hung open over a salmon-hued shirt; the sun stripe ended in a diagonal slit of gold across one perfectly pressed, blue pant leg. Into both pockets were jammed hands that were as immobile as the man.

A fish out of water, Jill thought. Something in his stance screamed, "I'm out of my element." Something in his stillness cried, "I'm scared."

She must have made some telling sound because he pivoted toward her. Moss-green eyes immediately meshed with blue. Curiously, at least it seemed so to Jill, neither said a word, but, oh, her mind ran rampant with thoughts.

He *had* been through hell. It was burned in his eyes. Yet there was a strength in those eyes, too. Maybe even a strength he didn't know he possessed. He looked older. Thinner. And his face was bronzed with the darkness that only long hours in the sun can achieve. There were wrinkles in his brow, from worry and from weather. There were also shadows, strangely becoming shadows, hidden in his cheeks. The thighs contained within the pants looked trim and taut, with superb muscular delineation. The part about his running must be true. She'd bet her law career on it. And one other thing was true as well: Ellen had been right when she'd said that Burke looked good enough to eat. Jill admitted this with no undue significance and nothing personal attached to it. It was all part of the honesty of her personality.

"Hi," she heard herself say.

"I wondered where you were."

"I've been out of the office. Interviewing a client who's suing his landlord because a bee in the landlord's geranium stung him. Claims he almost died. Claims also that the bee falls under the heading of a concealed weapon."

His response wasn't a smile, but it was the nearest thing to one that had crossed Burke Rawlins's face in a long time. "How are you going to plead the case, counselor?"

"I'm going to *bee* clever."

Burke groaned. "With a stinging, venomous attack against your opposition?"

"Naturally. I want a honey of a verdict."

Burke's lips twitched just an infinitesimal fraction. And so did Jill's. Privately, she was just shy of being elated. He might have walked with the devil, but the demon hadn't stolen his sense of humor. That fact pleased her.

"Is one of those for me?" Burke asked, nodding toward the cups she was still holding.

Jill glanced down at the forgotten coffee. "Oh, yeah," she said, thrusting a cup toward him. He withdrew his hands from his pockets and took it. She noticed that he was still wearing a slender gold wedding band.

Unasked, she eased into the leather chair across from his desk, he onto the desk's edge, where his legs spread in a slight vee. It was a pose they had assumed a thousand times, just as the comfortable silence that followed had been lived through countless times. Both took slow sips of their coffee. Both acted as though they'd seen each other only hours before.

"How are you?" she asked finally when she intuitively sensed the moment was right.

It never occurred to Burke to lie or sugarcoat the truth. Not with Jill McClain.

"I don't know," he answered with a shrug. Setting down the cup, he slipped from the edge of the desk and resumed his stance at the window. Several seconds rolled by, seconds in which the sun again noticeably sparkled in his hair.

"Take a guess," Jill urged.

He turned, his eyes finding those of the woman before him. "I guess I'm better. Or I wouldn't be standing here."

"Sounds reasonable."

"But I'm still . . . scared to be standing here."

"Sounds normal."

"Of course, I may be back only because I need money. A year and a half of bumming around leaves little in the coffers."

"Sounds prudent."

Both pairs of lips flirted with a grin. Burke's faded before ever being anything more than an essence.

"I'm all right," he said seriously. "Or at some point I will be."

"Sounds like the Burke Rawlins I know."

Something in his eyes said, "Thanks for the vote of confidence." Something in hers said, "You're welcome."

"So how are you?" he asked suddenly changing the subject.

She shrugged, much the same way he had, except that with her petite shoulders, it looked more as if she were dancing. "You know me. I'm always the same."

"Like the sun and the moon?"

"Nah," she said, as if insulted to be compared with such a shabby duo. "They wax and wane. I'm constant. Constantly confused, constantly overworked, constantly... whatever."

Burke's lips semigrinned again. "How's everything around here?"

"Well, let's see," Jill said, settling back into the chair. She crossed one sheer-stockinged leg over the other. For all her diminutive size, Jill McClain was proportioned in a way that immediately caught a man's attention, though she herself was totally oblivious to that fact. Burke Rawlins lowered his eyes to the shapely curves of her legs, then instantly shifted his gaze back to her face. "The Coke machine still doesn't work, Charles Evans is still complaining that he gets only the runt of the cases, Ellen's boobs are still out to here—" she made the appropriate gesture "—Ida is still in love with your dad and your dad still has absolutely no idea that she is."

Burke frowned. "You're kidding. Ida in love with Dad?"

Jill rolled her eyes heavenward. "Men! Blind as bats!"

"Well, I'll be damned," Burke said softly, pursing his lips and letting the idea sink in. "Speaking of the man who's as blind as a bat, did Dad tell you we're handling the *Stroker* case?"

Jill smiled. "Yeah."

"Does the smile mean you're pleased?"

"What do you think?"

"I think you're going to be working with someone who's rusty. You still pleased?"

Jill sensed a real vulnerability in the question. "Even rusty, you're one of the best lawyers in Boston. And you know it."

"We'll see," he added. "I am eager to get started." He laughed mirthlessly. "It's funny, but for the last year I haven't wanted to do anything, couldn't do anything, and now all of a sudden I feel that my only salvation lies in work."

"Sounds like a more positive approach."

"Yeah, I guess it does at that."

He took a slow step toward her, at the same time ramming a hand back into a pocket. Pant fabric splayed provocatively across his manhood. Jill couldn't help but notice, though she quickly glanced away.

"What does your schedule look like?" he asked.

She deliberately kept her eyes on his face. "Let me have today to rearrange some appointments and we can start in the morning."

"Good. Are you averse to working overtime?"

"Have I ever been?"

"No. I just keep thinking that one of these days there's going to be a man in your life who's going to resent the hell out of Rawlins, Rawlins, Nugent and Carson." He stopped. "Or is there already? I mean, a year and a half is a long..."

"No man," Jill interrupted, feeling peculiarly bereft by the truth of the statement. To cover that fact, she asked quickly, "Have you been following the case?"

"A little. But I'll need a lot of briefing. In fact, that's what I'm going to do this afternoon."

"Well," Jill said, finishing the coffee, rising and starting for the door, "let me get to work so you can get to work so we can get to work."

"Jill?"

She stopped and turned.

"Thanks for the coffee." The tenor of his voice suggested that he was thanking her for more than the caffeine.

"You're welcome," she answered, adding in a shades-softer tone, "I'm glad you're back." Their eyes held for a moment before Jill started for the door once more. Her hand was just wrapping around the knob when Burke spoke again.

"I see you're still not eating your Wheaties."

She hesitated. Turned. And tried to appear highly offended at his remark about her height—or lack thereof. She couldn't keep back a smile, though. "We've had this discussion before, Rawlins, but I see that I'm going to have to remind you that quality is better than quantity."

Burke said nothing; he simply fought his own smile. Slowly, though, each lost the battle. Mutual smiles emerged despite all attempts to the contrary. They were full smiles, smiles that showed not an inch of compromise. Burke thought how really pretty Jill's smile was and how his own felt really good. He also wondered just when the last time was he'd smiled. A year and a half ago?

Jill wondered why she'd never noticed before how really handsome Burke was when he smiled. He looked exactly as if he'd stolen some of the sun's beams and forced them to shine from his face and eyes.

Suddenly, Burke felt a little guilty standing there smiling. And more than a little guilty at enjoying the smile on Jill's face.

Jill suddenly felt a little awkward, as if she'd said what she came to say and was now wondering why she was still hanging around.

"Well, I'll . . . I'll see you later," she stammered.

"Yeah," Burke replied.

In a flash she was out the door and walking down the hall.

"Doesn't he look yummy?" Ellen whispered dreamily, a law book clutched to her ponderous chest in schoolgirl fashion.

Jill glanced up. "What?"

"Burke. Doesn't he look good enough to eat?"

"Yes," she replied, but her mind was not on the edibility of Burke Rawlins. Instead, she was thinking of Nicole Rawlins—model-tall, model-thin, gorgeous Nicole Rawlins. Nicole Rawlins who had been physically everything she was not. Jill made the honest assessment that petite women in need of Wheaties were not Burke Rawlins's type. She refused, however, to carry honesty a step further and ask why that fact carried with it the pricking sting of disappointment.

CHAPTER TWO

THE NEXT DAY dawned blue and beautiful, the perfect prelude to the weekend that was to follow. In the offices of Rawlins, Rawlins, Nugent and Carson, everyone worked with a thank-God-it's-Friday zeal, including Burke and Jill, whose work reflected the added fervor that only the *Stroker* case could inspire. Burke, in true workaholic fashion, was already ensconced in his office when Jill arrived; she simply moved into his, where they remained without interruption until lunch. That proved to be sandwiches from the nearby deli, which they consumed in record time. Then they went back to work, which they continued until a quarter to four when Jill took time out to take her sister's call. Mary McClain issued an invitation to dinner for the following evening, which Jill happily accepted, opting to wait until then to share her news regarding the *Stroker* case. She had simply told her sister that she had a surprise. Following the call, she and Burke did what they had done all day: they worked.

"Hungry?"

Jill glanced up from the script that was beginning to blur before her tired eyes. "What time is it?" she asked.

Burke angled his wrist and checked the gold watch nestled amid brown hair. The sleeves of his white shirt had been rolled up, his tie loosened to a benign noose, and his beige suit jacket abandoned. "Five till seven. You want to call down to the deli again, or you want to call it quits for the day?''

"What do you want to do?''

"I'll probably work on, but..."

"Pastrami on rye," Jill interrupted.

Burke half smiled and reached for the phone. Jill took the opportunity to ease her feet from the confining pat-ent-leather heels she'd worn all day. Flexing her toes, she tucked her feet beneath her and leaned lazily back in the corner of the leather chair. With her black linen dress, its square, biblike collar of white brocaded lace, and her reddish-blond hair, which was swept back from her face with black combs and allowed to sprawl freely about her shoulders, she looked a little like a calico kitten at the end of a long day of chase-the-mouse.

"You look tired," Burke commented as he hung up the phone and ran his hand around the back of his neck where he kneaded kinked muscles.

"So do you.'' She blinked against the gritty, dry feel of her contact lenses.

He shrugged. "I am a little. But it feels good to be back at work. And to be honest, it's been easier falling back into step than I thought it would be. Sorta like slipping back into a pair of old jeans.''

The latter comment brought a smile to his eyes, if not to his lips. It also brought the realization to Jill that she'd never seen Burke in jeans. She absently made the mental notation that he probably looked sensational in denim, especially since his leg muscles were now so perfectly honed. She instantly had the feeling that maybe she shouldn't have thought that, that maybe it was a little too personal for their impersonal relationship. She covered up the thought by telling herself she was just being honest and by asking, "Is the deli going to deliver our order or do we have to go after it?"

"They deliver until nine." Burke's brow suddenly wrinkled in question. "The building still has a security guard to let them in, doesn't it?"

Jill nodded. The twenty-six-story building, of which all of the twelfth floor belonged to Rawlins, Rawlins, Nugent and Carson, was usually vacated each weekday evening between the hours of six and seven, at which time a security guard went on duty in the main lobby.

"Good," Burke replied. Then, thinking of some other point he wanted to check about the upcoming trial, he launched into another discussion of *Stroker* versus *Stroker*. Suddenly, he stopped in midsentence. "You're not wearing glasses."

The statement took Jill, who was checking a deposition, by complete surprise. She glanced up.

"I've been trying to figure out since yesterday what was different about you." The question had occurred to him at numerous odd times, some of those odd times had been in the middle of work.

"Contacts."

His look was vague.

"I'm wearing contacts."

"Oh."

"I got them about a year ago."

There was a brief silence before he asked, "Why?"

"Why?"

"Yeah. Why?"

"In a word, Rawlins, vanity."

"Vanity?"

"V-a-n-i-t-y. You know—that thing that women are supposed to possess in abundance."

"But you always looked so . . . intelligent in glasses."

"There you have it," Jill answered. "Don't you know that all women my age are trying to trap a man? I'm thirty-four and getting desperate. Men don't want intelligent looking. They want glamorous, sexy. They want knockout in the looks department. Glasses just don't hack it. And heaven only knows that with my in-need-of-Wheaties size and my little-girl freckles I need all the help I can get." She was teasing. Or was she? she thought, as she remembered the feel of her empty bed. Had she had some subliminal realization a year before that she was only now confronting openly? Had she hoped that contacts would improve her chances of finding a man?

Burke smiled. "You have every right to be desperate. My God, thirty-four!" He said the number as if it were closely akin to the bubonic plague. "And you're so right. Men want looks, sex, glamour. And you look like a dog in glasses. A small, freckle-faced dog."

"Thanks, friend," Jill said, flipping the pencil in her hand across the desk in playful retaliation. Burke caught it in midmotion.

"Some men are turned on by intelligence, McClain." Burke Rawlins had been the only person to whom she'd ever made the statement that she'd love to shave off some of her IQ—which she knew to be above average—and add the figures to her height. "However it's packaged," he added meaningfully.

His remark made Jill uncomfortable. Her uncomfortableness stemmed entirely from the fact that she had the strong urge to ask if he was one of those men. It was an inappropriate question for their relationship. Or was what was inappropriate the fact that she wanted his answer to be yes?

Silence stretched into silence. Conjecture into confusion. At least in Jill's mind.

Suddenly the phone rang.

Jill glanced toward it as if it were her savior incarnate.

The call was the security guard checking out the deli messenger, and within minutes Jill and Burke were eating what everyone called the best sandwiches in town and drinking the last of the office coffee, which conversely had a reputation for being the worst in town. It was so bad that no one at the office would admit to making it. It just seemed to appear from nowhere.

Somewhere in the middle of pastrami on rye, Jill convinced herself that the discomfort she'd felt before the call had been the result of a long, tiring day. So what if she'd been tempted to ask him if he personally admired intelligence in a woman? Such speculation meant nothing. Absolutely nothing. They were simply friends talking.

Following the meal, they once more immersed themselves in work. It was just minutes shy of nine o'clock when Jill announced defeat. "Uncle," she called out, slapping the papers in her lap onto Burke's desk and reaching for her purse. "I've got to get these contacts out or go crazy. Or blind." Her eyes looked like a red-charted road map.

"They hurt?"

"When you wear them this long without a break, they become less than friendly."

As she fumbled in her purse for the case, Burke mumbled something unsavory about vanity. He also pushed back his chair, rose and walked toward the window. He rammed one hand into a pant pocket, while the other again rubbed weary neck muscles. He stared down at the city below. Car headlights bounced and bobbed as if transmitting silent signals of a secret code. They reminded him of other headlights that had come out of nowhere and changed his life. He could still hear the squealing of his brakes, could still smell the rubbery scent in the air. He could still feel the car skidding out of control and the panic that had rushed through him like some sinister drug. He could still hear the sickening sound of metal crashing with metal.

Jill watched Burke from behind tortoiseshell-framed glasses. She intuitively knew the darkness that had just claimed him. "I never told you how sorry I was about..." Her soft voice trailed off to a thin whisper.

He glanced back over his shoulder. Their eyes connected, and he made the silent acknowledgement that Jill had probably known what he was thinking. He also noted that she did, indeed, look intelligent in glasses. And pretty. But this latter was only a borderline realization, one that was forced out of prominence by what she had just said.

"Nicole?" he supplied. It had been the first time he'd spoken his wife's name aloud in months—eighteen months. He was surprised to find that saying it hadn't been as difficult as he'd thought it would be.

Jill nodded. "Yes." Leaving her shoes where she'd kicked them off earlier, she slowly rose from the chair and walked toward Burke. "In the beginning there was such chaos, and then you left Boston..." She again allowed the thought to go unfinished. "I started to write...later...but the time never seemed right. I guess I just didn't know what to say."

"You should have. Written, I mean. I would have liked hearing from you." He smiled slightly, and, Jill thought, sadly. "You could always cheer me up."

"Then I should have written. I'm sorry." What he'd said touched her. And pleased her, so that her heart glowed with a little bit of warmth. In that moment, she also realized just what a lucky lady Nicole Rawlins had been. For Burke's sake, she hoped his wife had realized that, too.

They were now standing side by side, both staring out the window and into the ebony night. Jill had eased her hands into the deep pockets of her black dress, and with both Burke's hands now bedded in his own pockets, they looked like an artist's rendition of man and woman in contemplation.

"I went a little crazy in the beginning," he said, speaking to her, himself, no one. "I thought I was going to die. And then, when I didn't, and I realized that I wasn't going to, that it just wasn't going to be that easy, I really did go crazy. That's when I started drinking." He took a deep breath and slowly exhaled. "But I couldn't get drunk enough to forget."

She angled her head toward him, admitting that the love he'd just spoken of was the kind she wanted in her life. "Is that when you started running?"

His eyes coasted to hers. It never crossed his mind to question how she knew of this athletic release. "Yeah."

"And did it help?"

"I've survived with reasonable sanity. I probably have the running to thank for that." He then offered her a glimpse of his soul and, had he been asked why he was doing so, he could only have said that it seemed right. "The nights were the worst. There's something about the night and grief that can bring the strongest man to his knees."

The words tore at Jill's heart. "I'm sorry," she whispered. It was a blanket apology, covering everything from the unfairness of Nicole Rawlins's death to the fact that life could be harsh enough to bring a man, a strong man like Burke Rawlins, a deserving man like Burke Rawlins, to his knees.

Their eyes lingered with not even a hint of awkwardness.

Her eyes were full of sympathy, Burke thought. Not pity, the way some people's were. But sympathy and understanding. Caring. And they were a shade of blue, a robin's egg, sky blue, that quite took one's breath away.

Burke's eyes were full of suffering, Jill thought. As though he had battled with too many warrior nights. But there was also a steely suggestion somewhere in the moss-green depths that the nights had not been the final victor.

Small. The word scurried through Burke's mind. He hadn't realized just how short she was. But maybe she seemed so short now because she wasn't wearing her shoes.

He was so tall, Jill thought. Why had she never realized how tall he was? Or was it because she stood only in her stocking feet?

She looked tired, he thought. As if she needed someone, some man, to take her in his arms and hold her.

He looked tired, she thought. Body tired. Soul tired. Suddenly, she had the urge to slip her arms around his waist, lay her cheek to his chest and tell him that everything was going to be all right.

The spell broke for each of them at nearly the same instant. Jill actually took a step back from Burke. And wondered what in the world had provoked her last crazy thought.

"I think I'll call it quits for the day," she said, the words superimposed on his, "Let's wrap it up."

They both smiled. He pulled his hands from his pockets; she pulled hers from her pockets. Crossing the room, she slipped into her shoes. Burke rolled down the sleeves of his shirt and drew on his jacket. In seconds they were walking down the hall toward the elevator. A quick ride downward and they were crossing the main lobby, their footsteps a hollow tattoo in the empty building.

"This is my first weekend back in civilization," Burke said, his voice cutting through the silence that had existed since leaving the office.

Jill heard the uncertainty, maybe the touch of fear, that tinged the statement. "Listen," she said, "my sister is having me over for dinner tomorrow night. If you'd like to come, you're welcome to. She wouldn't mind at all."

Burke didn't hesitate. "No, thanks. I think the beast is still too savage to take out."

"My sister teaches first grade," Jill said with a twinkle in her blue eyes. "She could have you tamed in two minutes."

Burke smiled, and there was a gentle crescenting of his full lips. "She probably could, but I'm going to pass anyway. But thanks. I appreciate the offer."

"Any time," Jill replied.

They reached the front door and exchanged good nights with the security guard, who let them out of the building. Once on the sidewalk, the March-night wind, still cold from its recent acquaintance with winter, sent them a chill welcome. Burke turned up the collar of his jacket; Jill huddled deeper into the light coat she'd thrown on over her dress.

"Could I give you a lift?" she asked, nodding in the direction of the car parked only a few feet away at the curb. She always left the car in the underground garage, but the attendant, who went off duty at seven, insisted on bringing hers out front if she was working late. It was a safety precaution and convenience she appreciated greatly.

"No, thanks. I have an apartment in the Prudential Center."

Jill suspected that the apartment, which was only blocks away, had been carefully selected because of its nearness. The rumor about his refusing to drive was obviously true.

"I need the walk," he added.

"Or run?"

He held up his briefcase. "With this? Are you kidding?" The running would probably come later, he thought. If the walls of the apartment insisted once more on closing in on him. If the past insisted on closing in.

"Well, good night," she said.

"Good night."

"See you Monday."

"Yeah."

He waited until she had unlocked the car door before starting off down the street. He had gone but a short distance when he turned and called, "Hey, McClain?"

She hesitated in her descent into the car. And looked up.

"I like your glasses."

Seconds passed. Jill's heart beat a strange rhythm. Which she ignored. "Yeah, I know," she finally called back. "They make me look intelligent." She knew that he was smiling because there was a wave of warmth undulating in the cool air. Then, just as suddenly as he'd spoken, he turned and moved off into the night. Jill watched as step after step took him farther and farther away. Burke was a solitary man intent on the solitary mission of surviving. She started to call after him, but stopped herself because she had absolutely no idea what she wanted to say. Instead, she crawled in behind the wheel, started the engine and pulled away from the curb.

In a very real sense, she felt as solitary as Burke and, though she was grieving over the loss of no one, the fact that she'd never had a beloved someone to grieve over was grief enough. Curiously, she suddenly felt as if she were on the same lonely mission of survival.

"WHAT'S THE SURPRISE?"

"Well, hello to you, too," Jill teased the next evening as she stepped through the screen door her sister held open and into the living room of a small, modest, yellow frame house. "Speaking of surprises," she added, ditching her purse on the blue, pink and yellow floral sofa and setting a bottle of white wine on the nearby kitchen cabinet, "I see you have one of your own." At Mary McClain's blank look, Jill jerked her head in the direction of the front yard. "The For Sale sign has a Sold plastered across it."

"Oh, yeah," Mary said in a voice that her fiancé proclaimed sounded like a husky June Allyson with a cold. Invariably when he said it, more-youthful Jill feigned ignorance and teased, "Who's June Allyson?" "The realtor came by yesterday afternoon and said it looked as if we had a buyer. A couple from Ballard Vale."

"That's appropriate," Jill said, thinking of the small upstate town of Shawsheen, only miles from Ballard Vale. Shawsheen had been their home until their parents' death. Only weeks afterward, Mary had moved the two of them to Boston. It was only as an adult that Jill had realized what courage it must have taken for Mary, who'd lived all of her life in a small town, to make that decision.

Mary smiled. "Yeah, I guess it is appropriate, isn't it?"

"Why did you move us from Shawsheen to Boston?" Jill asked as if she'd only this moment thought to pose the question.

The other woman's smile edged away, and she slipped into the kitchen and busied herself at the sink scraping carrots under running water. "Because I didn't want you growing up with a small-town heart."

Jill followed, plucked up a coin-shaped piece of carrot and plopped it into her mouth. She crunched down. "What's a small-town heart?"

"An unforgiving heart. A self-righteous heart. The result of a narrow worldview. I wanted you to see more of life, more of people. I didn't want you inhibited, constricted."

Jill frowned at the intensity of her sister's tone, and at the severity of the remark. Both seemed out of character. "Were you so inhibited and constricted in Shawsheen?"

Mary looked back over her shoulder and laughed, quickly, brittlely. "Of course not. You just asked why we moved and I told you. Besides," she added with a let's-change-tack hastiness, "I wanted to get you into a more progressive school system. With your IQ, I wanted the best education you could get." Mary McClain's bright brown eyes danced with a sudden teasing light that negated the seriousness of moments before. "I wanted you to go to law school, to be a rich and famous lawyer, so I could borrow lots of your money. Will you stay out of those carrots?" she fussed, swatting at the hand pilfering yet another.

"When you borrow money is the day pigs fly, and I guess I don't have to ask what's for dinner," Jill replied, knowing without any doubt that the meal would be her favorite—pot roast with potatoes and carrots, followed by a banana-nut cake.

"I guess you don't."

"So when are you moving out?" Jill asked, rummaging through a kitchen drawer in search of a corkscrew.

"I told the realtor that I couldn't possibly move out until the wedding."

"Antiquated, Victorian—these are just two words that come to mind. Did it ever occur to you, Miss Misfit of the twentieth century, to just shack up with Rob until the wedding? Where's the corkscrew?" she added, then tail-gated that request with, "And for goodness' sake, stop blushing."

"I am not antiquated—two drawers over—and I'll blush if I want to." And indeed that was just what she was doing. Just what Jill knew that she would be doing. A faint rosiness had seeped into a complexion that wore only the most minimal of makeup. With her sable-brown hair cut in a short blow-dry style, her big brown eyes practically filling her oval face and embarrassment splotching her cheeks, she, at fifty, looked in many ways younger than Jill. Jill often thought it was her sister's innate naïveté that made her appear so youthful, made her appear as if she were a throwback to a time that was simpler, a time less sophisticated and more pure. Then again, it might have been the hundreds of freckles sprinkled across her face. While Jill had a smattering of the tiny dark dots, Mary had a spill of them.

The two women were grinning at each other, as they spent most of their time together doing. Suddenly, Mary hurled a dishcloth at her. "You! You deliberately try to shock me."

"You wanted me to be uninhibited," Jill pointed out as she dodged the airborne cloth. It landed on the meticulously clean, but old, fruit bowl that had been their mother's. "Even moved me from Shawsheen so I would be."

"Maybe we should have stayed a little longer."

Sighting the corkscrew, Jill eased to one of four tall stools lining the wooden kitchen bar. She began to uncork the wine. "So where is this guy you won't move in with without benefit of ceremony?"

"Grocery store. I didn't have lettuce for the salad. Or more to the point, I had some, but was past its peak. Way past." The carrots were arranged by heaping handfuls into the broth simmering around the pot roast and the lid returned to the cooker. Mary slid to the stool beside Jill. Her jean-clad knee scraped against Jill's jean-clad knee. Both wore blue-trimmed sneakers that could have been identical. "He should be back any minute. So tell me, what's your surprise?"

Jill poured white wine into two glasses. "It's a doozy."

"Let me be the judge of that. You were the one who told me the new hairdresser was a doozy."

"Well, he was . . . is."

"He's a maniac with scissors. Would you just look at this?" Mary ran her fingers through her short hair in a way guaranteed to muss, had not the style been so short. This was a conversation that had transpired more than once in the past two weeks, and each player knew her part.

"It looks wonderful, Mary. Very chic. Very today."

"Very short," Mary supplied.

"Rob loves it," Jill pointed out in her favor.

"Why I let a woman who never gets her hair cut recommend . . ."

"I get it trimmed," Jill said, hand-tossing a russet-blond strand back over her shoulder as she spoke. Tonight, her hair fell somewhere between straight and curly, and one side was bunched back from her face with a currently fashionable clip.

". . . a hairdresser defies all logic," Mary mumbled to the end.

"Do you want to hear my surprise?"

"Of course I do. I'm just warning you that it better be a better doozy than the last."

"It is. Trust me." The self-satisfied smile that always seemed the forerunner of the statement appeared on Jill's lips. "I've been assigned to the *Stroker* case."

There was a pause as the words registered. Mary's hand tightened around the bowl of the glass. "The *Stroker* case? Isn't that the one where there's . . . an illegitimate child?"

"It's a lot more complex than that, but yes, there is an illegitimacy." As invariably happened, Jill's enthusiasm took over and her blue eyes began to sparkle. "Oh, Mary, every lawyer in town would love to sink his teeth into this one. There's going to be new ground covered, precedents set and possibly some restructuring of women's rights. Basically, it's a divorce case between a rich couple. We're talking mega-megabucks here. We're talking the old money of Louisburg Square," she said with the proper Bostonian grandeur to her voice.

"The fascinating part is that Mrs. Stroker is suing for damages that she claims are the result of the emotional and physical abuse she suffered at the hands of Mr. Stroker. She claims that he pressured her, even by rape, to get pregnant five times in the six years of their marriage. She miscarried each time. She claims he was obsessed with the idea of having an heir—which she never produced. And now, in walks a servant who claims he fathered her four-year-old child. I'm telling you, Mary, the case is fascinating. Absolutely fas—'' She stopped, aware that Mary McClain was not displaying the delight she'd expected. In fact, Mary looked only shades away from grim. "I thought you'd be pleased."

The disappointment-drenched words sobered like coffee administered to a drunk. "Oh, honey, I am pleased," Mary said, covering Jill's hand with her own. "Of course I'm pleased. Why wouldn't I be pleased?"

"I don't know, but you seemed . . ." Jill couldn't find the right word. Nothing as strong as upset would suffice, yet there was some negative emotion there. Troubled? Yes, Mary had seemed troubled at the mention of the *Stroker* case.

"What I seemed is outlandishly proud of you," she said in an effusive voice. "And not one thing less or more. I was just surprised that a case I've read so much about was yours. Usually I don't know anything about your work."

The brown eyes staring at Jill so honestly persuaded her in a matter of blinks that she had imagined Mary's reaction. What sense did it make, anyway, for Mary to be uncomfortable with a case that in no way concerned her? And surely she did have a right to be surprised at her little sister being assigned to it. After all, the little sister had been.

"I'm working on the case with Burke Rawlins," Jill announced, her enthusiasm back.

"Burke? Is he back?"

Jill smiled. "Yeah. Came in day before yesterday."

"How is he?"

"Better than he thinks he is. And he looks wonderful. Tanned, trim. He's been running a lot." Jill brought the glass to her lips and drank. "I tried to get him to come with me tonight."

"He should have." There was all the sincerity in the world in the remark. Though Mary had never met Burke, his tragedy had touched her the way it had many others.

Jill shrugged in that kind of nebulous way that really meant nothing. "I don't think he's ready to start socializing." Drawing the glass once more to her lips, she considered the subject of Burke. The result was she wondered what he was doing at that very moment. Eating? Running? Or maybe just staring at the four walls of a lonely apartment? The last thought appealed to some crazy urge in her to comfort. She quickly told herself that Burke did not need her comfort. Some part of her argued that maybe the need was hers. Maybe she'd reached the point in her life where she needed to comfort someone. Maybe she just needed to be needed. Not as a client needed a lawyer, but as a man needed a woman.

A sudden rattling sound at the front door shattered Jill's subtly disturbing thoughts. "There he is," she said at the sight of her future brother-in-law.

Rob Sheffield stood exactly one-quarter inch above six feet, had a head of sun-bleached blond hair that insisted on curling no matter how short it was cut and had coffee-brown eyes that were always smiling. At fifty-one, he had been divorced for ten years, a chemical engineer for twenty-three and for thirteen months on Jill's list of the most likable men she'd ever met. She had placed him on the list within thirty seconds of meeting him—and for lots of reasons, the most specific being that he was wildly, madly, unequivocally in love with Mary McClain.

"Hey, whatcha know, Blue Eyes?" As he passed Mary, a sack in his arms, he brushed a kiss to her lips. "Hi, babe."

"Hi," Mary returned, slipping from the stool and heading for the ringing phone.

"How are you?" Rob asked, scooping a now-standing Jill into his arms for a quick bear hug.

"Great," she answered, banding her arms about his waist. As she did so, she thought that Rob was tall, but not as tall as Burke. If she were to hug Burke this way, her head would rest whole inches from his chin. And Burke's shoulders seemed just a little wider. Maybe a lot wider. Maybe... Prudently, she let her speculations be corralled by Rob's next words.

"How's the law?"

"Never better. I'm working on the *Stroker* case."

Rob's eyes lit up. "Isn't that the one getting all the publicity?"

Jill's lips peaked as expected. "The same."

"Congratulations."

"Thanks." Rob's reaction was confirmation to Jill that she had been mistaken about Mary's initial response to the same news.

Rob Sheffield's attention was suddenly diverted from Jill to her sister, who was resetting an earring as she walked back to the kitchen. "Who was it, babe?"

Mary shrugged. "They hung up. Wrong number, I guess." As she passed by the grocery sack, she peeked in. "Do you two know anything about making a salad?"

Rob looked over at Jill with a feelings-crushed expression. "Do you have the feeling our culinary reputations have just been besmirched?"

"I do," Jill answered in a voice deeply aggrieved.

Rob turned back to his fiancée. "Do we know anything about making a salad? Do we know anything about making a salad?" He glanced once more toward Jill and, with a questioning expression that caused her lips to dance, asked, "Do we know anything about making a salad?"

Jill forced her lips into a stern line. "Of course we do."

"Of course we do," he repeated confidently as he started to rummage through the sack. He produced a couple of avocados, which he tossed in rapid-fire succession to Jill. She caught both. He then pulled out the lettuce. This he clumsily held in his right hand as one might a football. He raised his arm and took aim. He also began a sportscaster's coverage of the event. "It's Sheffield at the fifty-eight, positioning for a long, high-flying pass to McClain. And there it goes." The lettuce went sailing through the air in a high arc. "It's high. It's inside. It's aimed straight for McClain's talented hands, which are reportedly insured for $1.95. Sports fans, it looks like it's going to be a..." Jill caught the lettuce right before it struck a glass of wine; both Jill and Rob scrunched up their faces. "Touchdown!"

"All right!" Jill cried, made a few crazy steps of a victory dance and raised the lettuce in preparation for spiking the "football."

Mary cleared her throat.

Both Rob and his accomplice looked toward the sound. Jill slowly lowered her arm, while Rob uttered the words that produced a round of giggles from both women. "Oh, hi, coach," he said. "You know how to make a salad?"

Twenty minutes later, the salad was finished. It was at that point that the phone again rang.

"I'll get it while you two ogle your creation," Mary said, starting for the phone and automatically removing her earring.

"I think the composition is interesting," Rob commented, having now assumed the pompous role of art critic.

"Very definitely," Jill agreed, gazing down at the colorful bowl of sliced, diced and torn vegetables. "Don't you feel that the artist's statement is a pungent retort to those who would ask, 'Can you make a salad?'"

"I quite agree, Doctor of Art McClain. It's a subtle, yet unmistakably bold, statement of confidence. It says not only that I can make a salad, but that I can make a damned good one."

"I couldn't agree more. I..." Jill's eyes had strayed to her sister, the suddenly, pale-as-chalk face of her sister. "Mary?"

Rob Sheffield swiveled toward his fiancée.

"Mary?" Jill repeated.

The sound of her name seemed to drag Mary McClain from some dark planet. She was still clutching the phone to her ear with both hands. "What?" she murmured, her eyes vacantly meeting those of her sister.

"What's the matter?" Jill asked, taking instinctive steps forward. Rob did the same.

Their motion seemed to bring the room back into focus. "Nothing. Nothing," Mary repeated, dropping the receiver back into its cradle as if the plastic had suddenly grown hot. Her hand trembled slightly. "It was another wrong number. Just someone trying to sell aluminum siding." She appeared unaware of the contradiction in the two statements. "Well, if you two are through admiring your work, let's eat." She moved into the kitchen with all the zeal of an advancing freight train.

Rob caught her arm and turned her around. Their eyes met. "You sure you're all right?"

"Certainly I'm all right," Mary replied, her eyes never wavering, though she quickly pulled away and yanked the lid off the pot roast. "Jill, you put the salad on the table and Rob, you pour the wine."

Rob and Jill exchanged momentary puzzled looks before complying with Mary's orders.

The meal couldn't have been a more normal experience. Mary ate, talked, even laughed at all the appropriate times. They toasted Jill's involvement in the *Stroker* case, an involvement Mary seemed genuinely pleased with, and even made plans to have dinner together the following Saturday night. Once or twice, Jill caught Rob looking at Mary as if he were trying to decide if he'd only imagined her reaction earlier. It was an exercise in looking and judging that Jill could relate to, for she was doing the same thing. She concluded, as once before that night, that she'd simply misread her sister.

"I've gotta go," Jill announced a little before ten. She uncoiled herself from the sofa and reached for her handbag. "I know you two want to neck."

Mary did not give her usual groan and blush.

"Thought you never were going to leave," Rob teased, squeezing his bride-to-be's shoulders.

Still Mary didn't groan or blush—a fact Jill noted, just as she had noted her sister's quiet preoccupation all during the program they'd watched on TV.

"Are you sure you're all right?" Jill asked once more at the door.

"I'm positive," Mary replied with a weak smile. "I think I'm coming down with a cold, is all. We've had a rash of them this week at school."

The two sisters stared at one another, Jill searching for truth, Mary challenging contradiction.

"You take care of yourself," Jill said at last, then looked up at the man who stood behind Mary, his arms curling around her waist and drawing her back against him. "Better yet, you take care of her."

"You bet. Good night."

A few more words and kisses to cheeks and Jill was crunching down the cool grass and pulling open the car door.

"Bye," she called over the vehicle's closed sunroof.

"Bye," Mary returned and waved.

Seconds later, the couple watched as the car disappeared down the street.

Rob's arms tightened and his lips brushed Mary's ear with a worried, whispered question. "You okay, babe?"

Mary nodded, and nestled the back of her head deeper into his chest. It was only the night that saw the lone tear escape from the corner of her eye.

SIGHING DEEPLY, BURKE rested the back of his hand across his closed eyes. He should have taken Jill up on her offer of dinner at her sister's house, he thought for at least the dozenth time. If he had known how long and lonely his first Saturday back in civilization was going to be, he'd have jumped at the chance to protect his sanity. As it was, that thread-thin item seemed about to snap.

Burke rolled to his side and allowed the covers to slip to his waist. Absently, he trailed his fingers through the dark hair matting his chest and adjusted his hips to a more comfortable position. The feel of the soft clean sheets should have been lulling to his tired bare body, but instead, they curiously teased at his senses, reminding him that he was a man, a man who'd been a very long time without a woman. Increasingly, this fact was forcing its way into his consciousness and each time that it did, he rejected it—with guilt for having let it intrude at all, and with desperation because he knew that there was really no way, short of contradicting nature's design, that he could stop its intrusion.

With his usual dosage of guilt and desperation, he rejected the thought once more, replacing it with thoughts of how miserable the day had been. He'd wakened to a deafening silence and the threat of the eternally long day that loomed before him. After forcing himself to finish unpacking, he met his father for lunch, then stopped at the supermarket on the way back to the apartment. The act of grocery shopping had been, as it always was, depressing. It implied a domesticity he didn't feel. He really didn't live anywhere, and the fact that he had to go on eating, that he had to go on performing these stupid little duties just to survive irritated him, like back-rubbing the fur of a cat.

Survival.

There was that word again, Burke thought. But the truth was that he really did want to survive. He didn't want to want to, but he did. He had discovered that he couldn't change that aspect of human nature anymore than . . . anymore than a man could change basic physical needs. He again held the subject of sexuality at arm's length and forced his mind back to the topic of survival.

Because he had wanted to survive, he'd spent the rest of the afternoon and early evening working on the *Stroker* case. When he'd exhausted that, and himself, he'd tried to watch TV . . . but failed. Finally, the emptiness of the apartment had driven him back onto the streets. He'd run and run and run and, when his body had refused to go a step farther, he'd returned to the apartment. There, he'd showered and tumbled into bed. And proceeded to be restlessly awake.

He should have accepted Jill's offer.

Jill.

A slight smile curved his lips. She could always make him smile. She was a small bundle of irrepressible energy. Small... She was smaller than he'd remembered. Burke shifted and nuzzled his head into the softness of the pillow. He gave a quiet sigh as sleep stepped closer. She was small, but...womanly. His eyelids shut. And her hair was like a blaze of scarlet fire in a yellow summer sun. Her eyes...they were a man-tempting blue... blue...blue... Sleep danced around him with its foggy reality until thoughts were nothing but a surreal jumble.

Contacts...

Glasses...glasses...intelligent looking in glasses...

Jill...Jill...Ji—

Burke's breathing filled the room with its soft, contented cadence. For the first time in eighteen months, he had fallen asleep thinking of something, someone, other than his dead wife.

CHAPTER THREE

MARY MCCLAIN came down with a cold.

That fact greatly relieved Jill and persuaded her that her imagination had been overly vivid. The phone call on Saturday night had obviously been exactly what Mary had said: a wrong number. That issue settled in her mind, Jill was free to turn her full attention to the impending *Stroker* case. And she did, with Burke at her side, Monday night, until the wearying, wee-morning hour of one o'clock. They both had then crawled home to beds that, despite their fatigue, had seemed large and lonely.

Tuesday they again met with their client, Alysia Stroker, a women of tremendous integrity, average intelligence and minimal beauty. She had, however, a combination of attributes that blended into an attractive and compelling dignity. Jill wasn't surprised Wednesday morning to see the socialite's name once more splashed across the front page of the *Boston Herald*. She was surprised, however, to see that both she and Burke, as her lawyers, had been given inches of copy in the article. Apparently, anyone associated with the case was deemed newsworthy.

When Jill arrived at work later that morning, she found Burke in a quiet mood. She wondered if it had anything to do with the fact that the article had briefly, and tactlessly, she thought, mentioned Nicole Rawlins's accident. She didn't inquire, and Burke didn't offer to share.

"Don't tell me you two are working late again," Andrew Rawlins called from the doorway of Burke's office. It was a quarter to seven Wednesday evening, and two pairs of bleary eyes immediately glanced upward. As she had a countless number of times in the past hour, Jill blinked over sandy-feeling contacts.

"Hi, Dad. What're you doing here this late?"

"Finishing up some paperwork," the elder Rawlins said, stepping into the room and seating himself in the chair beside Jill.

She watched him cross one leg over the other in a way that ran the risk of being termed effeminate, but fell far short of it and into an area simply called grandly elegant. In truth, Andrew Rawlins, with his snow-white hair and Brooks Brothers suit, looked like a male model in search of a camera. As did his son, Jill thought, her eyes coasting to the man behind the desk. With Burke, however, the pose was altogether different. He sat negligently back in the leather chair with his right foot wedged in the space created between the desk and an open top drawer. His leg was bent at the knee and leaned masculinely outward, allowing a clear view of the taut muscles that resided beneath the oxford-gray pants. His sleeves were rolled up to reveal a dark dusting of hair, a replica of the brown coils spilling from the vee of his unbuttoned shirt. He looked both athletically fit and superbly attractive. And sexy?

Jill deliberately let her attention be swallowed up by the conversation.

"You look tired," the older man was saying. "I'd prefer you two not to be comatose when you try the case."

Burke's lips worked ever-so-slowly into a slight smile. "Jill and I are going to take turns being conscious in court."

The smile, the late-day teasing resulting from fatigue, was infectious. "To be honest," Jill said, "I'm praying hard to get fired."

"Never, Ms McClain, have your chances been so unlikely," Andrew Rawlins teased back. "How is it going?" he asked, his tone suddenly serious.

"Okay. Fine," came the two answers that managed to merge into one. Briefly, blue eyes met with green.

He does look tired, she thought.

Her eyes look glazed, Burke thought. *And she keeps rubbing her left one. It must hurt. Are the contacts...*

"Have you settled on a strategy yet?" the senior Rawlins asked.

Burke dropped his gaze from Jill's face at the same time he unwedged his foot and dropped it to the floor. Looking outside, he noted that the first star of evening was born in a blaze of silvered fury. He straightened and tossed the legal pad in his lap onto the desk. "We're going to take full advantage of the fact that Massachusetts allows the prosecution of husbands who rape their wives."

Andrew Rawlins nodded approval. "And can you win with that tactic?"

"There's no question in our minds," Jill said, "that Stroker raped his wife, if you define rape as sexual intercourse without consent. We'll also charge that his obsession for an heir took the form of other physical and emotional abuse."

"The rape is her word against his," Burke added, "but we have plenty of corroborative evidence concerning physical and emotional abuse—friends, servants, whose depositions we're getting."

"I repeat," Andrew Rawlins persisted, "can you win with that tactic?"

"I think so," Burke replied. "Especially since our client is seeking a fair settlement rather than the imprisonment of her husband."

"I think we have a better-than-fighting chance," Jill agreed.

Andrew Rawlins nodded again. "How does *Rideout* versus *Rideout* help you?" he asked, referring to a well-known rape-within-marriage case.

"Not at all," Jill said. "The verdict was in favor of the husband. Their cohabitation at the time of the rape was the determining factor."

"Mrs. Stroker claims she and her husband were estranged at the time of one of the rapes," Burke supplied. "And there's a New Jersey man serving time right now for raping his estranged wife."

"Excellent," the senior Rawlins said. "By the way, rumor has it that Judge O'Halleron's going to preside."

Both Jill and Burke groaned.

"Ole Banging Judge O'Halleron, huh?" Burke commented. "You'd think he'd retire."

Judge Timothy O'Halleron, baldheaded, full bearded, and florid faced, had the reputation of being the oldest, the most conservative and the most no-nonsense judge seated on any Massachusetts bench. So strict was he that his gavel was always in a state of motion, which had earned him the title "banging judge."

"I also hear that the mother of the illegitimate child will be bringing her own suit on behalf of the daughter later," the silver-haired Rawlins added, asking on the heels of the remark, "What about a court date?"

"Nothing's been set," Jill answered.

"Speaking of calendar dates," Andrew Rawlins said, now pointedly addressing his son, "have you made plans to attend the Bar Association dinner?"

Jill could feel the web-fine tension that suddenly wove around Burke.

"I really don't think I'm ready—"

"It's for a worthwhile charity," his father interrupted. "The Cancer Society—"

"I have no quarrel with the cause," Burke, too, interrupted. "I just don't want to—"

"You really ought to go, Burke." There was a paternal command in the older man's voice, along with an understanding look in his eyes that said, "Trust me in this, Son. There's never going to be a good time to pick up the threads of your life."

In the short interim filled with the two men's stares, Jill wished that she wasn't privy to such a private conversation. She also wondered what Burke's decision would be. And, if he went, would he take some—

"Why don't you two go together?" Andrew Rawlins said, machete-slashing through Jill's thoughts.

Her eyes flew to Burke's. Nothing there gave any hint as to what he was feeling.

"Or am I being too presumptuous to think you don't already have plans?" the elder Rawlins asked Jill.

She dragged her eyes from Burke to the man beside her. "No...no, sir. No plans other than attending the dinner." Though the event was still two weeks off, she'd had her ticket for months, had even already turned down, politely, of course, Charles Evans's offer to take her.

"You two are already linked together on the case—you can thank the ever-scavenging press for that. It would be perfectly natural to show up at the dinner together."

Jill knew what Andrew Rawlins was trying to do. He was trying to assure Burke that no one would misunderstand his being seen with his law partner. Which was true, of course. Only it strangely hurt to be considered a safe nonentity. Or did it just hurt to be considered a safe nonentity in Burke's life? Not wanting to answer that question, she glanced back at Burke . . . and waited patiently for him to say something. He didn't. He just stared at her. In the end, social decorum demanded Jill answer. "It's all right with me. Why don't I swing by and pick you up?"

Still Burke said nothing.

It was Andrew Rawlins who did. "Good. Then it's settled." With that, he stood. "I'm heading home. Why don't you two do the same?"

"Yes, sir," Jill said.

"Good night," Burke called after his father.

For a solid quarter-minute after the door closed, neither spoke. Except with work-tired eyes.

"I'm sorry Dad boxed you into a corner."

"He didn't."

"He did."

"He didn't!"

"McClain, you're in a corner."

"Rawlins," she said, gesturing around, "it looks like I'm in the middle of the room."

"You're in a corner. Daddy insisted that you take his little boy to the prom."

Both were now grinning. The masculine smile faded, however.

"I'm giving you a chance to back out."

The feminine smile faded as well, as she realized the truth of her reply: "I don't want to back out."

"There isn't some great guy waiting for your yes?"

"Actually, the only guy that asked me I said no to. Charles Evans."

"Evans? Is he your type?"

"Obviously not. I turned him down."

Burke gave a facial expression that indicated the logic of her answer. "Okay, this is your next-to-the-last chance to tell me to get lost."

"Next-to-the-last?"

"Now it's your last."

"I'll pick you up about seven-thirty, Rawlins. Now, what do you say let's finish up here and get eight hours of sleep like the rest of the world?"

"Suits me." He reached for his pad; she reached for a book. "Hey, McClain?"

She glanced up. "Yeah?"

"You getting me a corsage?"

A playful pencil sailed across the desk.

A few minutes later, and in regard to the last thing on the day's agenda, Burke asked, "You want to give the opening or closing remarks?"

"Opening," Jill said, blinking her left eye and automatically sending fingers up to rub it. "No, closing. No, opening." She blinked, rubbed, blinked again.

"With that kind of decisiveness, I'm certain our opposition is sleeping nights," Burke said, adding with a frown, "Is something wrong with your eye?"

"What?"

"Your eye. You keep blinking it."

"I think my contact's slipping."

"Slipping? They do that?"

"Uh-huh. You want to hand me the compact out of my handbag?"

"Where's your handbag?"

"On the floor. Over there. By the desk."

Burke reached for the rectangular piece of black leather and started rummaging through its contents in a way that was intimately familiar, though neither seemed aware of the fact.

"You want to hurry?" she asked, her eye now entirely closed and pain pinching her face.

Burke glanced up, his hands continuing to search for something round, something compacty feeling. "What's wrong?"

"It just slid into my forehead."

"Your forehead!" he said in a tone very much as the *Titanic*'s captain said "Iceberg!"

"Don't panic, Rawlins. Just get me a mirror."

Mumbling something crude, he simultaneously plunged into panic and through the purse's contents—a tube of lipstick, a wallet, Clorets and a chain full of jangling keys. "Well, I've at least solved the mystery of the missing continent of Atlantis. It's in this damned purse!"

"You're panicking," Jill accused, then moaned as the lens slid even deeper under her eyelid. "Hurry."

"Why in the world anyone would want to wear contacts is beyond me." He flipped over a checkbook and riffled through torn tickets to the Boston Philharmonic. "Why anyone wants to poke things in her eyes, why anyone . . ."

"Shut up."

"Here."

"Thanks. Can you hold it? There. No, up more. There."

Burke now stood between her and the desk, his hands trying to hold the oval of glass still. Jill, her eyelid pulled upward, was touching the visible edge of the contact with a tentative tip. The bulk of the lens did, indeed, appear to have drifted into her forehead.

"Does it hurt?" Burke asked, mimicking her grimace.

Jill gave him a withering look out of her good eye.

"Okay. Stupid question. My God," he said as she stretched the eyelid farther to reveal raw, pink tissue, "I've seen surgeries that involved less!"

"Got it," Jill said, sighing and withdrawing the culprit on the end of her index finger. She stored it in its case and glanced back up at Burke. He was still standing before her, still watching her.

"Your eye looks awful."

"It feels awful."

"Here, let me see." As naturally as the sky outside was darkening for evening, Burke slipped his finger to Jill's chin and tilted her head upward. "You ought to use some dro—" Their eyes met. His warm breath flooded across her cheek; her warm skin penetrated the layers of his loneliness to reach his starving senses.

Warm breath.

Warm skin.

Warm feelings.

Feelings that were too warm.

Burke was suddenly very much aware that he was man, and she a woman. It was the same basic realization that Jill had just made.

Dropping his eyes, he jerked away his finger as though her chin burned hot. He stepped back and cleared his husky throat. "You ought to use some drops when you get home."

He would have denied that something had happened between them, but denying the fact would have given the moment, the issue, more substance than he could deal with.

The removal of his hand from her chin left Jill with a feeling of abandonment. The reason why was inexplicable. And totally unexpected. It was also disturbing. As was the strange way her body had felt at his touch—as if everything feminine within her had awakened from a long sleep. "I will," she said, hastily stuffing compact and contact case back into her handbag. Refusing to look his way, she stood. "Well, I'm headed home."

Minutes later, as she walked alone from the building—Burke had insisted on finishing something she thought had already been finished—Jill felt it necessary to deny that anything had just happened between her and Burke. She couldn't help but secretly wonder, though, if for the first time in her life, honest Jill McClain wasn't lying to herself.

Lies.

As Jill left the office, Mary McClain sat staring at Jill's name in the paper and pondering the insidious power of lies. They were always such fragile untruths in the beginning, she thought, but as the years honed and tempered them, they took on a strength, mantled themselves in a force that quite literally gave them a life of their own. A dark life that instinctively fought to survive by refusing to let itself be destroyed in the act of revelation.

It had been her intention from the very beginning to tell Jill the truth. When she was old enough to understand. When she had lived long enough to know that right and wrong never dressed solely in the blunt shades of black and white. But each day had passed, the lie still intact, until it had been too late. The lie had begun to breathe life. And even if it had not, how could you tell the most innately honest person you knew that her life had always been a lie?

You didn't, Mary thought. Instead, you buried the secret deep, sharing it with no one but the night.

No one.

Yet somehow someone knew. Some strange male voice on the telephone knew. Someone knew her secret!

Mary forced her breath to a more even pace, forced herself to desert questions of who and why. Instead, she clung to the hope, feeble as it was, that the man wouldn't call again. He hadn't but that one time. Maybe if she wished hard enough, prayed hard enough...

The phone rang. Mary jumped. Stared. Listened to the loud, incessant intrusion.

Ring...ring...ring...

Please, Mary silently pleaded as she reached for the phone.

"Hello?" Her heart was beating so furiously that it roared in her ears, a roaring so loud that the male voice sounded like a whisper on the far side of a storm.

"Mary?"

Realization dawned, buckling her knees with relief. "Rob?"

"Who were you expecting, babe?"

"No one," she lied, closing her eyes and thinking on a wave of guilt that lying was the one thing she did well.

"YOU WANT A CUP of Charles River sludge?" Burke asked Friday afternoon as the hands on the clock crawled their way from four to four-thirty.

Jill glanced up and grinned. "Yeah," she said, slipping the tortoiseshell-framed glasses from her face and tossing them onto Burke's desk. She had worn glasses in lieu of contacts since Wednesday. She had no idea why, except that if pushed for an answer, she'd have to admit that it had something to do with what had happened

Wednesday—not the contact getting stuck, but the feel of Burke's hand on her chin, the feel of his moist breath against her cheek, the hot feel of sexual sensations vibrating over her body. "May I use your phone?" she asked, once more ignoring what she really didn't want to deal with.

"Sure."

Quickly, Jill punched in her sister's number and sat back to listen to the long string of rings. She was on the verge of hanging up when Mary answered.

"Hello?"

"Hi. Did I drag you from outside?"

There was the briefest of hesitations. "No. I, uh . . . I was in the back of the house."

"I was just calling to see if we're still on for tomorrow night." Jill smiled a silent thanks as Burke set a Styrofoam cup of thick, raven-black liquid before her. He moved toward the wall of windows where he stood sipping coffee and gazing out. Jill's eyes followed him before deliberately looking away.

"Certainly," Mary said with unfaked enthusiasm. In a world that had suddenly become unstable, the simple act of being with family was in and of itself stabilizing. Then, too, there'd been no other phone calls. That was cause aplenty for celebration. "I thought we'd broil steaks outside."

"Sounds like a great way to spend Saturday evening," Jill commented, and promised to bring a sinful chocolate dessert from her favorite bakery.

Saturday evening.

The two words echoed in Burke's mind with the overpowering force of a well-remembered and greatly-respected enemy. *My God,* he thought, *how am I going to get through another Saturday night? Another lonely*

Saturday night? It had been bad enough when he could run wild and free on the shores of the Atlantic, but here in the city the misery was amplified. He was like a beast in hateful captivity. And the four walls of that apartment, the four shrinking walls of that apartment, were like a cage. With his guilt the restraining iron bars, his bitterness the...

"Burke? Burke?"

The word penetrated his misery, and he meshed his eyes with Jill's.

"Mary wants to know if you'd like to come to dinner tomorrow night." Jill's palm spread across the receiver to insure privacy. "There's no pressure. If you don't want..."

"Yes."

Surprise flickered across blue irises. A little surprise even flickered across green. Jill's eyes still on Burke's, she spoke into the phone. "He said yes. Right. I'll tell him." After a proper goodbye, she replaced the receiver. Seconds crept by. "I'll pick you up about six."

"Six o'clock," he repeated.

"Oh, Mary said to dress casual."

He nodded. "Casual."

She nodded and stupidly repeated, "Casual."

Why had things suddenly turned so awkward? As if the two of them weren't good friends? As if the two of them didn't spend almost all their time together anyway? As if either one of them could possibly misconstrue the evening as a date?

"Why don't I dress casual?" he asked, covering the awkwardness with humor.

Jill grinned, suppressing her discomfort in the same manner. "Suit yourself. I'm gonna dress casual."

HE DRESSED CASUAL.

Jill noted the fact the moment Burke pushed from the side of the apartment building and sprinted toward the car she was pulling alongside the curb. She noted it as he eased in beside her, noted it as she negotiated Saturday-evening traffic, noted it as he unfolded his long frame from the car and started up the sidewalk, she at his side, toward Mary McClain's little yellow house.

As his joggers shuffled up the steps, Jill remembered once speculating that Burke probably looked sensational in jeans. Probability had now moved into the realm of certainty in a way that would have pleased Levi Strauss. To say nothing of Mrs. Strauss's pleasure. Even the ordinary red sweatshirt, its long sleeves pushed to the middle of Burke's hairy arms, molded his chest and shoulders in a way that was arresting.

"Am I dressed too casual?" Burke asked under his breath.

"What?"

"Did I overdo the casual?" His eyes made a quick assessment of her pertly creased navy slacks, plaid shirt and white sweater carelessly but stylishly tied around her neck.

"No. You look . . . great." *And sexy,* some part of her mind tossed in just for the perverse heck of it.

She pulled open the screen door and motioned him into the cool, shadowy interior of the house. They were immediately met by Rob Sheffield.

"Hey, Blue Eyes," he said, swooping to plant a kiss on Jill's cheek. Without waiting for a proper introduction, he swiped his hand down his jeans leg and extended it to Burke, who had to juggle Jill's cake and his bottle of wine to reciprocate. "Hi. You must be Burke."

"Guilty," Burke replied. "And you're Rob."

"Equally guilty."

"Sorry about the hand. I've been playing in the charcoal. By the way, how do you like your steak cooked?"

"Medium obliterated," Burke replied. All three smiled.

"Hi," singsonged a low and throaty feminine voice.

"Hi," Jill called back and watched her sister advance wearing an apron that read Kiss the Cook. "Mary, I'd like you to meet Burke. Burke, Mary."

Mary McClain likewise extended her freckle-sprinkled hand, accompanied by a sincere smile. "I'm so glad you could come."

"Thank you for the invitation." Burke's lips tilted upward. "I confess you're nothing like what I was expecting. I thought you'd be..." He stalled.

"In need of Wheaties like me?" Jill supplied.

"Petite," Burke substituted with a teasing look in Jill's direction.

"I'm the only small fry in the family," Jill said. "At least as far back as the family photo albums go. Makes you wonder about genetics, doesn't it? Here, give me that," she said, taking the cake box out of Burke's arms and missing the look that sprang into Mary's eyes. "The wine's Burke's," she called out, heading for the cabinet.

There was a moment's hesitation in which Rob waited for his fiancée to take the wine bottle being offered. When she didn't, he did. "Great. We were just wondering if we had enough."

The simple movement snagged Mary's attention. She glanced up quickly, guiltily, at Rob, who was watching her with thinly disguised interest. Suddenly, she smiled as if nothing in the world could possibly be wrong and waved behind her. "Why don't we go into the backyard?"

The backyard was very much like the house: small and unpretentious, but immaculately kept. At that hour of evening, the golden sun was bidding farewell to a fair sky, and the late-March air was chilling to a pleasant nip. Charcoal squares glowed gray and red in a grill, and the refreshing sound of a tin can being drawn from chunks of ice filled the silence along with the musical chords of an eager cicada.

"Want a beer?" Rob called to Burke from the cooler.

"Yeah."

"Jill?" Rob asked.

"Later," she answered, automatically starting to help Mary with the few things that needed doing.

Although the weather was cool, they decided to eat outdoors. A red-and-white checkered cloth was draped over the redwood table, and plastic plates in assorted bright colors were laid out. As Jill wrapped corn on the cob in foil, Mary readied the steaks and put the finishing touch to a potato-and-cheese dish.

"He's nice," Mary whispered over the sound of crinkling foil.

"Uh-huh. Very."

"He's also nice looking."

Jill glanced up at her sister, then across the yard to where Burke, beer can in hand, stood talking to Rob. At that precise moment, Burke smiled at something the other man said. He also ran a hand into the back pocket of his jeans, drawing attention to the masculine curve of his hips. The gorgeous, sexy, wake-up-every-female-in-the-area curve of his hips. "Yes, he is," she admitted honestly, adding, just as candidly and for the benefit of the gleam in Mary's eyes, "We work together. Nothing more. So don't go indulging in sisterly matchmaking."

"Sometimes people who work together..."

"He's married," Jill interrupted, her gaze once more finding Burke. As he tipped the can of beer to his lips, the gold band on his finger glinted mockingly in the day's fading light. "His wife's dead, but he's still very much married." The realization hurt. She didn't ask herself why.

"And if he weren't?" Mary asked.

Jill's eyes lowered from Burke to her sister. "We're friends. We're co-workers. Nothing more." It was the truth. Totally. Completely. Wasn't it?

Seconds later, Mary carried the potato-cheese casserole into the kitchen, leaving her question behind to nag Jill. It was still nagging—what *if* Burke wasn't grieving over his wife?—when she heard a familiar male voice at her side.

"Hi."

"Hi."

"Looks good," he said of the four-layer cast-calories-to-the-wind chocolate cake that now presided in all its fattening glory from the middle of the table. He stretched, scooped a dash of chocolate icing that the baker had let drip onto the paper doily decorating the cardboard bottom, and licked it from his index finger.

Jill watched as his lips closed over the pad of his finger and sucked at the icing. She briefly saw the tip of his tongue. The sight ignited a warmth and slow-spread it throughout her body. Instantly, as if seeking sanctuary, she raised her gaze to his eyes. In the sophisticated denial pattern of human beings, she ignored what she'd just felt.

"Chocolate and beer?" she asked with an appropriate face.

"Nicole always said . . ." He stopped.

Curiously, so did Jill's heart. Just a little bit. Nicole's name was as sobering as a splash of cold water to the spirited question she'd just been entertaining. What if Burke wasn't grieving over his wife? The answer was simple: Forget it, because he is. With logical precision, everything fell back into proper perspective.

Jill smiled, understandingly, encouragingly. "What did Nicole always say?"

Burke studied the blue eyes behind the glasses. The kind, comforting blue eyes. The blue eyes he'd so closely looked into the night her contact slipped. He let the thought drift away because there was something decidedly disturbing about remembering that night. "She said my stomach had all the delicacy of a garbage disposal."

Jill's smile spread. "And here I though you athletes watched what you ate."

"Athlete? You've got to be kidding. I run purely for therapy. Usually right after I've devoured a ton of junk food."

"You don't enjoy running?"

He gave the question serious consideration. Finally, he shrugged. "Yeah, I guess I do."

"But not enough to enter the Boston Marathon next month?" she teased.

He laughed—a low, all-male sound that reminded Jill of thunder on a still, summer day. "Not on your life. I'd get trampled before the first watering hole."

"Me too."

"You run?" he asked, again bringing the beer can to his lips.

She shook her head, swaying the ponytail she'd opted for that evening. "Not really. Sometimes I feel guilty about not exercising, usually right after a TV commercial where the woman is shadow-thin and exists on crunchy cereal and workouts. Then I'll jog or run or walk for a couple of days."

"We'll run together sometime," he said.

It was a simple statement, with no underlying meaning, and yet Jill's stomach somersaulted. She told herself she was hungry. "Yeah, right out of town if we lose the *Stroker* case," she teased.

He grinned down at her. "We won't."

She grinned up at him. "You sound confident, counselor."

"I am. I'm working with the best lawyer in the city."

"Thanks," she said, pleased that Burke respected her professional capabilities.

The compliment curiously slowed time.

His eyes were a remarkable shade of green, she thought. The kind of green that probably darkened in moments of passion. And his mouth . . . She dragged her eyes away. "I think I'll get a beer too," she said, glancing over toward the cooler. At the sight of Mary and Rob seriously engaged in interpreting the message on her sister's apron, Jill added, "Then again, maybe I'll wait."

Burke's gaze followed Jill's, and both watched as Rob's lips moved over Mary's in a slow rhythm. When their lips disengaged, he whispered a question to which Mary shook her head a reassuring no. He then grazed her cheek with a knuckle before lowering his mouth once more to hers. Even at a distance, one could see that the kiss was gentle and sensual and begging for closer intimacy.

A longing, knife-sharp and strong, speared both Burke's and Jill's bodies. The scene reminded Burke of what he'd lost, Jill of what she'd never had. Instinctively, neither able to help it, their eyes met. But held for only seconds. Because looking into each other's eyes only seemed to intensify the painful longing.

Without any real thought to the act, Burke shoved his can of beer forward, indicating for Jill to take it. She did. And took a swallow. At the exact spot where his lips had been. The spot was warm. And malty-tasting. Like his mouth? Jill again banished the thought of his mouth, handed the can back with thanks, and leaned against the edge of the redwood table. Burke joined her. Together, they watched the stars appear in the sky.

Neither spoke for a long while.

In the deep silence, a siren wailed. Burke automatically searched out the guilt in his heart. He found it, crouching and ready to spring as always. But tonight it didn't. For once. The beauty of the night, the tranquility of the night, had momentarily diluted its power. As had the friend at his side.

"I'm glad I came tonight," he said softly.

Jill's eyes met his. Blue and green. Sincerity and sincerity. "I'm glad you did, too."

JILL'S GLASSES LAY ABANDONED on the redwood table. Fine wisps of reddish-blond hair escaped from her ponytail and wafted about her ears and neck, and her shirttail was pulled from pants that had lost their crease. Even with the chill in the evening air, even with the white sweater now encasing her arms, a thin dotting of perspiration lay across her upper lip.

Burke's hair, more golden than brown in the outside lights, slashed across his sweat-damp forehead, while his breathing was a husky rasp that sent his chest heaving in and out. A smile, which would have measured somewhere between that of a boy's and a man's, tugged at the corners of his mouth.

"So you want to play dirty, huh?" he asked.

"That's the problem, Rawlins," Jill taunted, rubbing her grass-stained palms down her pant legs. "You and Mary are playing, while Rob and I are dead serious."

That comment brought instant disagreement from Mary, instant agreement from Rob. It brought laughter from everyone.

After dinner, someone—none of the four would take credit for the idea now—had suggested touch football. As the game progressed and the close competition became heated, the mild rules of touch football had given way to a more rambunctious form of the game. In fact, Jill had just tried to trip Burke as he'd spectacularly caught Mary's pass in midair.

"C'mon, let's get down and get dirty," Jill said, adding, "This is the tiebreaker, right?"

"Right," a trio of determined voices answered.

The two teams broke into huddles, Burke and Mary whispering low, Jill and Rob gesturing in secret ways.

"Let's play ball!" Rob called, clapping his hands together.

Burke and Mary gave one more whispered exchange before getting into position.

Jill made hunkering preparations to hand the ball off to Rob, who stood behind her. Her and Burke's eyes collided, head-on and with a smiling threat.

"Ninety-two, forty-seven, hike..." Rob called out, only to be interrupted by the muted ringing of the telephone within the house. He straightened. "I'll get..."

"No!" Mary cried. Three pairs of eyes swerved toward her. The panicked electricity in the air could have made hair stand on forearms. "I mean, let it ring. If it's important, they'll call back." Seconds passed slowly. The look on Mary's face was one of pleading.

Jill and Rob exchanged quick glances, but it was as though neither could settle on an opinion. Even Burke had a look of uncertainty.

The phone rang again and again. Then it stopped.

As if on cue, as if deeply relieved, Mary smiled. "C'mon, let's play," she said, falling back into a bent position with the fingers of one hand resting on the grass.

Jill, Rob and Burke hesitated, then one by one slipped back into place. Moments later, the game was in progress and all but the score forgotten.

Jill handed off to Rob. Rob ran to the right. Jill circled to the left, right in front of Burke. He segued at the last moment and zeroed in on the ball headed straight for Jill's tummy. Her hands grabbed it. His hands grabbed it. Their feet became tangled, their legs laced.

Shrieking and giggling, Jill fell to the grass.

Laughter rumbling in his chest, Burke followed.

And in the exact time that it took the unexpected to happen, one large male body sprawled across one petite feminine form.

CHAPTER FOUR

JILL'S SENSES STUNG with awareness.

The heaviness of Burke's body. The damp, clingy feel of his sweatshirt. His heartbeat shattering against her own. She was also assailed by the sudden invasion of smells—that of crushed, spring grass merging with a masculine cologne and the more masculine fragrance of sweat. Sweat. She could almost taste—her tongue moved restlessly behind her lips—the salt in the perspiration slicking his forehead. She even fantasized that she could hear the sound of the moist bead that dripped from his temple onto her cotton shirt. Without question, she felt it, even as she felt the lower portion of his stomach laid bare against hers, even as she felt the snap of his jeans pressed against the slight mound of her womanhood.

Even as she felt the exquisite proof that he was a man.

Woman. The message registered in Burke's mind with all the speed of rain-chased lightning. He felt curves and hollows that were indisputably feminine, curves and hollows and rounded breasts that he hadn't felt against his body in so long that he had almost forgotten the feel. Almost. He also smelled perfume, something light and airy and as elementally honest as its wearer, and he heard the smothered, rushing sound of breathing. His? Hers? He didn't know. Perhaps it was a combination of both.

Realization slowly dawned that they were staring into each other's eyes, and for the briefest of unguarded moments his gaze plunged deeply into hers. She was startled by the raw, hungry need she saw in him. And by the raw, hungry need unleashed in herself. So startled that her reaction was uncensored. She wanted, more than the next beat of her heart, to shift her legs, to spread them, to welcome him between them as woman was meant to welcome man. Only some innate sense of propriety stopped her. That and the fact that she'd never felt any need so strongly, so strongly that it was frightening. And stunning. And a thousand other baffling emotions.

"Hey, are you two all right?" Rob called out in concern as he jogged toward them.

Reality slapped them with its cold hand.

Burke blinked, Jill's gaze shifted to Rob Sheffield, and, when she looked back, a curtain had fallen across Burke's eyes. They were now neutral, impersonal, blank. Hers turned a pale shade of confusion. Had she only imagined the desire in his eyes?

Pulling to his feet, and without making eye contact, Burke reached out his hand. Automatically, Jill took it. He tugged. His hand was warm—and trembly?—touching hers so briefly that she almost stumbled when he let go.

Somehow he'd managed to hold on to the football, which he now tossed to Rob.

"Your point," Burke said in a voice that sounded foggy and thick.

"Okay!" Rob hollered, spiking the ball and grabbing Jill around the waist for a crush-your-ribs hug. "Guess we showed 'em, huh, Blue Eyes?"

"Yeah," Jill said with a forced smile. Her eyes sought out Burke. He wasn't looking at her. In fact, he seemed determined not to look at her.

"You two want to play a catch-up game?" Rob asked Burke and Mary. It was Burke and Jill who answered, however.

"I don't think..."

"It's getting kinda..."

Burke's and Jill's eyes met. Fully. For just a second.

"It's getting kinda late," Jill repeated.

"C'mon, guys. It's only a little after ten," Rob pointed out.

"We've been putting in long hours at the office," Jill explained.

After a couple more protests from Rob—Jill was later to realize that Mary had seemed so distracted that she'd never once insisted they stay—they were allowed a gracious departure. Jill had promised to call soon. Burke had promised to visit again. Jill had thought his voice lacked sincerity.

The drive back possessed all the silence of eternity. Burke sat stonily, rarely glancing Jill's way. She, on the other hand, felt as fidgety as an expectant father. On the rare occasion when they did speak, there was an awkwardness in the exchange.

As they passed by the Boston Common, which by day was filled with crisp activity but by night was as quiet and still as the inside of the car, Burke said, "Your family's nice." As he spoke, a renegade image flashed through his mind. It was the image of a small, sensual woman trapped beneath him. He instantly fought the memory.

Jill gave him a quick glance. He sat, ankle squared to knee, staring straight ahead. "Yes." Firm, she thought, his body had felt firm and strong against hers.

Minutes later, as the Boston Public Garden came into and out of view, he added, "When are they getting married?'' Burke remembered beautiful blue eyes drowning in his . . . and shook his head.

"May," Jill answered, remembering the feel of his stomach rubbing against hers, the feel of his manhood nestled snugly, promisingly, against her.

"I, uh . . . I appreciate the invitation tonight." He recalled soft, tempting lips resting so near his own . . . and breathed deeply, shattering the unwanted vision.

"Did you get enough to eat?" she asked, blatantly wondering what it would be like to kiss him.

"Are you kidding?" This time he did look at her, briefly, and grinned, slightly.

She dragged her eyes from his mouth. "Good." Which probably described the way he kissed.

"I liked the cake." *. . . and the way you smell . . .*

"I got it at this great little bakery on Newbury Street." *Would he be a tender lover? A demanding one?*

"I'll have to get the name of it. The bakery, I mean. Sometime when the old chocolate tooth is aching." *Ache, ache . . . God, he ached!*

"Sure. Just let me know."

"Okay."

"Okay."

End of subject. End of stupid subject.

Didn't you feel what I did! she suddenly wanted to scream. Doesn't your body still tingle with need? Sweet heaven, what's happening to me?

God, what's happening to me? Burke questioned frantically. He forced thoughts of Nicole into his mind, thoughts of Nicole's laughter, thoughts of Nicole's beauty, thoughts of Nicole making love to him.

"Burke?"

He glanced up sharply. And noticed that they were pulled alongside the curb in front of his apartment building. He noticed also that Jill was staring at his hands. He glanced down...and to the sight of his fingers turning, turning, turning, the gold wedding band. Abruptly, his fingers stilled. His eyes found hers. Even in the night's shadow and shade, she could tell that his irises darkened.

"I, uh...I enjoyed the evening," he said.

"Me too."

"Thank Mary again for me."

"I will."

Hesitation.

"Well, good night," he said, throwing open the door.

"Good night," she called after him.

Once on the outside, he hesitated again and, bracing his arm across the top of the car, leaned down to stare into the open window. Before he could analyze why it seemed so necessary to say so, he said, "Drive carefully."

Cars passed. Somewhere there was the muted chatter of people. The light at the corner turned from red to green and back to red again without Jill or Burke realizing the passage of time.

"Well, good night," he said again, this time pushing from the car.

Jill watched as he walked toward the entrance of the multistory, chic complex of apartments. She watched as he jogged the last few steps and disappeared inside the building without even a backward glance. She watched the suddenly empty doorway.

In that moment, she cursed her own honesty because it forced her to painfully lay the cards on the table. She was attracted to Burke Rawlins. Strongly. The admission instantly brought to mind the lyrics of an old song that asked the question: How long has this been going on? She had no idea how long, had no idea whether it had begun his first day back, whether it had begun at some point during the long hours they'd worked, and laughed, together; whether it had begun the night her contact lens had slipped, or whether it had started only a half hour before, when his body had lain intimately against hers. Perhaps it had always been there, just waiting for the proper catalyst to spark it to life. She couldn't honestly pinpoint its inception. She just knew that, at this moment, she recognized the attraction. She thought she even sensed Burke's attraction to her, but couldn't be sure she hadn't fancifully imagined it. One thing was certain; if it was real, he was denying it. Vehemently. Completely. With every ounce of strength he had. Either way, it translated to the same stark reality. She had just entered into a one-sided relationship.

HAD SHE OR HADN'T SHE?

The question became a litany during the next week. Each time Jill asked it, however, she came no closer to an answer. One minute she did indeed believe she had imagined, out of wishful thinking, the flicker of desire in Burke's eyes, while the next minute she was certain she'd seen it. If something mutual hadn't happened that few seconds he'd had her pinned to the ground, why had he participated in the virtual silence that had prevailed on the drive back?

Simple, she'd taunted herself. Maybe he had sensed her desire and felt awkward about being its cause without being able to be its cure. Maybe he'd felt something all right. Maybe, sprawled atop her, he'd been reminded of Nicole and how much he loved and missed her. Maybe... Jill conceded that there may be a thousand, nerve-shattering maybes.

The atmosphere around the office gave no clue as to Burke's feelings, though Jill sensed a subtle change in him and their relationship. While they still worked together as compatibly as ever, Burke seemed quiet, moody even, and less willing to engage in the teasing she had been getting so accustomed to. He seemed all business, though that business no longer involved working late. In fact, he'd made lame excuses both times she'd suggested it.

But if Jill sensed a change in Burke, she likewise sensed a change in herself. Though it was as delicate and slight as a mist of warm rain, it was still present. She felt somehow...different after her bold response to his body on hers. Almost as if she no longer knew herself. Her reaction had been stronger than any she'd ever experienced with a man. With no questions asked, no holds barred, she had been willing to make love to him. And what's more, it had seemed the perfectly natural thing to do. All of this was now demanding a new perception of a man she'd such a short time before considered only a friend. The adjustment made her feel strange. Especially around him. Which only added to the disquieting feeling of change.

Change. It seemed to be in the air. Even Mary seemed different—again, in a way too subtle to pinpoint. She had become edgy, jumpy—traits she'd never exhibited before. Most of the time Jill passed the change off as premarriage jitters. Occasionally, when worry insisted on having its due, she wondered if it could be something more. Though what that "more" could possibly be, she had no idea.

When Friday rolled around, Jill was relieved. She badly needed some rest from the emotionally draining week. As she was leaving her office for the day, she ran into Burke and his father. The two of them were planning dinner together. Jill had shown them her dinner companion, a book on rape, which she wanted to read in hopes of gaining some insights into the case she and Burke would be defending. They'd parted in the main lobby of the building, and as Jill had walked alone to the underground garage, she'd had the unsettling feeling that Burke was watching her. She hadn't had the courage, however, to turn around to confirm or deny her hunch. She didn't know whether she was more afraid to learn that he was or that he wasn't.

By seven o'clock, she had eaten a sandwich, bathed, and settled in bed with a law book. She adamantly refused to think of Burke Rawlins. At a quarter to ten, tired from reading and weary from constantly shoving Burke out of her mind, she reached for the phone and dialed her sister's number. She got a busy signal.

"WHO IS THIS? What do you want?" Mary whispered, cold sweat blistering her forehead at the sound of the strange male voice. It was only the second time she'd heard it, though it was the thousandth time she'd imagined the call. She'd prayed that she wouldn't hear from him again, but she'd known in her heart that she would.

"It don't matter who I am," the low, slow, gravelly voice replied. "It's what I want that counts." He allowed a meaningful pause. "I want money. Five thousand dollars in small bills..."

"I don't have that kind of money!" she cried.

"Sure you do," the voice said so softly, so soothingly, that that in and of itself leant an air of malignancy to the conversation. "If you don't, lawyer Jill does. Or maybe that fiancé of yours..."

"How do you know about..."

"About Rob? Oh, I know everything about you. Everything important. Like that little secret of yours. C'mon, Mary, five thousand and I'll forget all about your past."

"Don't ... please ..."

The voice became firm. "Five thousand by Friday. Leave it on a bench in the Public Garden." The stranger spent the next few minutes identifying exactly which bench in exactly which section of the park. And exactly when to leave the money. "You will show, won't you, Mary? 'Cause if you don't, I'll have to talk to Jill. And I don't think you'd like that." The phone went dead.

"Wait!"

The dial tone hummed a loud, irritating tune.

"Wait," she whispered. "Please wait." Tears sprang into her eyes as she eased onto the sofa. The receiver slid forgotten from her hand. Within seconds, the tears turned to soft weeping, which quickly gave way to a deluge, a deluge spawned by guilt and regret. All the while, the phone dangled ... and whined its monotonous message.

AT 10:15 p.m., the busy signal still beep-beeped in Jill's ear. She smiled. Rob. It had to be Rob. The smile faded, leaving behind an undisguised look of longing. She suddenly felt singular in a coupled world. The thought inevitably led to thoughts of Burke and to the groove-worn litany. Had she imagined his desire or had it been the real thing? And how many kinds of a fool was she for asking the same question over and over?

OVER AND OVER, footsteps pounded the sidewalk, jarring the night's silence and replacing it with the huffing sound of breath being sucked in and out of a deep chest.

Racing against the wind, Burke emptied his mind the way he'd tried to keep it empty all week except for selected thoughts and memories. Right now, he registered nothing but the feeling of exhaustion—how many miles had he run? Ten, twelve, fifteen?—and the torment of unrelenting pain, pain in his chest, pain in his legs, pain in every inch of his body. Good pain. Desired pain. Because pain allowed nothing, no unwanted thoughts, to share its spotlight.

He had no idea how many hours he'd run that week, nor how many miles he'd logged. He knew only that every evening after dinner, he'd taken to the streets. Those hours when he wasn't running, he had deliberately hugged thoughts of Nicole to himself. He'd forced himself to remember every minute of the nearly five years they'd shared together—the first time he'd seen her, the first time he'd kissed her, their wedding day, that first night they'd spent together as man and wife, the accident. *The accident.* He relived that memory again and again because it was the most potent, the most powerful, the most punishing. And he felt the need to be punished. He could never clearly define why, though he knew it had everything to do with Saturday night.

He slowed his pace, from running to jogging to walking to finally collapsing against the side of a brick building. With eyes closed, he bent at the waist and planted his hands just above his knees. His breath was fast and short and agonized. Long moments passed while he steadied it to a slower, more even rhythm. At last he opened his eyes. His gaze fell to the wedding ring. But it wasn't an image of his wife that filled his mind. It was an image of Jill—and how good she'd felt beneath him.

In punishment of the betraying thought, he ran another mile.

MILES AWAY, on the sleazy side of Boston, in a two-room efficiency apartment that had rust stains in the chipped porcelain sink and cracks in the Naugahyde sofa bed, a man sat staring at a photo. The man in the picture was of short stature, had a youthful face and was wearing a newly issued, crisply creased khaki uniform. Across the back of the photo, written in a woman's small neat script was: "May 2, 1951—Tommy, leaving for Korea."

"That's wonderful, Tommy, you made straight A's again."

"Lenny, did you hear that your cousin made the swimming team?"

"He's never been a minute's trouble since we took him under our roof."

"It was like losing a son. He was such a fine boy. So proud to be going off to war. He was going to go to law school, you know."

The man in the two-room efficiency apartment shook his head, ending the intrusive, shoutingly silent dialogue. With a careless flick of his thick wrist, he tossed the snapshot into a cardboard box that held all the worldly possessions of his recently deceased mother. He gave a snort of laughter. A cardboard box. It wasn't a whole helluva lot to show for seventy-two years. But then, Maude Larimer hadn't been a worldly woman. She'd been a woman of principle and good deeds. Good to everyone but her own son.

Anger coiled inside the man's stomach, and he rummaged more persistently through the cardboard box. He'd probably been through the contents a hundred times since the nursing home had signed them over to him, but there was something therapeutic about touching the left-behind mementos. The touching was a validation that he was alive. His mother was dead. Straight-A, fine-boy, perfect Tommy was dead. But he, Lenny, was alive.

He shoved aside a small, worn book of poetry and rifled through the bundle of letters, held together with a time-cracked rubber band, that he'd sent her over the years, most asking for money, which she'd never sent. There was even the childish valentine, with his crudely written young name, that he'd given her in the second grade. That was the first year he'd flunked school, and he could still remember the licking he'd gotten. From both her and Poppa. But somehow hers always hurt worse because it was his momma that he'd wanted to please. Because pleasing Momma had been impossible for him to do from the day he was born.

His fingers stopped at the brown-tinged obituary dating back to 1951. He knew what it said. He'd read it a dozen times. He read it once more.

Private Thomas Jacob Wilson, son of the late June and John Wilson, was killed June 1, 1951, in the service of his country. For valorous actions which resulted in his death . . .

"... He was posthumously awarded the Medal of Honor. Interment was in Arlington National Cemetery," the man said aloud by rote, even though he'd already tossed the column back into the box.

He lived perfect. He died perfect. He was just goddamned perfect!

"Don't you talk that way about your dead cousin. And don't you swear in this house, Leonard Larimer," he heard his mother's voice saying as clearly as if it had been thirty years before.

"I'll say any damn thing about Tommy that . . ."

The crack of a remembered slap had silenced him.

"If perfection means having a sense of decency, then Tommy was perfect."
Perfect

The man laughed hollowly. As it turned out, Thomas Jacob Wilson was as human as any man.

Reaching for the one dog-eared letter that he'd found at the very bottom of the cardboard box, a letter postmarked Boston, he opened it. A strange handwriting confronted him. The letter was dated January 13, 1952. It began:

Dear Maude,
The child was born yesterday. It's a girl. I think she's going to have Tommy's eyes . . .

Leonard Larimer stared for a long while at the letter. He stared and wondered and brooded over why he'd been allowed to live his life thinking that Thomas Jacob Wilson had been perfect.

BURKE FLEW to New York the following Monday morning. He remained there all week. The trip was unexpected and had to do with another case that the firm was handling. Burke had volunteered to do the footwork on this second case while juggling the ongoing *Stroker* case, which as yet had not been scheduled for trial.

The fact that he had volunteered for the trip so readily led Jill to a bold conclusion. She had been right in believing that he had responded to her that Saturday night at Mary's house—something that Burke was literally running away from. She faced one other fact as well. It really didn't matter that she had seen a seed of desire in his eyes, because he was in no way emotionally fit to deal with it. He was a man married to a dead woman, and a dead woman was a far more formidable opponent than a live one. In fact, so formidable that Jill had no intention of entering into competition. She'd never played at no-win games, and she didn't intend to start now.

Furthermore, she told herself, it was important to her to keep the old Burke in her life. He was her friend and co-worker, and she didn't want to complicate a simple issue. She would just file that Saturday night under the heading What Might Have Been Had Things Been Different. She didn't bother to file the feeling of unfairness she felt.

The Bar Association dinner was at eight o'clock Friday night, and Burke's plane taxied to a stop at exactly two minutes of seven. With his briefcase in one hand and a garment bag in the other, he rushed through the corridors of Logan Airport and grabbed the first phone he saw. He shoved a coin into the slot and dialed Jill's number. As he waited, he wished for the dozenth time that he hadn't committed himself to the dinner. Or was it that he wished that he hadn't committed himself to the dinner with Jill? Some secret part of his heart asked, and in so doing, declared the week away a dismal failure.

Jill had just stepped from the tub and into the warmth of a terry bath sheet that swallowed her whole when the phone rang. The jingling cut short the thought that had flitted in and out of her mind all day. She wished she wasn't going to the dinner. She wished even more vehemently that she wasn't going with Burke. She didn't bother to analyze that this was contradictory to the new attitude she'd adopted.

"Hello?"

Her voice was warm and womanly and not a damned thing like he'd remembered. It was a thousand times better, ten thousand times better, a hundred thousand...

"I'm running late," he said, his voice somewhere between choked and husky.

Jill's hand slid to her stomach where it splayed against the sudden hollow feeling. It seemed like forever since she'd talked to him. "Hi," she said, her tone softening.

"Hi. Look," he said, turning his back to the man dialing the phone beside him, "the plane just got in, and I'm still at the airport."

"Want me to pick you up later than planned?"

"Yeah. What about eight-fifteen?"

"Fine. It doesn't matter if we arrive late."

"Come on up instead of waiting for me at the curb. There's parking in the back."

"That's all right. I'll just wait..."

"I don't know how long it'll take me to get a cab. Then I've got to shower and shave and dress. Come on up."

The mention of showering and shaving and dressing brought to mind images that deepened the hollow feeling in Jill's stomach to cave proportions. She felt a rush of warmth, but ignored it.

"Okay," she said, forcefully holding on to the resolve she'd made that week. "See you at eight-fifteen." She paused. "How did everything go in New York?"

"Fine. How's everything here?"

"Quiet. We sent our troublemaker to New York."

One side of Burke's mouth tilted upward. It was the first time he'd smiled in a week. It was funny, but Jill McClain was fast becoming the guardian of his good mood.

"See you later," he said.

"Right. Oh, Rawlins...what's your apartment number?"

She could tell he was still smiling. "After that comment about troublemaker, I ought to make you look for it."

"Troublemaker," she reaffirmed.

"Five-eighteen," he said, and hung up.

Her own lips curved into a smile. The smile slowly faded. God help her, she couldn't wait to see him again.

As Jill was piling her hair into a loose knot atop her head and applying frosted shadow to her lids, Mary McClain was boarding the subway. She carried a large tapestry bag that had a plain grocery sack inside it. She was frightened.

As Jill patted glittery gold dust on her bare shoulders, Mary exited the subway and walked toward the Boston Public Garden. Evening shadows were falling, painting the sculpted landscape in watercolor shades of gray and lavender. Mary's heart quickened, and she asked herself why she just didn't tell Jill the truth, instead of emptying her savings account and perpetuating the lie in a way that made her sick to her stomach. The answer was immediate. Jill would never forgive her for not telling her in the beginning, and if a note of this sordid song leaked to the press, they'd have a heyday, especially with Jill already getting coverage because of the trial. No, she thought, she had no choice. She'd forfeited that luxury years before.

As Jill slipped her dress over softly curved hips, Mary searched for a wooden bench under a crooked elm tree bordered by pansies and tulips.

As Jill donned gold sandals with three-inch heels, grabbed her gold filigree clutch and headed out of the apartment, Mary glanced quickly about her and practically threw the grocery bag onto the bench. She knew he was watching. She could feel him—like a tainted, unclean mist rising off stagnant water. She walked, walked, ran—she couldn't stop herself—until she emerged back onto the street. Gasping for breath, she slowed her pace and smiled nervously at the couple coming toward her.

As Jill parked the car and started for Burke's apartment building, Mary turned the key in the lock of her front door. Stepping inside, she closed the door behind her and leaned back against it. She sighed and closed her eyes. Thank God it was over!

Jill ran her eyes over the metal numbers tacked to the doors. Five-eighteen. She stopped, hesitated, then rang the doorbell. A swarm of butterflies launched into flight in her stomach.

"It's open!" a voice shouted from within.

Turning the knob, Jill pushed the door inward. She stepped inside. And told the butterflies to settle down.

"Be with you in a minute!" The voice came from what Jill surmised to be the bedroom.

"Don't you know you shouldn't leave your door unlocked?" she asked, looking around her. Her immediate impression was that of a small, but expensively nice, apartment in a neutral color scheme unquestionably chosen to please a great many tastes rather than express any individual one.

"Yeah, well, I was kinda hoping someone would break in and steal this damned tux! Look, fix yourself a drink if you like. The bar's in the kitchen."

Jill's eyes automatically drifted in that direction. She saw a couple of nearly full bottles of liquor and a garment bag haphazardly thrown across the width of the bar. A briefcase sat on the floor. The abandonment of bag and case suggested haste.

"No, thanks," she called back. "I'm fine."

"Make yourself at home."

"Right," she said, but stood exactly where she was, somewhere between the kitchen and the back of the sofa, somewhere between wanting to see him and not wanting to see him.

Her eyes, however, continued to scan the room, and she made brief, almost disjointed, observations. Cream-colored carpeting. Sage-green furniture in plaids and paisleys that decorously blended. Dark wood, fireplace, burgundy accents, a photograph of...Nicole. Pretty. God, she was so pretty! In a classic kind of way. Jill suddenly felt so...ordinary. So little, so drab and ordinary. So unable to compete in a competition she'd already sworn she wouldn't involve herself in.

"Damn!" Burke swore.

Jill's eyes shifted to the bedroom door.

"Do you know anything about cuff—" their eyes met, solidly and as thirsting men drink water "—links?" The last word was nothing more than a sibilation of sound.

Burke felt as if some giant fist had just walloped him in the stomach, while Jill felt as if someone had just carved out her insides and carelessly tossed them aside. Both would have sworn that the room's oxygen supply had dwindled. Dwindled dangerously.

Jill McClain was stunningly beautiful. The thought raced through Burke's mind with the intensity and speed of high-voltage electricity. Even as he thought it, his eyes began a slow perusal just to confirm the fact. Golden-red hair, which strangely reminded him of the color of the tea roses his mother used to grow, swirled on top of her head with dangling wisps falling at brow and ear and neck, while her cheekbones rode high with a natural grace that shamed the artifice of apricot blush. Her eyes sparkled the blue of a sky just washed clean by rain—she was wearing contacts, he noted—and her lips gleamed a bronzy color that blended with her dress. Her dress. Burke's eyes slid over the glittery gold-lamé dress, from its high cowl neck to its long sleeves to its belted waist to its straight, floor-length skirt. A slit ran provocatively up one side. Once he'd finished the journey, he confirmed his original finding. She was beautiful. Stunningly beautiful.

Handsome, Jill thought as her eyes roamed over the man before her. His sandy-brown hair shone with healthy highlights, his cheeks with the gloss of newly shaved skin. His eyes were a deep dark green that in that moment suggested a forest, a primeval forest. He wore a black tux and a pristine white shirt that made a boldly attractive color contrast, a contrast that somehow lent strength and authority and . . . sensuality to the man wearing it.

She had missed him, she admitted honestly.

It had been a long, lonely, smileless week, Burke admitted, even though the realization caused him a painful pang of guilt.

The silence had lengthened until it was now almost embarrassing.

Jill forced her eyes to Burke's wrist. His other hand was holding the folds of the shirtsleeve together. "Do you need—" she cleared her throat "—some help?"

Burke lowered his eyes. He seemed genuinely surprised at the difficulty he was experiencing with the cuff link. "Yeah," he managed to say.

Laying her handbag on the bar, Jill stepped forward with a gentle sway of her hips. The motion didn't escape Burke's attention. "What's the problem?"

"The, uh . . . the cuff link. I got one, but . . ."

The words trailed off as Jill's fingers started to fumble at his wrist. With a skill that defied trembling, she took the onyx-and-gold cuff link he offered—their fin-

gers touched, scoring two bodies with hot, sizzling feelings—and penetrated the slit of the highly starched cuff.
In so doing, she inserted her finger under the cuff's edge.

She felt the prickly feel of pasty starch and the warm
feel of skin. Skin covered in a mat of hair that stimulat-
ingly felt between silky and crisp. She even felt a raised
vein on the back of his hand.

Burke experienced the feel of warm, warm skin and the
feel of her nail lightly scraping back and forth. When she
bent her head to fasten the cuff-link clasp, a tendril of
hair, which curled just at her ear, brushed against the
back of his hand. The gentle abrasion had all the subtlety of a ton of bricks tumbling onto his senses. He had
the sudden need for exercise. Like running around the
world.

"There," she said, her breath washing across his hand.

Like running around it twice, he amended.

She looked up into his eyes. He looked down into hers.

"Thank you." His voice was reed thin.

"You're welcome." Hers was soft like snowflakes on
a velvet landscape.

Time dragged. Both forced breath into their lungs.

"Well, are you ready?" he asked, stepping back. With
this distancing of his body from hers came the sudden
feeling of more oxygen in the room. He experienced the
heady feeling of optimism. The night was going to be
okay.

"Sure," she said, turning and walking the few steps it
took to retrieve her handbag.

Burke's eyes fell to Jill's back. Jill's bare back. The
dress draped in a perfect and wide U that exposed every
inch of skin from neck to waist. Every inch of beckon-

ing skin. Burke realized his optimism had been premature.

Oh, God, he thought, *it's going to be a long evening.*

CHAPTER FIVE

THE CHAMPAGNE WAS EXPENSIVE and effervescent, the veal they'd been served at dinner had been cooked to a succulent perfection, and the orchestra was now playing the finest and purest of notes. Burke noticed none of this. Nor did he notice the rich appointments of the Copley Plaza Hotel—not the gilded ceiling, not the Waterford crystal chandelier, not the marble-top tables, nor the antique furniture.

In truth, his whole world had been reduced to a woman's back. Jill's back. Jill's smooth, cream-colored back, sprinkled with reddish-brown freckles and gold dust. The latter glittered provocatively in the right light.

Burke drew the glass to his lips and swallowed a portion of the chilled and tasteless champagne. Twenty-three, he mused sarcastically as he watched the man, a good-looking jock type from another law firm, brush Jill's back with his fingertips. That was the two-dozenth—give or take a feel—man to touch her. He'd never realized before just what open season it was on a woman's back. And all of the touching fell within the perimeters of propriety. It was the most natural thing in the world for a man to assist and guide a woman by placing his hand at any number of spots from neck to waist. In fact, hadn't he almost done it a half-dozen times himself? It was also apparently socially acceptable to lingeringly touch a woman for a fraction of a second during the course of conversation. As long as a man didn't salivate noticeably doing it.

Twenty-four. Burke watched as Charles Evans, dressed in a steel-gray tux and pink shirt, stepped to Jill's side and made the score an even twenty-four. Burke marked the event with another mouthful of champagne. Then checked his watch. He had been right. It had been a long evening. And it was growing longer by the minute.

"Cape Cod."

Burke inclined his head to the woman at his side, the woman he was supposed to be having a conversation with, though that presupposed that he was paying attention. Which he wasn't. "I beg your pardon?"

Harriet Cummings, a prominent corporation lawyer and an individual with the reputation of always knowing whom to call if you wanted to wade through the city hall's records at a run, pulled a gold case from her evening bag. "Do you mind?" she asked, indicating elegantly shaped cigarettes. Burke nodded that he didn't. "I said, I adore Cape Cod. Did you buy or rent a cottage there?"

"Rented," Burke said, his gaze once more magnet-drawn to Jill. She, too, glanced up. Their eyes grazed, then raced away as if they'd been caught in a naughty indiscretion.

"It's so nice to have you back practicing law."

"It's good to be back," Burke answered absently.

"I understand you and Jill McClain are involved..." Here, Harriet Cummings paused to light her cigarette. Burke's head jerked to attention. "...on the *Stroker* case." A curl of white smoke climbed upward through carnelian-red nails.

Burke felt foolish. "Yes. Yes, we are."

"It promises to be an interesting case. Every legal eye in Boston..."

Burke again tuned out the voice. And cast his legal eye once more on Jill. She stood in profile, but he could still see her back. It was then, as his eyes were traveling over the endless expanse of the ivory skin contained within the fashionable U, that the question came to him. What did a woman do for a bra when she wore a dress like that? Automatically his eyes lowered to the gentle swells thrusting against the gold-lamé fabric. Jill shifted her stance. Nothing. A woman did nothing. At the sudden realization of what he was thinking, a wave of self-disgust flooded him. Cresting on the wave were droplets of guilt. My God, what was he doing? In answer to the question, he amended the score to twenty-five.

Burke drained his champagne.

Just as Jill drained hers.

Was it her imagination or had every woman in the room singled out Burke? Even as she asked the question, she saw Harriet Cummings stroll away, only to be replaced by yet another woman. This one Jill didn't know, though she was tall and willowy and gorgeous. Just like... She refused to acknowledge Nicole's name.

"He's yummy looking, isn't he?" Ellen said wistfully at Jill's elbow.

Jill was irrationally irritated. "Remind me to teach you a new word Monday," she said, and stalked away.

Ellen's surprised eyes were almost the size of her augmented chest.

The evening progressed. Strangely. One moment, Jill and Burke seemed to withdraw from each other, the way they had for the past couple of weeks. It was a discreet distancing, both physical and emotional. At those times, Jill sensed a sultry, smoke-thick tension in the air. Did he feel it too? Or was she simply projecting her own feelings? Then, at other times, the old Jill and Burke renewed their acquaintance, the old Jill and Burke who knew how to talk and tease and be friends.

It was during one of these latter periods that Jill, fresh from a talk with Judge O'Halleron, eased over to Burke's side and said, "I thought there would be nothing left of you by now."

One of Burke's brows hiked upward.

"If Ellen tells me one more time how yummy looking you are..." she said, leaving the threat unfinished. "She's been devouring you with her eyes."

The comment caught Burke entirely off guard. He laughed. The sound was one-hundred-percent male. Jill's one-hundred-percent feminine heart flopped over. She cursed herself for the weakness.

"She thinks anyone with matching chromosomes is 'yummy.'"

"That's a distinct possibility," Jill said.

"Has she been surgically augmented again?"

Jill shrugged offhandedly. "Can you buy anything bigger than a size forty-two?"

"Why do women do that?" he asked seriously.

"Naturally not every woman's reason is the same, but I think it's fair to conclude that a good many women do it to be more appealing to men."

"But breast size has little to do with being appealing. There are a lot of things about a woman that are sexier."

Like what? she had the sudden urge to ask.

Like a perfectly flawless back, he had the sudden urge to volunteer.

The mood had changed again, this time evolving into an intimacy that neither had expected, that neither knew quite how to handle. And for that matter, neither knew how to break eye contact. Nor did either want to. Except that staring at each other was becoming more and more awkward as the seconds ripened into a mature silence.

In the background the orchestra began a slow song. People two by two, migrated to the floor. As they did so, they passed by, and around, the couple standing and gazing into each other's eyes.

Casting caution to the wind, Jill allowed herself the luxury of imagining what it would be like to dance with Burke. She imagined the feel of his arms around her; she imagined the feel of his body only inches from hers; she imagined that for the span of a dance they were a couple. A normal couple. She knew, though, that they weren't. Normal or otherwise. And that he had no intention of asking her to dance. She told herself that she really didn't want him to. It was best in view of her non-involvement policy. Yet she fantasized that she heard him ask her.

"Would you like to dance?"

She heard the words as clearly as bells ringing on a still day, though his lips made no movement. Fantasies were strange things, she was concluding when she heard the question again.

"Jilly, you wanna dance?"

The spell tumbled, wish over wish . . . and she looked up into the expectant eyes of Charles Evans.

"Wanna dance?"

"I, uh . . . sure," Jill said with a half smile. Her eyes briefly connected with Burke's. His blank eyes matched his expression. "Excuse me," she all but whispered.

Burke made no reply, but watched as Charles Evans guided Jill onto the dance floor. His hand caressed the middle of her back. It rested there as he took her into his arms. Burke had a flash sensation of what that hand must be feeling. Warm, smooth, soft skin. Skin soft like silk. Or intimate like whispers at midnight. He dismissed the thought. Just the way he shoved aside the thought that Jill, with her petite figure, and Charles Evans, with his medium height and athletically stocky build, made a nice-looking couple.

You could have asked her to dance, some part of his heart accused.

No, you couldn't, another part, presiding over emotional survival, answered.

Charles Evans stared down into Jill's face, said something, and she laughed.

Burke reached for another glass of champagne. His third. But who was counting? he sneered.

She danced well, he thought. Even at a distance he could tell that. The way her feet moved, the way her shoulders swayed, the way her hips... She danced well.

Evans's hand slid downward, to a spot just shy of the small of Jill's back. Exerting a pressure there— which Burke could almost feel—he turned her. As he did, the slit of her skirt parted. In that brief wink of fabric, Burke saw a shapely, silky leg.

He took another drink. A hefty belt. And went with the stream-of-consciousness thoughts bombarding his brain. *She'll marry a man like Evans someday—a bright, successful, handsome man—and have his kids. That's the way it should be. The way it should have been for me and... Did Evans hand shift lower? None of your business, Rawlins. None of your bus... Wonder what he just said to her. And what is she saying to him?*

Burke took another drink.

Evans's hand, not crudely but in the tradition of man making a move on woman, glided onto the rounded fullness of Jill's hip.

Just moments before Burke had wanted Evans to get his hand off Jill's bare back. Now he wished he'd return it. He told himself he had no right to wish anything, but he did.

The music trailed off. The dancing couples halted. Charles Evans's hand gradually, reluctantly, fell away from Jill's body. They spoke briefly. Laughed. Evans spoke again. Burke could tell he'd made some comment about Jill's dress. A compliment, no doubt. She thanked him.

The music, once more a slow song punctuated by the weary wail of a saxophone, recommenced. Jill started away from the floor. Charles Evans gently grabbed her arm. He spoke, then jerked his head backward toward the already slow-swaying couples. He smiled enticingly, temptingly. Irresistibly?

Burke drained his champagne, set the glass on a nearby table, and stepped forward. He told himself not to be impulsive. He then ignored his own command.

"C'mon, Jilly," Charles Evans was saying, "one more." He was tugging at her arm as he spoke.

Burke had the irrational—and strong—urge to physically remove Evans's hand. But he didn't. Instead, he said, "How about that dance you promised me?"

Jill's eyes flew upward. And met Burke's. His were a shade somewhere between jade and jealousy. Hers simply registered a shade of surprise.

For a minute it looked as if the trio had been frozen in space and time.

Finally a grinning Charles Evans unwrapped his fingers from Jill's arm and spoke. "Hey, if the boss wants to pull rank, it's okay with me. Just make sure my file indicates my cooperativeness. Better yet, my paycheck." His grin widened and there was a sense of expectancy on his face as he waited for the other two to join in the humor. They didn't. They were still staring at each other, totally oblivious to the fact that the rest of the world was inhabited. Giving his blessing to something already decided, Charles Evans said, somewhat awkwardly, "Yeah, sure. Go ahead. I'll catch you later, Jill."

Jill never remembered stepping into Burke's arms. It was just that one moment she was standing alone, while the next she was swallowed up by the most incredible warmth. A massive warmth. A sheltering warmth. A warmth that spun itself around her in fiery, candent threads.

He was so tall!

She was so petite!

Jill's arm strained to reach his shoulder. Burke's hand strained to stay away from her back. Instead, he clung to her side where the fabric acted as a buffer between bare skin. It was a clumsy arrangement, but one he considered necessary—the way he considered air and water necessary.

"You lied," she said, her eyes finding his after a few seconds. "You never asked me for a dance, so how could I have promised one?"

"So sue me for perjury."

"Know a good lawyer?"

They smiled at each other. Genuinely. With no barriers between them.

Playfully, Jill thought that she might not know a good lawyer, but she knew a lawyer who looked good. And felt good. That observation was followed by the thought that, if she wanted to be good to herself, she'd stop thinking along those lines. Those counterproductive lines. To put backbone in the issue, she deliberately let her eyes find the hand entwined with hers . . . and the wedding ring encircling the third finger.

It was just a dance, she reminded herself. Nothing more. Why then did the hand holding hers, the warm hand, seem like so much more than a casual dance partner's? And why did she simply want to melt against, and into, his strong body?

"I see the cuff links are holding," she said, chasing the thought away.

He muttered something inflammatory about cuff links and their inventor.

This time they avoided each other's eyes, as if fearing they'd see reminders there of those unsettling few minutes at his apartment.

"Are you tired?" she asked moments later. The question was addressed to the smartly tied black bow of his tux. "I mean, you've had a rough day. What with New York this morning and Boston this evening."

"Yeah," he answered. "I am tired."

She looked up, past the tuck of his neck and the square of his cleanly shaven jaw. The smell of a richly scented, tempting cologne reached her nose. "We'll leave whenever you like."

Like. He tried to ignore it but he liked the color of her eyes. He liked the fresh sweet fragrance that he was beginning to associate with her. He liked the way her gold dress swished in a faint, teasing rhythm.

He cleared his head of the disturbing thoughts. "Whenever. I'm with you."

Perhaps it was the height difference, perhaps it was the fact that they were tired, but more probably it was the fact that they were staring more than dancing, whatever the cause, Jill missed a step.

"Oh!" she gasped, grabbing the lapel of his tux. In a totally spontaneous act, Burke's hand tightened, shifted, grazing the bare skin of her back.

Hot!

The touch was the ultimate definition of hot. It seared, scorched, burned until its reality lay as ashes at their feet. From the ashes rose hunger.

Burke's eyes deepened to the color of smoky emeralds. Jill's darkened to the hue of an ocean in the hush of night.

Each waited, breathing suspended on an airy, uneven note.

He told himself not to do it, not to lay his hand full on her back, but, sweet heaven, he couldn't help himself! It was what he'd wanted to do all evening. Denying all wisdom, defying his will, his fingertips brushed her skin, easing ahead like scouts on a daring mission. She shivered. Or did he? Slowly, slowly, his eyes still fastened to hers, he eased the length and breadth of his hand against her back. At a spot shy of shoulder and straddling spine.

There was an unwanted sigh. A shudder. A falling from control. For him. For her. For both.

Jill's eyes fluttered. Somehow their thighs connected, and the tips of unconfined breasts skimmed against a solid male chest. Hearts raced. And for one brief, breath-held second, he lowered his eyes from hers to her lips.

Lowered.

Held.

Wished for...

"Your wife."

The word chilled like a ruthless winter wind. Burke's eyes flew upward...to those of... He scoured his brain

for a name. His brain responded with Ted. Yeah, yeah,
Ted Something-or-other. He worked with Harriet Cummings. Burke's brain volunteered, mockingly, the fact
that the music had stopped. He didn't dare ask it how
long ago. Instead, his eyes raced once more to Jill's.
Quickly, guiltily, he drew his hands from her and stepped
backward. The hand that seconds before had held her, he
jammed into his pocket. It still felt warm, Jill-warm.

". . . sorry," Ted Something-or-other was saying.

"Thank you," Burke answered absently.

"Glad you're back."

"Yeah. Thanks."

The man and his dance partner moved on by, leaving
Jill and Burke alone in a sea of people. Their eyes met.

Guilt. It flowed from every pore of his being. She
could see it as clearly as if it were written across his still-
smoky irises. And his eyes were smoky, smoky from a
hunger he'd felt for her. That was what hurt the most.
She now knew beyond a doubt that he was attracted to
her, yet that attraction had only the power to cause guilt.
Not joy. Not pleasure. Just guilt. Monumental, unadul-
terated guilt. And something more, something she saw
bubbling to life. Anger. Unless she was very much mistaken, he was angry with himself . . . and angry with her.
With himself, for wanting her; with her, for making him
want her.

"Burke . . ."

"I'd like to go," he said with a steely softness. There
was no doubt as to where. Home. Safe home. Home
where he could wallow in guilt and assuage it with anger.

Jill didn't object. She suddenly wanted out, too; out
where the night air could cool her fevered senses. With
Burke behind her, she stepped from the dance floor and

toward the door. She was through it and into the mo-
saic-tiled foyer of the hotel when she heard her name
being called.

"Jilly?"

She stopped, almost colliding with Burke in the process.

"Hey, you two aren't leaving, are you?" Charles Evans asked. There was an incredulous look on his handsome face.

Both Jill and Burke exchanged glances.

"Yeah," she said. "It's, uh . . . it's been a long day."

"I'm tired," Burke said, then added something about
New York and late planes.

"C'mon, you guys. It's early."

"No, really, we . . ."

"We'll see you Monday."

When it became obvious that the two were leaving,
Charles Evans half skipped to Jill's side. "Look, I was
going to ask you later, but . . . well, I have two tickets to
the theater next week. I was wondering if . . ."

"Charles, I don't . . ." she said, still slowly heading for
the door.

Sensing a rejection, the man added, "Why don't I call
you about it tomorrow?"

"I don't . . ." Jill stopped—her words, not her steps.
She couldn't turn him down so rudely. Charles was a nice
man, and she didn't want to hurt his feelings. She even
managed a smile. "Right. Call me."

Burke's hand snaked from behind and pushed open the
entrance door. Jill had a quick glimpse of a starched
white cuff against the black of tux and the tan of skin.
Dark hair swirled at the sculpted wrist. She also caught
a flash of a gold band. For the first time, the sight of it

caused a ripple of anger. *Good grief,* she asked herself, *just how long is the man going to wear the damned thing?*

At the hotel entrance, Burke gave the parking attendant a description of the car. During the wait, neither spoke. Minutes later, Jill pulled the car into the flow of Saturday-night traffic. The drive from St. James Avenue to Burke's apartment was short and, just as it had been the night they'd returned from Mary's house, silent.

Jill would have paid a large sum of money to know what Burke was thinking. For that matter, she would have paid a lot to unscramble her own thoughts and feelings. One emotion she felt clearly was frustration. She was attracted to him. He was attracted to her. It should be simple, but it was everything but. A sudden thought occurred to her: surely he could no longer deny the attraction. Could he? She glanced over at the man hugging the far side of the car. His face was stern, his features set. She sighed. Not only could he deny it, he probably still was denying it—at least on some plane of thought. This realization shoved her once more in the direction of anger. How long was the man going to grieve? She admitted, grudgingly, that hers was an unfair, an insensitive, question.

She also admitted that it was unfair how good his hand had felt on her back. This pushed the anger button once more, so that when he finally spoke, she answered with an irritation that matched his.

"Jilly?" He said the word in an almost snide tone.

She threw a quick glance in his direction. His eyes were waiting for hers. "So he calls me Jilly?" Her tone said, "Make something of it, buster."

"Are you going out with him?"

She shrugged, when in fact she hadn't the least desire to date Charles Evans.

"He isn't your type."

"Who said?"

"You did."

Their eyes locked. Neither could read what lay in such secret depths.

"Oh," she said finally and sheepishly.

Neither spoke again until she pulled the car parallel to the curb in front of Burke's apartment building.

He reached for the door handle, then hesitated.

"I, uh—" he brought his eyes to hers "—I appreciate your coming by for me."

She nodded, sending wisps of pale hair into delicate motion. "No problem." A lifetime passed before she swallowed and added, "Burke..."

"No," he said, his voice, his eyes, full of pleading. "Please don't."

She wanted to say, "We need to talk. Can't you see what's happening between us? Can't you feel it?" In the end, however, she said nothing. She simply watched as his eyes withdrew from hers, and he opened the car door and got out. Though he walked tall and erect, she could see the guilt sitting squarely on his shoulders. In fact, it was beginning to make permanent grooves.

It was illogical, it was irrational, it was nothing of which she was proud, but in that moment she hated Nicole Rawlins. Why, why, wouldn't she let Burke go? The answer was simple. The answer hurt. Nicole Rawlins wasn't holding on to him. He was holding on to her. Because he loved her.

TEN MINUTES after Jill pulled away from the curb, Burke had changed into running gear and had hit the Boston sidewalks. With no real destination in mind, he found himself on Newbury Street, where he jogged past elegant boutiques and expensive specialty shops that had long ago closed for the evening. The buildings, most old brownstones that were once home to high society, looked out through dark, sleepy windows at the stranger in their midst. Some, their doorways curved into yawning arches, even seemed to smile, understandingly and with the wisdom of the ages, at the stranger's restlessness. At a quarter to one, tired, sweat dripping from brow and limb, Burke entered his apartment. He deliberately moved Nicole's picture from the living room to the bedroom, showered, then fell naked onto the bed. He was still awake, however, at three o'clock. Dammit, he wondered, why couldn't he forget the feel of Jill's warm skin?

As Burke was swearing, Jill was tossing. She floundered and flounced, her white cotton gown alternately caught at her ankles and riding her hips, until the pale-morning. At three minutes after the hour of five o'clock, she dozed off and slept until early afternoon, at which time she awoke with a throbbing headache. As she took two aspirins, muted the ring on the telephone and slipped back beneath the covers, Burke once more took to the streets. He ran until he pulled a groin muscle, then limped home to a hot shower and another restless day and sleepless night.

Both he and Jill awoke Monday morning with a powerful irritability.

JILL'S HEELS STRUCK the hallway of Rawlins, Rawlins, Nugent and Carson, with a force that sounded like bullets spewing from a gun. Her lips were sliced into a severe slit and anger fire-danced in her blue eyes.

"Hi," Ellen said as she passed by. "Wasn't Saturday night fun?"

"I tried to call you yesterday," Charles Evans said.

"Do you have change for the Coke machine?" the receptionist asked.

Jill answered no one. In fact, no one's remarks had registered. Her full attention was on the papers in her hand. The red-pencil-corrected, words-marked-out, words-written-in, papers in her hand.

Without knocking, which was totally uncharacteristic, she threw open the door of Burke's office and stormed in. From his place behind the desk, where he sat scribbling notes with one hand and holding the phone to his ear with the other, he glanced up.

Angry. She was angry, he thought. On the heels of that came the realization she had never looked more beautiful. Her reddish-blond hair, in curls and held back from her face with turquoise-colored combs that matched her unstructured jacket, fairly bounced with energy as she moved, while her eyes shone a piercing, though pleasing, blue. Beneath the beige tailored blouse and beige skirt lay the back, the legs, the breasts that had been degrees of bare and braless Saturday night. The quick memory-image that Burke received in his brain led him to a silent curse.

It was a curse that Jill echoed. "What in hell is this?" She sailed the papers onto his desk. They fluttered, seemingly alive with their own irritation.

"Let me call you back," Burke said calmly into the phone. It was a calmness that piqued Jill's ire even more. With a twist of his wrist—his uncuff-linked wrist, Jill noted and hated herself for the memories that bombarded her—he replaced the receiver, stared briefly into Jill's flashing eyes, then down at the papers strewn across his desk. He recognized them for what they were: the only bit of work he'd done that weekend. "If I were guessing," he said, still in a voice that qualified as unemotional, "I'd say it's your opening speech to the jury."

"Wrong," Jill said in a frigid tone. "It's your opening speech to the jury. Oh, it used to be mine before your little red pencil went wild."

"You asked for my comments," he said, his own voice now slipping into the anger he'd nursed all weekend.

"I didn't ask you to rewrite it!"

"And I didn't re..."

"When did you do this?" she interrupted.

"What?"

"When did you 'give your comments'?"

"What has that got to do..."

"When, counselor?"

"Yesterday!"

A look of *I knew it* crossed Jill's face, and she sighed in utter disgust. "Oh, Burke, that's so contemptibly beneath you."

With that, she turned and marched from the room.

It took Burke exactly fifty-seven seconds to gather up the papers and limp into Jill's office. He found her standing and staring out the window.

"Are you implying what I think you're implying?" he asked, throwing the papers down on her desk. One sheet swooped to the floor like a glider coming in for a landing.

She whirled at the sound of his voice...and wondered if she was going to faint from the utter handsomeness of the man. His toasty-brown jacket, tan vest and brown slacks fit him to perfection, to heart-stopping perfection. With effort, Jill quelled her thoughts.

"And just what are you implying that I'm implying?"

"That I've allowed my private life to influence my professional life."

Jill saw her advantage...and, like a good lawyer, took it. "And just how is that possible? How could I be implying that your private life is influencing your professional one?"

"You know damned well what I'm talking about," he said, the fingers of one hand dipping inside his jacket to splay at his waist. "You're implying that what happened Friday night..." He stopped, realizing the corner he was trapped in, the corner he'd trapped himself in.

Jill moved in for the kill. "Just what did happen Friday night, Burke?"

She could feel the hurt the question caused, the guilt it stirred. For the briefest of seconds she felt sorry for him. But the second passed. Dammit, she was hurting, too!

He took an instinctive step backward. "Nothing," he said hoarsely. "Nothing happened."

"Liar," she accused, with a softness that took the sting from the accusation.

His face filled with a vulnerability that tugged at Jill's heart.

"Burke..."

"Don't!" he whispered. Turning, he walked—limped—from the room.

"Burke!" she called after him.

He didn't stop, he didn't answer, he simply fled. He had made it back to the safety of his office, but was only midway into the room, when the door burst open for the second time. He whirled around. Green eyes clashed with blue.

"I'm sorry, Burke," she said. "But you're not going to run away this time."

"What are you talking..."

"If you won't tell me what's going on . . ."

"Nothing's going . . ."

". . . then I'll tell you."

"Jill, don't . . ."

"You're attracted to me," she said, her innate honesty refusing to let her speak less than the truth. "And you're eating yourself alive with guilt because of it."

The words hung in the air, as threateningly as gray clouds in a blue sky.

From where she stood, Jill could actually see Burke's Adam's apple bob in a slow swallow.

"You're wrong," he said, the denial barely audible.

"Am I?"

"I just said you were."

"Then prove it," she said, walking resolutely toward him.

"W-what do you mean?"

She now stood directly in front of him, all ninety-one pounds of her.

"Just what I said. Prove you're not attracted to me." Standing on tiptoe, she slipped her hand around the back of his neck. "All you have to do," she whispered, drawing his lips to hers, "is not respond."

CHAPTER SIX

SHE TOOK HIM by surprise.

The result was that soft, stunned flesh met hers before he could react in any way. There were milliseconds of pliancy, milliseconds of a warm intimacy, glimpsed promises of what Burke's kiss could be like, before she felt his resistance. His lips stiffened, yet, curiously, took on a blankness. Likewise his body tensed, yet donned a passivity. A willed passivity. A strong-willed passivity. He did not pull away, however, when he most assuredly could have. Did it mean anything? Jill responded as if it did.

Her mouth moved surely, purposefully, against his. Ignoring his nonparticipation, she parted her lips and slow-drove them into his. In a tempting, circular, relentless rhythm, she seduced him with every bit of expertise and feminine wile she knew.

Don't, don't, don't! Burke chanted, steeling himself against a reaction. He told himself that he didn't want this kiss, that he hadn't longed for it all weekend, that he hadn't longed for it maybe even longer than that. One part of him asked why he didn't pull away, while another part tried to conjure up an image of Nicole. Brown hair, blue eyes. No, no! Nicole's eyes were brown. The blue eyes belonged to...

Jill moved closer, meshing her body with his until her breasts flirted with the breadth of his chest. She placed her right hand against his cheek. It felt smooth and warm and angular. Her fingers at his chin, she tilted his face downward at a more convenient angle to hers. Opening her lips even more, she deepened the kiss. *No!* he cried silently, while Jill mercilessly sent the tip of her tongue to tasting the seam of his mouth.

Even with his mouth suctioned to hers, he gasped. It was a raw intake of air. His hands knotted into tight, painful fists at his sides.

"Kiss me," she ordered raggedly against his lips and slid her tongue forward until it met his. It was half command, half plea. It was wholly irresistible.

With a deep-throated groan, Burke surrendered. He grabbed her shoulders and hauled her against him. Her breasts flattened against his chest until he could feel every fiber of her jacket and a small, hard button of her blouse—or was that the hard nipple of her breast? The latter thought destroyed him. Splaying one hand across her back he tangled the other, fistlike, in the red-blond thickness of her hair. Primitively. Almost punishingly. His mouth opened, wide, wider, and assumed the control she'd only moments before been exerting.

He couldn't help himself. He didn't try to help himself. He simply felt. God, was it so wrong to feel again? Everything masculine about him cried *No, no!*

His tongue darted forward, curled with hers, then plunged deep inside the cavity of her mouth. There, he stroked and washed the walls in sensual designs.

He moaned.

She moaned.

She coiled her arms more tightly about his neck. And came closer at the very moment that he sought to draw her closer. His hands ran the length of her back and intimately slid onto her hips. The secret place between her thighs sweet-throbbed; his maleness blossomed against her stomach. Hard and noticeably.

Jill felt her head spinning, swirling. She felt everything in her opening up—her mouth, her arms, her womb, her heart—to receive the fullness of him. She felt...she felt... God, she didn't know how she felt! Out of control. Wonderfully out of control! And she could feel Burke's loss of control, too. His kiss had turned deep and savage—fire and windswept fury. And God, she liked it!

Alive...alive... The words blared in Burke's head. Dear God, she felt so warm, so womanly, so *alive*!

Heads tilted, lips ground together, tongues clashed and claimed.

In the end, the kiss didn't burn itself out. It simply got too hot to handle. Physically and emotionally.

In the middle of the most sweetness, the most sensuality either had ever known, Burke tore his mouth from hers. Gasping, chests heaving, astonished at the intensity of the emotions ravaging them, they just stared. Wide-eyed, moist lipped. With their hearts bare and vulnerable. Ultimately, he released her. She stepped backward. As if claiming the space, the distance, to gain some perspective.

Perspective. The need for it was settling about Burke's shoulders, like cold chunky flakes of a winter snow. Slowly, and all too predictably, the guilt straddled his back once more. It was now magnified. Tenfold. A hundredfold. The look on his face, the look of confusion and defeat and self-loathing, knifed at her heart. Sweet heaven, what had she done?

Her trembling fingers rose to her lips, her already swelling lips. She worked her mouth, but no words came out. She took another step backward, then another, and suddenly she was running from the room…and from her supreme folly.

JILL SHUT THE DOOR of her office and leaned back against the hard wood. She closed her eyes. Her heart was still pounding a too-quick cadence, her body still tingling from Burke's kiss, and she was still feeling like a fool. A first-class fool. She had confronted the situation with her customary honesty, but where had it gotten her? In one irrevocable step, she had destroyed the relationship she and Burke had…with no promise of a new one to replace it. And she had single-handedly caused Burke pain. She'd seen it in his eyes, seen it in the tortured paleness of his face.

Pushing from the door with hands that shook, she headed for the expanse of windows and stood staring down at a bright, midmorning Boston. From twelve stories up, the people in the streets looked tiny, unreal, doll-like. They looked devoid of the spectrum of human emotions. Yet they dreamed, wished, hurt, cried, loved… Loved. Was she falling in love with Burke? She had no idea. She knew only that what she'd felt minutes before she'd never felt in any other man's arms. In fact, she'd never even come close.

Her fingers trailed to her still-wet lips. They were… bruised. In exactly the way her emotions were.

She was standing, fingers on lips, heart in throat, when she heard the door open. Snatches of hallway conversation darted in before the loud symphony of silence resumed. She didn't turn around, but she knew that Burke stood behind her. She felt him. Felt also a requickening of her heartbeat, a reheating of her body's warmth.

"We have to talk," he said. The words sounded as if they'd been laid bare until they were raw; bone, blood raw.

Jill glanced over her shoulder...met his eyes, his hazy eyes...and realized that one side of her hair had tumbled loose. Running her fingers through the mass of curls, she groped for the anchoring comb, but couldn't find it. She'd lost it. Where, she had no idea. Maybe...

"Here," Burke said, handing her the comb.

Their eyes touched briefly before she reached for the turquoise adornment. They clumsily avoided contact. "Thank you."

Turning, she gazed back out the window. With unsteady fingers, she threaded the comb's teeth through her hair and secured the renegade tresses. Burke watched, fascinated against his will, before stepping to her side. He stared outside with her.

"You, uh...you have...lipstick..." she said after a few seconds.

Burke looked at her and when she didn't reciprocate, he ran a hand into a back pocket and pulled out a white handkerchief. He wiped it across his mouth—once, twice—before repocketing the cloth. He vaguely wondered if her mouth was as tender as his.

For long seconds, time was but a canvas on which was painted emotions—bold, red streaks of uncertainty and regret, splashed with the cooler colors of doubt and frustration. And dominating all were the myriad black shades of guilt.

"As a lawyer, I, uh...I've been trained to deal in facts," Burke finally said, never taking his eyes from some distant spot on the far horizon. "Facts substantiated by evidence." He nervously shifted his weight from one foot to the other. "All the evidence points to the fact

that I find you—'' he swallowed and amended roughly
"—that I want you."

Jill said nothing. She didn't know what to say. She
knew only what she was feeling: a sense of relief that he'd
at last admitted to the attraction, yet a sense of pain that
it was hurting him to do so.

Suddenly, his laugh bounced about the room in a sharp
staccato burst of sound. "It's kinda hard to deny it when
I practically threw you to the floor of my office." Anger
once more informed his tone. Was it directed at him or
her? Probably at them both.

"Burke, it was my fault. If I hadn't . . ."

"It wasn't your fault."

"Yes, it was."

"It wasn't."

"It was!"

His eyes caught hers in a blistering glare. "Dammit,
Jill, you didn't force me to get hot and hard!" The words
were blunt, to both sets of ears. He rammed his hands
into his pant pockets. Jill wondered if the gesture was
meant to hide any lingering evidence of his response. His
voice was lower-pitched, though no more calm, when he
added, "I could have pushed you away. I obviously chose
not to."

Memories of minutes before assailed them. Jill remembered the way Burke's mouth had smothered hers,
the way his tongue, with its velvety roughness, had caressed her own, the way his male body, hard and full of
sensual strength, had pressed intimately, unashamedly,
against hers.

Burke remembered the incredible feel of her soft body
clinging to his, the way her lips were malleable, but mas-
terful, the way she wasn't afraid, or embarrassed, to show
her desire. She would be an aggressive lover—he knew

that—and he found that fact... He stopped himself short of the word exciting. It was too late, though. Guilt was already slithering through his body.

"I, uh—" Burke raked his fingers through his brown hair "—I have to be honest."

"Please do."

"I'm...I'm not sure of the reason...I mean, I'm attracted to you, but I don't know..." He hesitated, unable to express himself.

"Don't know what?" she prompted.

"I don't know if it's because I haven't..." He stopped once more and this time he swore. "How can you always be so damned honest?" he asked, knowing that what he had to say would hurt her.

"What are you trying to say, Burke?"

His eyes grazed hers. "Jill, I..."

"Just say it."

"I haven't been with a woman since...Nicole."

Jill let the words sink in, along with their implication. "And you aren't certain that the attraction you feel for me isn't simply because you just need a woman."

He felt some innate need to protect her, even from himself, and fought against the desire to pull her back into his arms. "Yes," he whispered.

The admission caused a dull pain in Jill's heart. She accepted the pain, however, squarely and with dignity. "I suppose that's a possibility, isn't it?"

He saw the emotions tearing at her, witnessed the prideful tilt of her chin and the honest square of her shoulders—the square of her dainty though strong shoulders. In that moment he'd never respected anyone more. He also admitted what he guessed he'd known all along: Jill McClain was a woman of substance. A woman a man could walk with, trust in and lean on, as the inconsistencies of life dictated.

"Jill, I . . . I don't know what I'm feeling." He sighed, adding irritably, "I don't want to feel anything. I don't want to have . . ." He stopped.

"Needs?"

"Yes!" he answered, his voice harsh, ragged, impatient with the humanness of his body. "Yes," he repeated in a calmer tone, "but I can't seem to stop them. I wanted them to die with Nicole, but . . ."

"They keep insisting on reminding you that you're alive?" Jill offered, hoping she'd scored at least a shallow point.

She had. His eyes said so. They said, too, that he rejected the easy excuse.

Burke drew in a deep breath, knowing that there was one more thing he had to say. It was the only thing he could offer Jill. Admitting it, though, would add one more layer to his guilt. "I want you to know something," he began. "I said that I may be attracted to you only because I hadn't . . ." He paused, drawing in a richer lungful of air. "The truth is that no one else . . . I mean, no other woman . . . I haven't felt this way with anyone else."

The words warmed Jill's heart. Even more so because she knew how difficult it had been for him to say them. "Thank you for saying that."

They stared into each other's eyes, both feeling the other's pain, both wanting to ease that pain.

"Jill . . ." he began, but couldn't find the words to convey what was in his heart.

"I want you," she said with her typical frankness. "I want you in my life. For one simple reason. I care for you." She smiled, sending her lips into a subtle curve. "I don't know when it happened. I just know that it did, that right this moment it's fact.''

Her honest admission disarmed him. ''Jill, I . . . I have nothing to offer you. I'm still tied to the past. I'm caught somewhere between being dead and alive. I'm neither.''

''Because you choose to be,'' she said bluntly.

''No. Because I deserve to be.''

Her smooth brow wrinkled. ''What does that mean?''

Burke glanced away, somewhere to a past that owned his soul. ''I killed my wife. If it hadn't been for me . . .''

''You can't be serious,'' Jill interrupted. ''My God, Burke, that's the oldest guilt trip in the world. Surely, you're too intelligent to believe . . .''

''It doesn't matter whether it's rationally true or not! It's what I feel. In the night. When I'm alone. When it's just me and those damned headlights that came out of nowhere! I should have done something, I should have seen it coming, I should have . . .''

''Died with her?''

Their eyes collided. ''Yes, dammit! Yes!''

''That's the stupidest thing I've ever heard,'' Jill said, her own emotions string thin and quivering. ''I never knew Nicole, but I can assure you she'd be livid to hear you say that! Love doesn't chain, Burke. It frees.''

Long seconds passed, with the electricity of passions popping in the air.

''Can't you see that you're paying for a debt that you don't owe?'' she asked at last. ''Can't you see that you're cheating yourself?''

''That's better than cheating you.'' Their eyes lingered, neither knowing what to say or do. Finally Burke whispered, ''I'm sorry.''

He was already at the door when Jill spoke. ''Burke?''

He turned.

"One of these days you're going to have to face the fact that Nicole's dead, that you're alive and that neither fact is your fault."

He said nothing. He simply stared at her for the span of an uneven heartbeat, then opened the door and disappeared

THAT AFTERNOON, tired and in need of inspiration, seemingly every employee of Rawlins, Rawlins, Nugent and Carson converged on the refreshment alcove at the same time.

"Sugar?"

"Yes, please."

"Could you hand me the creamer?"

"Yeah. Hey, where's the creamer? Anybody seen the creamer?"

"You're stepping on my foot!"

"This darned thing ate my quarter again!" Thud, thud, pound!—a fist walloped the Coke machine in the stomach.

Jill eased her way through the mob, headed for the coffeepot. "Hi," she said to Ida Tumbrello, who was just pouring out a cup of the murky liquid. "Any left?"

"Are you kidding? This stuff is so strong it reproduces itself."

"Still no one taking credit for making it?"

"Terrorist acts people will admit to; this coffee, no way."

Jill laughed and reached for a Styrofoam cup.

"See you later," the older woman said, forging a trail back through the crowd.

"Right," Jill answered, smiling at the ritual that she'd been told was almost ten years old. Every workday at four o'clock—not a minute before or after—since the death of Andrew Rawlins's wife, Ida Tumbrello had poured her boss a cup of coffee, carried it to him and had then spent the next ten minutes—not a minute more or less—discussing anything that came into their heads. Jill had often wondered if it was during these ten-minute sharings that Ida had fallen in love with Andrew Rawlins. Or had she always been in love with him? The question led her to thoughts of Burke. Had she always harbored these feelings—whatever they were—for him, but always kept them carefully hidden? Even from herself? She had no answer.

"Ooh, excuse me," Ellen said, now slinking through the crowd in a white sweater that looked as if she were packing a pair of Alps. "That soda looks yummy. Does anyone have a quarter I can borrow?"

All the men's hands rushed to their pockets.

All except one man's. Burke stood mesmerized at the sight of the woman pouring the coffee. He'd avoided Jill all day. Now he questioned the prudence of his decision. The impact of seeing her again after long hours had practically emptied his lungs of air. How had he worked beside her for so long and never realized how beautiful she was? How desirable?

As if sensing someone watching her, Jill glanced up. Her eyes instantly gravitated to Burke's. The solid ground beneath her feet seemed to shift.

"Will you pour me some coffee?" he asked, mouthing the words over the chaotic din. "I can't get through."

She nodded, poured another cup—were her hands trembling?—and wove her way through the throng. She almost collided with Charles Evans.

"Careful, Jilly!" Charles cautioned, his hand automatically grasping her shoulder. Burke's gaze shifted from her face to Charles Evans's hand. His stomach tightened.

"Sorry," she said, moving by. A few steps more and she stood before Burke. Handing him a cup, she said, "Be careful. It's—" their fingers brushed, causing their eyes to instantly meet "—hot." The word had all the consistency of vapor. As if choreographed to do so, eyes lowered to mouths.

Warm, she thought. She could still remember how warm his mouth had felt against hers. And how demanding. She wondered if it was her imagination or if his lips were a little swollen.

Soft, he thought. Silky soft and tasting of honey and passion. He wondered if it was his imagination or if her lips were swollen. My, God, had he kissed her that hard?

He forced his eyes back to hers. "How's the work going?"

She shrugged. "Okay. I just made some changes to my opening speech."

Her comment was just one more thing to make him feel like a heel. "It was fine. I shouldn't have..."

"No, you had several valid criticisms."

"Use what you want. Throw the rest out."

"Have we heard anything more about a court date?"

"No. Rumor has it, though, that we will soon."

"Good."

Charles Evans, a cup in his hand, stepped to Jill's side. He took a sip of his coffee and grimaced—whether from the taste or the tongue-searing heat wasn't quite clear. "I'll pick you up around seven-thirty."

Jill's eyes briefly met Burke's before shifting to the man beside her. "Fine," she answered with entirely no enthusiasm, though she did make a noble effort.

"What did you do to your leg, Rawlins?" Charles Evans asked.

No response followed. Burke's attention was fully on Jill. She sensed it and refused to look up.

The heat of Charles Evans's stare finally penetrated Burke's consciousness. He glanced over. "What?"

"I saw you limping. What did you do to your leg?"

"Pulled a muscle."

"Running?"

"Yeah."

"I did that once. Trying to get into shape for summer camp when I played college football." For the next couple of minutes, they listened to graphic details about Charles Evans's once-wrenched muscle. "Well, gotta get back to it," he finally said, strolling off... after a smile at Jill.

A silence descended.

"I, uh... I'm going to the theater with Charles."

What she didn't say was why. He had cornered her at noon, repeated his offer of the theater, and when it appeared she was going to turn him down, he asked if it was because of Burke. Jill had been stunned. What did he mean? He had shrugged, saying that it had crossed his mind that "the two of them might have something going." What with "leaving the dance early and all." The "and all" Jill was afraid to question. Had Charles Evans sensed an undercurrent? Not wanting a rumor started, she had agreed to go. She couldn't help but wonder if she had agreed for one other reason, as well. A human reason. A feminine reason. Had she hoped to make Burke jealous?

"When?" Burke now asked.

"Wednesday evening."

"I see." His voice didn't sound quite full. "Actually, that's good. I, uh...I hope you have fun." Their eyes held for seconds longer before Burke added, "Well, I've got some phone calls to make."

Jill watched as he walked—limped—off. Why hadn't she noticed the limp before? But then, the time she'd spent around him that morning had been occupied with either anger or...

"Burke?"

He turned.

"Does it hurt? Your leg, I mean."

"Yes," he answered. In some secret-dark corner of his mind, he admitted, however, that the pulled muscle hurt little compared to the knowledge that Jill would be spending Wednesday evening with another man.

WEDNESDAY NIGHT it rained—marblelike drops that splattered against the windows in a restless rhythm. Or was it just that he was restless? Burke mused.

Barefoot and bare chested, wearing only a pair of worn jeans, he forced himself to stop roaming the room. He plopped onto the sofa. Picking up the latest issue of *The New Yorker*, he paged through it, bypassing an article on the economy and one on foreign markets. With a deep, impatient sigh, he chucked the magazine back onto the coffee table. He reached for the remote-control panel of the TV.

Black brightened to color, silence to sound. A woman with shapely legs touted the miracle feel of a brand of panty hose. She was followed by a man selling microwave-oven popcorn. They were followed by a man from outer space who knew all about fabric softeners. Burke said something foul about commercials and silenced the TV. He rose and headed for the kitchen. There, he poured himself a bourbon and water, only the second he'd had since returning to Boston.

Slanting the glass, the amber liquid flowed over tinkling cubes of ice to reach his lips. It was smooth but strong. It was also ten-thirteen, he noticed, his eyes catching the hands of the watch on his uptilted wrist.

Was she home yet?

He downed the drink, trying to wash the question away. Shutting off the lights in the front of the apartment, he walked to the bedroom where he shucked his jeans and slipped into a hot shower. Minutes later, wet and warm, he stepped out of the frosted-glass stall, grabbed a towel and a bottle of liniment, and headed for the bed. Haphazardly drying his body, he threw the towel to the floor in a careless heap and dropped onto the mattress.

Bending his left leg at the knee, he uncapped the liniment and poured a puddle of white into his palm. He leaned against the headboard and spread his bent leg. With a firm pressure, he rubbed the lotion into his sore, but healing groin muscle, the moistness plastering the dark hair on his inner thigh into copious swirls. The pungent-smelling cream penetrated deeply, leaving behind a menthol-cool feel.

It felt good. Real good. Only one thing might feel better. A woman's hand—Jill's hand—doing the rubbing. The thought brought an instant reaction. His breath quickened. His heartbeat raced. His body became aroused. All of this was tailgated by a rush of guilt, which he tried to absolve himself of by deliberately focusing on the picture of Nicole that stood on the nightstand. It was his favorite picture of her, taken only months before she'd . . . died. It was her smile that made the picture so special. That so-full-of-life smile. She'd been happy. He knew he'd made her happy. He knew also that she'd loved him. That realization suddenly filled him with a satisfying warmth.

"Love doesn't chain. It frees."

The words reminded him of the woman who'd spoken them, and Burke glanced at the bedside clock. 10:33 p.m.

Was she home yet? Would Evans kiss her good-night? Was he at this moment tasting her lips? Was he . . .

Burke swore, rolled from the bed, and flung back the covers. Impatiently, he shut off the lamp and slid between the cool sheets. He planted his hands at the back of his head and dared himself to think an unwanted thought.

Darkness. Rain. Thunder. Lightning that ribboned across the tender sky. Ticktock . . . ticktock . . . ticktock . . . Burke angled his head toward the clock. 10:34 p.m. Only one minute had passed. One damned minute!

"I want you in my life. For one simple reason. I care for you."

"Jilly?"

"So he calls me Jilly?"

Jilly . . . Jilly . . . Jilly . . .

A vision of Charles Evans's mouth closing over Jill's jumped into Burke's mind. He swore again. Without turning on the lamp—somehow the darkness sanctioned the act—he yanked the phone from the hook.

Thunder growled a low, provocative sound just as the phone rang in Jill's bedroom. Not bothering to switch on the lamp, she stretched, searched for and finally found the receiver. Her gown, short and pale-yellow satin, rode upward to almost the middle of her stomach. She wore nothing beneath it.

"Hello?"

Her voice carried through the line like a breeze tiptoe-
ing over the top of a lacey-leafed tree. Burke's stomach
suddenly felt weightless. "Hi."

Jill's stomach jumped into her throat. "Burke?"

"I, uh . . . I'm not calling at a bad time, am I? I mean,
Evans isn't still . . ."

"No. He's already gone."

Relief flooded Burke, but disappeared as quickly as it
had come. Had Evans kissed her? Had they done more
than kiss? Evans was a healthy, normal male . . . A
thought crossed Burke's mind. With Evans's athletic
build, and Jill's petite size, would he hurt her if they
made love? A large man would have to be careful not to
crush her with his weight. And at the moment his body
fitted itself into hers . . . Burke deliberatcly fought the
powerful thought. "I was just calling to tell you that we
have a court date."

He told himself that the news could have waited till
morning at the same time that disappointment claimed
Jill. *Stupid, why did you think he was calling? Because
he was jealous?*

"I got a call right after you left the office this afternoon."

"When are we scheduled?" she asked, trying to sound
professional.

She didn't have to sound so damned businesslike,
Burke thought, suddenly irrationally disappointed that
her response hadn't been more that of a woman than a
lawyer.

"Monday. Bright and early."

"That's good. We're ready."

"Yeah, we'll beat their socks off."

"Might even win the case while we're at it," Jill teased.

Burke's lips slanted into a smile, and he turned to his side. The sheet wrapped tightly around his hips. It hurt. But then the slightest pressure hurt these days. He ran his hand the length of his bare stomach and, tugging, loosened the sheet. "Yeah," he answered, but the word struggled to escape.

There was a sudden silence.

Was he in bed? He sounded all warm and mellow and stretched out.

Was she in bed? She sounded relaxed and sultrily lazy. He wondered what she slept in.

Burke cleared his throat and told himself to hang up. Instead, he asked, "How was the play?"

Jill pushed to her elbow, her hair fanning about her like a red and gold, delicately spun curtain. "Good. It was a musical comedy."

"One of those where the guy breaks into song just as he's about to kiss the girl?"

The question sent funny feelings scurrying over both bodies.

"Yeah."

There was another awkward pause filled with the sound of thunder.

"It's raining here," he said, still resisting hanging up.

"It's raining here."

Burke grinned. "What a coincidence, huh?"

Jill rolled once more onto her back and smiled, the corner of her mouth curling into the pillow. "Yeah." The silence pleaded that he wouldn't hang up just yet. "How's your leg?" she asked, assuring a few more seconds.

The question made him aware of the hot menthol still stinging his thigh. It also reminded him of what he'd earlier wished Jill's hand was doing—rubbing, stroking,

caressing... He banished the thought to a hot spot in hell.
"Almost well. I'll be running again by the weekend."

"Good. Where do you run?"

"Anywhere. I just start out."

There was another interlude of silken silence. This time
it was too uncomfortable to tolerate, especially after the
wayward turn of Burke's last thought. He also had the
incredible urge to ask if Charles Evans had kissed her
good-night. If he didn't hang up, he couldn't guarantee
that he wouldn't.

"Well, I'll let you go. Just wanted to tell you about the
date."

"Thanks. See you tomorrow."

"Yeah. Good night."

"Good night."

For a long time after Jill hung up, she lay quiet and still
in the dark. One moment she told herself that what he'd
called about could have kept till morning; the next, that
she was just trying to give herself hope where none was
really justified.

Burke, on the other hand, tossed and turned, relent-
lessly and in madman fashion. At a point near midnight, his anguished cry filled the room. It was the
tortured sound of entrapment. He was caught somewhere between the cool, distant memories of Nicole and
the warm, vibrant memories of Jill.

FOR THE REMAINDER of the week, the rain continued.
Sunday morning, however, the sun rose with a brilliance
that was dazzling. Bostonians thanked it by flocking out-
of-doors.

Her hands still dirty from potting a blood-red geranium, Jill had just stepped from the patio and back into
the kitchen when her doorbell rang.

"Coming," she called, wondering who it could be. She wasn't expecting anyone. And it was only—she glanced back at the clock on the kitchen wall—nine-thirty-five.

Opening the door the inch slit that the chain lock allowed, she peeked out. She saw a man, bare except for a pair of blue nylon running shorts and a pair of running shoes. The latter were even sans socks. Jill's immediate impression was of lots of tanned skin, a mass of dark chest hair and sweat everywhere.

The man peered back through the slit . . . and waited.

Jill unlatched the door and pulled it open. She looked up into Burke's moss-green eyes.

"Don't ask me what I'm doing here," he said. His breathing was still wild from running and, combined with the seriousness with which he spoke, made his delivery as eloquent as any ever exhibited by statesman or orator.

In truth, he had no idea why he was there. He had just started out running. Somewhere along the way, he'd realized he was running to instead of away from something. He was running to Jill. He didn't want to analyze why. He didn't want to make a big deal out of it. He didn't want to feel guilty because of it. He just wanted to see Jill. Surely there was nothing wrong in just wanting to see Jill...on a pretty Sunday morning...when he was feeling good.

"If I can't ask you what you're doing here, can I at least ask you to come in?" She was smiling. It was a smile that she felt all the way to her soul because, suddenly, the Sunday-morning sun shone brighter.

Burke grinned as he hiked both hands to his hips. "Yeah. You can ask me in." He stepped in as she stepped back. "I promise not to puddle on the floor," he said, referring to his sweat-drenched state. "I also promise to stay a safe distance from your nose."

"Did you run all the way from your apartment over here?" she asked in disbelief. Involuntarily, her eyes scanned his wide chest. It was glistening a bronzed color beneath the sheen of perspiration. The chest hair was wet and matted and almost begging her to touch it. The sight did curious things to her stomach, all of which she blamed on the small breakfast she'd had.

"No, I took a cab part of the way," he teased. "Of course, I ran it, McClain. It's only five, six miles."

"Only?"

"Piece of cake."

"Looks like a piece of coronary to me."

"Don't let the . . . gasping fool you," he said still gasping. "C'mon, let's go," he said, when he caught his breath.

"Go?"

"Come run with me."

"But I . . ."

"C'mon, you promised."

Jill remembered the discussion they'd had at Mary's. "I think that was sort of a loose arrangement along the lines of maybe someday we'll run together."

"Well, let's firm it up."

"I'm not dressed." But then, neither was he, she thought as her stomach did funny, turnover things.

"Go trade the jeans for shorts."

"I'm dirty," she protested, holding up a hand. "I was potting some flowers . . ."

"Trust me. You'll be dirtier."

She hesitated. "Burke, I . . ."

"I'll take it easy with you." The words had an intimacy that both chose to ignore. When she still stood riveted to the same spot, Burke ordered. "Go, woman! My muscles are cooling!"

Twenty minutes later, Jill thought she was going to die. Her breath felt like a knife slashing at her chest, and her legs felt like... her legs felt like nothing. They had gone from aching to paining to numb. Dead numb. Let's-bury-these-legs-and-get-it-over-with numb.

"I quit," she gasped, stopping, slouching her shoulders and heaving in place.

Burke, too, stopped. "Yeah, me, too," he agreed. "We'll walk back." As he spoke, he bent at the waist, hands to knees, held the position a moment, then raised himself and started walking in small cooling-down circles.

Jill noticed that he gave in to his left leg. "Did you hurt your leg again?"

He glanced up, sweat running off and down his forehead. "It's okay. Probably should have taken it a little easier the first time out, though."

"You're an idiot," she said.

"Flattery, McClain, will get you nowhere."

Both smiled into the glare of the sun.

Burke noticed that Jill's blouse clung to her sweat-dewed body. In fact, he could see the outline of her bra. He could also remember the feel of her breasts against his chest. They had felt good and no amount of wishing they hadn't could change that fact. Not even Nicole could change that fact.

Jill noticed that Burke's shorts were so wet across the back that they were plastered to his rear. In front, they were... She tried not to notice what they were in front. She could remember, however, and very vividly, what his front had felt like flush against her own. The words satisfyingly hard came to mind.

Burke kicked his feet.

Jill fiddled with her hair. Her damp hair. In fact, it was so damp that it was frizzed.

"I know now why you don't see runners with loose long hair," she said, trying to drag the moist strands from her face.

Without thinking, Burke reached out a finger and shoved back a wisp from her exercise-reddened cheek. Her skin was hot...sweet...soft. They both felt the touch as if it were the most intimate contact. Burke's eyes tumbled into hers. They were blue...deep...so deep a man could lose himself and never care. He swallowed...and lowered his eyes to her mouth. Her provocatively curved, woman's mouth. Which he suddenly longed to do all kinds of manly things to.

Time stopped. Bodies pulsated. The smell of desire and sweat permeated the air.

"Did he kiss you?" Burke heard himself asking and couldn't have been more stunned if he'd just asked someone to shoot him. Suddenly, the answer to that question mattered more than he could have ever believed possible.

"What?"

Burke's finger inched nearer her mouth, almost touching the corner now. "Evans. Did he kiss you?" he repeated hoarsely.

Jill's stomach felt gutted—at Burke's nearness, at the question. "No," she whispered, shaking her head. The action brushed his finger across her mouth. Both would have agreed that the touch was devastatingly sensual.

"But he tried, right?"

"Burke..."

"He tried, didn't he?"

"Yes."

The obvious question was, Why did you stop him? It was what was on the tip of Burke's tongue; it was what Jill expected. Both were, therefore, surprised when, after what seemed like an eternity's delay, he simply stepped back and asked, "Will you drive me back to my apartment?"

She did. On the drive, she settled on an answer as to why he hadn't asked the question. The answer was simple. He'd known the answer and didn't want to hear it. It was too uncomfortable for a man fighting to stay uninvolved.

"Burke?" she called softly after he'd thanked her and opened the car door.

He swiveled in the seat, his eyes meshing with hers.

"I didn't let him kiss me because he wasn't you."

The comment produced the anticipated reaction. "Jill, please . . ."

"I won't fight Nicole for you, Burke. But neither will I make it easy for you to turn your back on me."

The words hung in the air like a silken threat. Burke heard it, felt it. And couldn't honestly say that he wanted Jill to make it easy.

CHAPTER SEVEN

MONDAY MORNING, in one of the hallowed rooms of the red brick courthouse, the trial began. With only slight exaggeration, it could have been said that all of Boston was in attendance. Publicity-seeking reporters sat alongside professionally interested lawyers who tried to hide their envy that they weren't at the head tables. Sprinkled among these were friends and family of those involved and, liberally lacing all of the above, were spectators who were there simply out of curiosity. All eyes were riveted on the principal players.

David Gareth Stroker III, wealthy looking and with the quiet arrogance of class, was wedged between his top-gun counsel, while Alysia Wainwright Stroker, looking proud and regal, sat between Jill and Burke. In the front row, and highly visible, sat the Strokers' former servant, a woman in her mid-twenties who was pretty despite the modest way she was dressed. Beside her, looking more like a princess from a fairy world than a child from an illegitimate union, fidgeted a beautiful blond-haired, blue-eyed little girl. The young woman's lawyer had obviously pointed out the advantages of keeping the child in the press's eye.

"All rise," the stocky, basso-voiced bailiff recited. "This court is now in session. The honorable Timothy O'Halleron presiding."

Burke and Jill exchanged a quick glance. Jill gave a thumbs-up sign of victory, which Burke returned along with a smile. By tacit agreement, the discussion of personal issues would be shelved for the duration of the trial. That fact, however, did not keep Jill from remembering the fur-matted chest hidden within the perfectly fitting navy suit, nor did it keep Burke from recalling the long hours he'd lain awake the night before, mulling over Jill's parting remark. More and more, he wasn't certain that he wanted to turn his back on her. More and more, his body longed to intimately know hers. More and more, he longed for some tenable reconciliation between the past and the present. "Longed for" as in "desperately needed," because he felt on the precipitous edge of an emotional explosion.

For the next two days, the plantiff and the respondent waged war seating a jury. That done, on the third day, at 11:32 a.m., Jill rose to deliver her opening remarks.

Burke, his elbow on the chair arm, his fingers at his lips in a casually studious pose, watched as she approached the jury box. Her hips swayed slightly, femininely, beneath the white linen skirt, while the copper-colored blouse, nestled beneath a matching white jacket, managed to stunningly contrast her eyes and to memorably complement her hair. The latter was piled atop her head. She looked chic, professional and—he squirmed in his seat—sexy. Burke banished the thought before it could sear his body and soul.

"Ladies and gentlemen of the jury," she began with a confident, I-know-we're-going-to-be-friends smile, "the task that lies before you is a serious one. In the course of this trial you will be asked to examine your heart, your conscience . . ."

Conscience. The word, as though it were hollow, wafted weightlessly on the air and reached the ears of the man sitting three rows from the back in the spectators' gallery. He wore a wrinkled, gray plaid shirt and a sullen expression. He'd arrived at the courthouse early that first trial morning so there'd be no chance of his not getting in. He'd wanted to see firsthand the woman with Tommy's eyes. He'd wanted to see visible proof of Tommy's imperfection. Each day since, he'd returned, as if watching her, hearing her, somehow bleached his own imperfections.

Conscience. The word bumped and banged around inside Leonard Larimer's mind. He should feel remorse for what he'd done to Mary McClain. He knew that. As a human being, he knew that. As the son of a saintly woman who'd more than once crammed conscience down his throat, he knew that. He knew, however, that, like one anesthetized to pain, he felt no guilt. Not even the tiniest bit. In fact, he could never remember feeling guilty about anything. All he'd ever felt, and in staggering proportions, was the unfairness of life. Beginning with a mother who'd never loved him, a cousin who'd taunted him with his perfection and a series of other life events whose sole purpose seemed to be to take the wind out of Lenny Larimer's sails.

"You bring on your own problems," he could hear Maude Larimer pronounce in that sanctimonious way she had. God, how he hated her when she said that!

Like it was his fault he wasn't smart and couldn't get good grades and go to law school. Like it was his fault he hadn't died a hero in some stupid war. Like it was his fault that once he'd finally made the police force, they'd kicked him out without even listening to his side of the story and forced him into one barely-make-ends-meet night-watchman job after another.

"It was your fault they fired you, Lenny. Your temper's too quick. You shouldn't be anywhere near a gun. Your fault . . . your fault . . ."

Leonard Larimer thought of the gun back in his cubbyhole apartment. His lips curled into a twisted semblance of a smile. His mother wouldn't approve of the gun. Which was just fine with him. He liked to do things she wouldn't approve of. And he knew for certain she wouldn't approve of what he'd done to Mary.

His mind scurried back to weeks before when he'd found the letter in the bottom of the box. His first reaction had been, Why hadn't she told him that Tommy wasn't perfect either? That reaction had soon given way to the need for revenge. He'd wanted to hurt his mother the same way she'd hurt him. All these long, lonely years. The only way he could do that was to hurt Tommy. Which meant he had to hurt something Tommy loved. And God, how he'd loved Mary McClain! Because of that, he had to make her suffer. It wasn't his fault. She owed him. Tommy owed him. His mother owed him. Life owed him.

Hell, maybe even Tommy's little blue-eyed bastard owed him!

Leonard Larimer's attention was snagged by the words Jill was just then speaking, with such eloquence: "... You owe it to my client, you owe it to all women, you owe it to yourself, to listen openly and fair-mindedly to the evidence the plaintiff presents and then render your verdict intelligently, conscientiously." Her hands on the railing, she leaned forward. She paused for the proper effect. "That's all Alysia Wainwright Stroker asks of you, all the state of Massachusetts asks." Another dramatic pause and then she pushed from the railing and headed back to her seat.

A hush descended over the courtroom, as if no one wanted to sully what had just been said.

Finally, Judge O'Halleron broke the silence. "Since we're so near the hour of twelve, we'll break for lunch. Court will resume at 2:00 p.m. sharp."

A pound of the gavel, an "All rise," and the courtroom erupted into chatter.

"How about some lunch?" Burke asked, turning to Alysia Stroker and Jill. Both women agreed and, after Burke and Jill closed their briefcases, the trio started wading through the crush of people.

"Mr. Rawlins, what are your opinions on the trial so far?" asked a reporter as he stuffed a mike beneath Burke's nose.

"No comment," Burke replied, unruffled.

"Ms McClain, feel you've got a sympathetic jury?"

"No comment," she answered.

"You just addressed the jury," the reporter persisted. "What kind of vibes were you getting?"

"Please," Burke said nicely, but firmly, "could we pass by?" Jill felt Burke's hand at the small of her back as he nudged her and their client on through the throng. His hand felt wonderfully comforting, in a way that no man's hand ever had. It also evoked tingly sensations. "By the way, McClain," Burke added, leaning close to her ear, "your opening remarks were excellent."

She glanced up, ignoring the fact that he was so very near. Or at least giving it a good try. She smiled with a sudden impishness. "Thanks. I had some good input from a colleague."

Burke responded with a grin.

Then, as if both simultaneously remembered what had happened following their argument over her speech, their smiles faded. Their eyes lingered where those smiles had been. Briefly lingered. Before each pushed the past away in favor of the present.

Borne along by the sometimes shoulder-to-shoulder crowd, they were approaching the door of the courtroom when Jill felt the sharp jab of an elbow to her arm. She jerked her head upward...to a thick, square chin that could have used a shaving...to gray eyes that could have used softening. Jill had the immediate impression of cold. Ice-cold. A cold that marched like an army of icicles up and down her body.

"Excuse me," she said politely, not knowing whether it was he or she who should apologize.

"That's all right," he answered in a low, slow, gravelly voice. "Nobody's perfect."

Jill was never conscious of lowering her eyes from his—they were almost mesmerizing—but seconds later, she stood in the courthouse hallway, now swamped by news-craving reporters.

"Ms McClain, what do..."

"Mr. Rawlins, do you think..."

"Mrs. Stroker, are you pleased..."

"Ladies, gentlemen," Burke said, "could you let us through?"

With some pushing and shoving, the three finally emerged on the other side of the press crowd, which was now surging toward Mr. Stroker and his legal entourage with the same unending zeal.

"It's going to get worse before it gets better," Burke said of the press coverage.

Jill agreed. As she walked on down the hall, she threw a quick glance back over her shoulder. The man in the gray plaid shirt was gone. For some crazy reason, she felt relieved.

BY THE END of the week, Jill realized just how prophetic Burke's statement had been. And not only about the press. The entire trial apparently was going to get worse before it got better. Judge O'Halleron, in his ultraconservative posture, had banged his gavel so repeatedly, and had sustained so many of their opponent's objections, that the plantiff had not been allowed to introduce all of its evidence concerning the rape. The net result was that it was simply Mrs. Stroker's word against her husband's, and with the defense making David Gareth Stroker III out to be such a philanthropist, such an outstanding member of the community, it was hard, if not impossible, to accept him in such a brutal role.

"Damn!" Burke said Friday afternoon when O'Halleron's gavel had pounded the trial to a close for the weekend.

"Do we have problems?" Alysia Stroker asked.

"No, no!" both Jill and Burke assured. "None we can't handle," Jill added, placing a comforting hand on the woman's arm.

"You're paying us to worry," Burke said with a smile that melted Jill's heart if not their client's. "You just go have a restful weekend and be back here first thing Monday morning."

Minutes later, Burke and Jill watched their client walk away, surrounded as usual by a sea of reporters.

"Damn," Burke repeated. "I understand O'Halleron's position, but..."

"...Damn his position," Jill filled in.

"Exactly," Burke agreed, adding, at the sudden loss of Jill's attention, "What's wrong?" His eyes sought out the object of her interest. It was the Strokers' former servant, today in court without the child. The young woman's eyes looked fully into Jill's, then skittered away, almost nervously. Shouldering her handbag, and without glancing back, she started for the door. "What was that all about?"

"I don't know," Jill said, "but that's the second time today I've found her staring at me." Even as she spoke, Jill became aware of the man in the gray plaid shirt. He, too, was making his way toward the door. His eyes were cold-burning into hers. "Then again, maybe I'm just being paranoid."

"What do you mean?"

"The guy at the door, the one in the gray plaid shirt, he's been watching me all week, too."

Burke glanced across the room, but caught only a glimpse of a broad back as the man disappeared through the door. His eyes shifted back to Jill. Just as hers shifted back to him. Some carefully bridled emotion slipped its reins. "There's no mystery to that," he said, his voice lowering to a rumble. "Every man in court has been watching you."

The words bound her in a gentle captivity. "Have you?" The question was direct and typically Jill.

"Yes." The answer was direct and atypically Burke. Somewhere in the back of his mind, he told himself that he'd been spending too much time with her. Another part of his mind told him he wasn't spending enough time with her. Not in the intimate way he'd like. In the end, guilt rained down, but more in a shower than the deluge he'd come to expect. The guilt he did feel was offset by the relief he felt at speaking the truth.

Jill simply felt the strong need to be kissed. Because of that, she unconsciously moistened her bottom lip with the tip of her tongue.

Burke's eyes heated and hazed.

"At least O'Halleron's consistent." A voice cut through the sultry moment.

Jill and Burke jerked their heads around. Strangely, both were grateful for Andrew Rawlins's intrusion. Their attention quickly reverted to the trial. It was only later, as Jill drove home alone, that she allowed Burke's remark, and the look in his eyes, to penetrate her thoughts. The memories brought an afterglow that hugged her body in its rich, golden arms. Small though it was, she had scored a victory. If Burke walked away from her, he wouldn't do so totally unscathed.

FRIDAY NIGHT, all day Saturday and well into Saturday night, Jill studied trial transcripts, looking for any way to get the edge over their opposition. She and Burke spoke once by phone, but the conversation stayed well within the perimeters of business, possibly because Andrew Rawlins was present at Burke's end, possibly because Burke wished it so. The latter thought depressed her.

By Sunday afternoon, Jill needed a break, both from the case and from thoughts of Burke. She decided to check on Mary whom she'd called several times during the week only to get no answer. One thirty-minute drive and several ringings of the doorbell later, she used her own key and entered the house. She found Mary in the attic, knee-deep in boxes and dust and memories. A musty smell of the past filled the air.

"Let me guess. You're having the world's biggest junk sale," Jill said, bracing herself on the skinny stairway and poking her head through the opening in the floor.

Mary jumped, sighed in relief, and smiled. "Hi," she said, feeling love and pride in equal proportions the way she always did at the sight of Jill. "And I'll have you know, this is not junk," she said with a careless swipe of her hand that left a sooty smudge on the end of her nose. "It's first-class memorabilia. That's why I'm carefully boxing it and moving it over to Rob's."

Jill slipped through the hole and into the small room that was used solely for storage. "You mean your possessions can live with him without benefit of marriage, but you can't?"

"Don't start on me," Mary teased with an ear-to-ear grin.

Jill returned the smile. "You look wonderful," she said, adding, "I've been worried about you."

Mary gave an uncomfortable laugh. "C'mon, you know I always go a little crazy toward the end of school."

"That isn't for quite a while," Jill pointed out.

"So I got a head start this year." Eager to drop the subject, she said, "I'm feeling wonderful. Really, I am." Now that the nightmare is over, she added to herself. She tried not to let her thoughts travel in that direction, though she couldn't help but wonder where her hard-earned five thousand dollars was . . . and what kind of person would be so inhumanly cruel. She also wondered how he'd found out something that she, and her parents, had worked so hard to keep a secret. But the whole ugly mess was over. She was packing it, and the past, up just as she was packing up her things and transferring them to Rob's house. Only she wouldn't take the malignant part of the past with her. The move, the marriage, was going to be a new beginning, and she refused to give voice to the niggling worry that blackmailers—God, what an ugly word!—were notoriously greedy people. "I'm feeling wonderful," she repeated, because it felt good to say so and because saying so kept dark thoughts at bay.

"Want some help?" Jill asked, folding her jean-clad legs onto the floor in an Indian-style position.

"Do I look stupid? Of course, I want some help." She pushed an empty box forward with her foot and nodded toward the columns of old paperback books. "Here, start with these and then you can sort that junk—that memorabilia—behind you."

Both women giggled.

"I tried to call you this week."

"I've spent a good part of it over at Rob's."

"That's what I figured." Jill frowned and blew the dust off a yellowed mystery novel. "Do you ever throw anything away?"

"Sure. Those little wires that you tie the bread wrapper with. I can't figure out anything to do with them."

"And you can this antiquated copy of *Murder at Midnight*?"

"Have you ever seen another copy of it?"

"No, but . . ."

"I rest my case." On the heels of that, and with an enthusiasm that bubbled like champagne in her veins, she added, "You want to go shopping for a wedding dress with me next Saturday? I thought maybe just a knee-length dress, a chiffon or a silk, in a pastel color. Do you think I'd look better in pink or blue?"

When there was no answer, Mary glanced up from the bric-a-brac she was packing. Her eyes met the tear-glassed eyes of Jill.

"I love you," Jill said, smiling sheepishly at her own sentimentality. "I don't think I've said that in a long time."

Mary's heart constricted into a tight knot. "Why now?" she asked in a voice grown husky. She remembered exactly the last time Jill had told her she loved her. Just the way she remembered every time she had.

Jill shrugged. "I don't know. It just seemed real for the first time—that you and Rob are getting married, I mean." She looked embarrassed, but was too honest not to add, "I have these crazy, mixed feelings all of a sudden."

"What do you mean?"

"I want you and Rob to be happy, you know that, but it suddenly seems as if I'm losing you. It's just been us for so long." She wiped her hand across her runny nose. "This sounds like I'm not happy for you, Mary, and I really am. I swear it," she added, as if genuinely perplexed by her emotions.

Mary leaned forward and placed her palm against Jill's cheek. It felt warm, and a single tear ran beneath her fingers. She fought the urge to take her in her arms and comfort her like a moth... She stopped. She had never allowed herself to acknowledge the word. Silently or aloud. It was part of the bargain she'd made. "I love you, too. And you're not losing me."

As Mary knelt looking into Jill's sea-blue eyes, her own eyes glistened. She'd fight every devil in hell if need be to keep her secret safe. Nothing, no one, must ever be allowed to destroy Jill's feelings for her. And if Jill knew the truth...

"Sisters forever?" Jill asked with a tentative smile.

"Sisters—" the word was always comparable to cutting out her heart with a rusty knife "—forever." Mary forced her hand from Jill's cheek. Deliberately she went back to packing. "Now, are you going shopping with me?"

"Yes," Jill answered, relieved to have the subject once more emotionally neutral. "I think you'd look pretty in blue. Maybe even a soft lavender. Or what about..."

They were lost to girl talk, clothes talk, wedding talk.

"How's the trial going?" Mary asked during the first lull in conversation. "By the way, I planned on going to the trial Friday after school, but a parent stopped by unexpectedly." Mary seldom ever attended Jill's court sessions—usually they conflicted with her own work schedule—but she had stayed away from this case primarily because of the illegitimacy issue...and because of the madness happening in her own life.

"I wish you could have, but I understand."

"I did see your picture in the paper. You looked annoyed."

"I was. The press was badgering my client. As to how the trial is going," Jill said as she continued stacking books into the box, "the answer is somewhere right next to nowhere."

"Problems?"

"Not if we could hide the judge's gavel. He won't let us introduce some valuable material about the rape. Alysia Stroker has a sister we want to testify, but the defense, and Judge O'Halleron, insist that anything she says is simply what Alysia Stroker said to her, which is true, but—" Jill sighed "—it's been a frustrating case. All the way around."

"How so?" Mary asked, starting to stuff another box with fruit jars.

"It's just that...it's just that it's reminded me how we human beings love to make things black and white, and how things never really are. You know what I mean?"

Mary's hands paused ever so slightly. "Yes. I know what you mean."

Jill gave another deep, reflective sigh. "I don't know, Mary. My heart goes out to Alysia Stroker and to the former servant...Paula Keszler, I think her name is. And the child. Here Rawlins, Rawlins, Nugent and Carson are defending Alysia Stroker and, if we win, she'll be awarded a huge settlement. But what about Paula Keszler? Doesn't she deserve something? After all, she did have the man's child. And what about the child?"

"What about her?" Mary asked, falsely busying herself with packing.

"She is the product of an unwed union..."

"You make it sound so sordid," Mary interrupted.

"It's certainly no social stigma to be illegitimate anymore, but it's bound to be something of a burden to carry. Plus, there's no question that the child's the product of a notorious trial. No, the child has her own set of problems now and deserves some kind of compensation."

"Surely all that'll be addressed in the next trial," Mary said, straining to keep her voice natural.

"Oh, yeah. I can't help but wonder, though, why Paula Keszler's waited this long to identify the father."

"Maybe she saw the money slipping away and..."

Jill frowned. "No, I don't think so. She doesn't look money hungry to me." Shrugging, she added, "Who knows? I wonder if she was eventually planning on telling the child who her father was."

"Maybe she didn't want her to know," Mary said, suddenly feeling the cloying heat in the attic. Why hadn't she noticed how hot it was up here before?

"Does a parent have the right to decide that? Surely the child should know who her mother and father are, if for no other reason than the genetic problems that can arise. I mean, what would happen if—" Jill stopped at the sight of Mary's pale face "—Mary, are you all right?"

Mary smiled faintly. "It's just a little warm up here. Aren't you a little warm?"

"No, but..."

"How about a soda?"

"Sure," Jill said, concerned. "You stay here and I'll go get us two."

"No, I'll go..."

"Stay put. I can scramble down faster than you."

"Is that a reference to my age?" Mary teased, feeling better now that the subject had changed.

"No, just a testimony to my shrimpy size."

A few minutes later Jill returned, bearing canned drinks and an oscillating fan. Within a short time, giggles were once more filling the air.

"Well, I've gotta run," Jill said just as the sky was turning the gray of gloaming. "Want me to take my box down as I go?"

"Yeah, just set it anywhere downstairs."

"Okay," she said, throwing in the last of the books, scrapbooks and photo albums that were piled behind her. As she did so, a black-and-white photograph, age worn and faded, fell onto the floor. Jill picked it up...and stared down at a young man, short in height, wide in smile, who was dressed in spanking-new military khakis. She turned the picture over. "Who's Tommy?"

The cola can clinked against the floor, and a brown puddle spread into a fizzing lake. Immediately the two women tried to contain it with old rags that had previously been used to fight the dust.

"I've got it," Mary said, her voice strong only because she willed it so.

"It's no big deal," Jill said, assuming that the tension in the air had to do with the spilled drink. "The cola didn't get on anything," she said as she sopped it up with her rag. "So who's Tommy?"

Mary forced herself to glance down at the snapshot. It was a snapshot she'd seen a thousand times, one she'd carried in her wallet for all the youthful years of her adult life. "Tommy... Wilson. He, uh... he used to be a neighbor in Shawsheen."

"I don't remember him."

"No... no, you wouldn't," she said, deliberately averting her eyes. "He died in Korea and his family, his aunt, moved away shortly afterward."

Satisfied completely with Mary's explanation, Jill negligently tossed the picture into the box with everything else and hoisted the cardboard monster into her arms. "Well, I'll phone you next week."

"Right," Mary answered, and watched as Jill negotiated the stairs.

"Bye," called Jill.

"Bye," Mary replied, closed her eyes and slumped back against the wall. Her heart was pounding so hard that it hurt. Or maybe the pain was nothing more than the accumulative effects of deception.

Downstairs, the phone was ringing. As fast as she could with the box in her hands, Jill hastened toward it, knowing that Mary wouldn't even hear it, let alone reach it in time. Bracing the box on the back of the sofa, she grabbed the receiver.

"Hello?" she said breathlessly.

There was a slight pause. "We need to talk about your daughter again," the low, slow, gravelly voice said.

"You have the wrong number," Jill said politely and recradled the phone. Fitting her hands once more beneath the box, she lifted it and sat it by the front door. She then opened the door and stepped out into the night. In no way did it cross her mind that she'd heard the caller's voice before.

LATER THAT NIGHT it rained, a slow, drizzling, lazy kind of rain that streaked windows in wet and wistful messages. Burke lay in bed trying not to think of Jill, Jill lay in bed trying not to think of Burke, while both their bodies betrayed them with heavy, aching needs. Rob sat pouring over some business reports that he'd promised himself he'd finish before calling Mary. Mary sat on the sofa staring down at the picture of Tommy Wilson. It had taken a long time, but the hurt of his loss had healed, leaving behind only a pleasant memory of a fine young man's love.

When the phone rang at a quarter to nine, she smiled, tossed the picture onto the coffee table and reached for the receiver.

"Hi, darling," she said without preamble, "did you finish the reports?" Whether it was the long pause or the raspy breathing that first alerted her, Mary didn't know. She knew only that a black, cold fear crawled up her spine. She swallowed, low and hard, and tried to speak. "Who... who is this?"

"I saw her, Mary," the low, slow gravelly voice said. "I even spoke to her at the courthouse."

The fear changed pace. It now chased up and down her spine.

"No," she whispered, suddenly sick at her stomach to think he might have been near Jill. Not her Jill near something so... vile.

"It'd be so easy to tell her."

"You promised," Mary pleaded, knowing full well he'd never made any such promise. Had he intended to play this game all along?

"I've been thinking. I don't think five thousand's enough. I want another two, Mary."

"I don't have another two thousand!" she shrieked. She felt the ugly, jagged petals of hysteria blossoming into a dark flower. "I gave you all I had!"

"Get it," he said curtly. "By Friday."

"I can't..."

"Then I'll just arrange a little talk with Jill."

"Listen," Mary said, her mind whirling for a solution, "I, uh...I'm selling my house. If you could wait..."

"I've waited a lifetime, Mary. Friday. Same place. By three."

"No, listen," she pleaded, grasping the phone until her knuckles turned white, "I could give you more..."

Click. The dial tone whirred in Mary's head. It was joined by the heavy pound-pound of her heart that echoed sharply in her ears.

This time, there were no tears. Calmly, she replaced the receiver and stared vacuously into space. Finally she quietly lay down on the sofa and drew her knees to her chin in a fetal position. Slowly, she began a monotonous, chilling, rocking motion. There she lay, long after the rain stopped, long after the phone rang and rang and rang Rob's call, long after the nausea in her stomach had eased to a dull pain in her head.

THE NOTE CAME at the eleventh hour of the trial and as Jill was feeling more helpless than she'd ever felt in her life. All week the trial had gone badly for the plantiff, and Thursday afternoon, with only both sides' closing remarks left, Jill had been reduced to her last legal option. She was praying for a miracle. It came in the form of a slip of paper handed her by the bailiff. With a frown, she glanced behind her. Her eyes met those of Paula Keszler.

Giving her attention once more to the paper in her hand, she unfolded it and read the message. Jill's heart leapt. She forced herself to read the message again, more slowly, just to make certain she hadn't misread it. She hadn't. Looking over at Burke, who wore a quizzical expression, she passed him the note and, scraping back her chair, stood.

"Your Honor, the plantiff would like to call one last witness."

Judge Timothy O'Halleron, with his stern brown eyes, his long, pointed, russet-colored beard and his black judicial robes, looked more like an eighteenth-century Quaker than an instrument of the law. "Your request is highly irregular, Ms McClain."

"Yes, sir. The plantiff appreciates that fact, but something vital has just come to our attention."

"Is the witness you want to call in court?"

"Yes, sir."

Every eye in the courtroom, especially those of the defense, began scanning the sea of spectator faces.

"Your Honor, the defense objects."

Jill's eyes sought Burke's. His prayer entwined with hers as they awaited the judge's ruling.

It came after a long, contemplative silence. "Overruled."

Both Jill and Burke let out an audible sigh.

"Call your witness, Ms McClain."

"Your Honor, the prosecution calls Paula Keszler to the stand."

Low murmurs undulated like sea waves across the room. Moments later, Paula Keszler, her eyes wide, her hands trembling, sat in the witness chair.

Jill walked slowly toward the young woman, smiled her most reassuring smile and said, "Ms Keszler, I want to ask you only two questions. Is David Gareth Stroker III the father of your child?"

"Yes," came the hushed reply.

"Speak up, Ms Keszler," the judge admonished.

Paula Keszler quickly glanced in the direction of the man giving the steely-timbred command. Her gaze returned to Jill. "Yes," she said in roughly raised compliance.

"Ms Keszler," Jill said, choosing her words carefully, "were you and David Gareth Stroker III ... lovers?"

Silence. Followed by a "No."

"Ms Keszler, please speak ..." Judge O'Halleron began.

"No!" she cried, then lowered her voice. "No, we were not lovers."

"I'm afraid I don't understand," Jill said, understanding exactly what she was doing. "You say your child is his and yet you say that the two of you weren't lovers. How can that be?"

The courtroom was dead silent; everyone awaited the answer.

Paula Keszler looked up and over at the socially prominent, the personally powerful, defendant. Fear danced across the irises of her gray eyes. Then, proudly, fearlessly and in a voice that carried the width and breadth of the room, she said, "He raped me."

The courtroom burst into chatter. Judge O'Halleron hammered his gavel.

"Ms Keszler, I'm curious," Jill asked. "Why haven't you come forward before now?"

This time there was no hesitation. "Because he threatened me."

The courtroom went wild again. Judge O'Halleron went wild with his gavel.

Exactly forty-nine minutes later, at three minutes of five o'clock, the jury returned its verdict. It found in favor of Alysia Wainwright Stroker. At the reading of the verdict, chaos reigned supreme. Reporters converged, family converged, lawyers, those connected with Rawlins, Rawlins, Nugent and Carson, and those not connected, converged. Hugging and handshaking became the order of the day.

In a matter of minutes, with laughter and talk and shouting engulfing them, Burke and Jill found themselves facing each other. They smiled.

"We took it right to the wire, counselor," Burke said.

"It was about to fall over the wire," Jill answered, her face radiant.

His smile widened, her smile widened, and suddenly she was in his arms, all sixty inches of her pressed tightly against all six-plus feet of him, his hands splayed across her back, her hands against the nape of his neck. Bodies blending, they hugged triumphantly. Pulling back, their eyes met. Like swimmers from high, treacherous cliffs, blue plunged into green, green into blue. Their smiles vanished.

Whether it was the exhilaration of their victory, the adrenaline speeding through their bodies, or simply feel-

ings that had been too long suppressed and denied—
whatever the reason, their senses heightened to an al-
most-unbearable state. Smells of cologne and perfume
intoxicated to the point of faintness, eyes inhaled images
of the other's face, ears devoured every shallow nuance
of breathing. And bodies burned, blazed, raged with a
passion that was so palpable it was almost a taste on the
tongue.

Because of their surroundings, because he was burning to cinders, Burke slowly released her. Because of their
surroundings, because liquid fire sizzled in her veins, she
stepped from his arms. Neither, though, could break eye
contact.

"Mr. Rawlins, how do you feel?" a member of the
press asked.

The word horny sprang to Burke's mind.

"Ms McClain, were you surprised?"

"Yes," she answered weakly, adding to herself, *I had
forgotten how wonderful his arms felt.*

"Do you think the verdict will have any effect on future rape-within-marriage cases?"

The seriousness of the question forced Jill and Burke
to unlock their gazes.

"Uh, yes, as a matter of fact," Jill began to explain.
Burke followed suit. Once again, their private life was
placed on hold. And there it stayed for the next hour as
they fielded questions from the press.

At 6:00 p.m., the two of them made their way to Jill's
car, which had been parked in a nearby underground garage.

"You sure you don't mind giving me a lift?" Burke
asked.

"No, of course not."

Both avoided looking at each other. Both walked discreet distances apart. Both bodies were taut with restraint. Burke felt on the sliver-thin edge of the explosion he'd sensed coming. Jill just felt Burke in every cell of her being. Along with need. And desire. And some warm feeling that kept ribboning in and out of her heart.

Within minutes, they were inside the car. Still without looking his way, she started the engine. She cupped her hand over the floor shift. Before she could slip it from Park to Drive, Burke's hand covered hers. Quickly. Spontaneously. Without imprisoning thought. For long seconds, with her heart pounding a too-fast rhythm, Jill just stared at the hand blanketing hers—at the suntanned skin, at the dark hair curling over the cuff of the white shirt, at the vein almost visibly throbbing at his wrist. Slowly her eyes traveled the length of his navy jacket, over the width of his shoulder, up to his silvery-green eyes.

He, too, was staring. At her hair piled atop her head in a way that left her neck open and vulnerable. At the man-eating blue of her eyes. At the curve of her lips. At her incredibly soft-looking lips. Her lips that were beckoning, calling, pushing him over the explosive edge.

Suddenly he tumbled.

Groaning in abject defeat, Burke wrapped his hand around the back of her neck, pulled her forward and crushed her mouth with his.

CHAPTER EIGHT

AT LEAST ONCE in every human being's life is born the moment when thought is the captive of feeling. As Burke's lips met Jill's, his moment was born. God help him, Nicole forgive him, guilt be damned, he had to have Jill's mouth or die! With that elemental thought, he kissed her deeply and savagely.

His lips were commanding and desperately seeking. Caught off guard by the power of his kiss, Jill leaned forward and anchored her hand against his chest. She parted her lips beneath the persuasive pressure of his. Her immediate acquiescence fired his blood until it was a scalding liquid need pumping through his restless body. He felt the need gravitating to the most supremely male part of him. He hurt. He ached. He wanted her. As always, and out of habit, he cursed his reaction, and yet, curiously and for the first time in a long while, he also treasured it.

Placing both hands on the satin skin of her neck, he pulled her closer. Her breasts were soft orbs plumped against his chest. Her nipples peaked impertinently. His chest was a solid hard wall that strained against her.

Fast and furiously, slow and leisurely, he took her sweetness and, when he took all that he thought he could without bruising her lips or causing his body to explode with desire, he took more because there had been altogether too many long nights without knowing the infinite mystery of a woman.

Long, sensually quiet moments later, both Burke and Jill gasped for air. Their lips tore far enough apart that breathing was possible, yet touch was still maintained. At least between bottom lips. Eyes closed, Burke rested his forehead against Jill's. Both hearts pounded wildly, like stallions stampeding over dry, barren earth. At last, heartbeats slowed. Yet still they didn't pull apart.

"Burke..." she whispered against his lips, sending tickling, tingling shivers of motion purling across the flesh of his mouth. The sound also sent shivers of molten emotion lapping over his body. He shuddered.

"Shh..." he answered as he started to nibble and tease the tender skin of her lower lip. He pulled it inside his mouth and gently worried it with his teeth. He didn't want to talk, he didn't want to think, he just wanted to feel. He just wanted to kiss her.

His teeth bit and nipped. His tongue flicked across the fullness of her lips, imprinting them with a slick shiny wetness. The same tongue darted into the tight corner of her mouth before outlining the feminine curves of her upper lip.

His hand slid beneath her chin and tilted her head upward. Flirting with the seam of her lips, he eased his tongue forward. The tip of his met the tip of hers. The sensitive points touched, rubbed, stroked. The tip of hers danced with his; his curled around hers. She opened her mouth for him to come inside. Maddeningly, he didn't. Instead, he withdrew his tongue entirely and settled his lips back on hers. He kissed her softly, slowly, teasingly, until her head lolled back against the seat in abject surrender. Languidly, he pulled his mouth from hers and opened his eyes.

God, she was beautiful, he thought as he watched her tawny-lashed eyes slowly drift open, too. Her eyes were blue...and smoky with passion. In the split of a second, fully aware that the devil guilt might demand payment, he made the decision.

"Burke..." she tried again.

He interrupted her by placing his fingertips at her lips. "Let's celebrate our victory in court."

She hesitated before nodding. "Okay," she said finally, though it was obvious she'd rather have discussed the intimacy they had just shared. "What do you have in mind?"

"Steaks and champagne." He paused, meaningfully, and as his eyes darkened to jade moons at midnight. "At your place."

HAD SHE MISUNDERSTOOD? she thought two hours later as they sat across from each other at her small table. Had she read into his suggestion of dining at her place more than he'd intended? When she remembered the sultry look in his eyes on first seeing her when she'd walked back into the kitchen after releasing her hair from its topknot, she thought no. She thought no again when she remembered the moment they'd accidentally bumped into each other while preparing the meal. The blatant desire that had shimmied across bodies and stabbed deep into irises had been obvious. At least she'd thought it had been. Now she didn't know. Maybe she was the only one who'd grown so weak she could hardly stand. How else could she explain the fact that Burke had made no further attempt to touch her in any way?

"Would, uh...would you like something else?" Jill asked, laying her fork on the side of the almost untouched plate of food. The action produced a clatter that jarred her dancing-on-edge nerves. "I think there's more..."

"No. No, thank you," Burke answered, swallowing the last bite of his steak. It had been a hard-won battle of man over beef, but finally he'd gotten it down a throat that seemed to grow tighter by the minute. Just the way another part of his body was growing tighter and tighter and... "Everything was good," he said in a cloudy voice as he shifted in the chair.

"Yes," she agreed, running her finger up the stem of a champagne glass. An almost-empty champagne glass. The tiny sparkling bubbles, which she fancifully imagined were laughing at the adolescent awkwardness the two adults were exhibiting, had been about the only things she'd been able to choke down.

"You didn't eat much," he pointed out.

She shrugged and smiled. "I wasn't hungry. I guess the day was too emotional." Interestingly, the comment brought to mind thoughts of the kiss, not thoughts of the trial.

The same thoughts jumped into Burke's mind, where they played careless havoc and caused that part of his body already tight to grow even tighter. He swallowed. "Yeah."

"I, uh... I wish I had some dessert to offer you, but..."

"I don't need anything," he said, silently adding, except you. *God, do I need you!* He shifted in his chair again, trying once more to ease, or at least to accommodate, the escalating ache.

She laughed nervously. "I don't either. I'm gaining weight as it is."

The feel of her body drawn flush against his flooded his mind—rounded breasts a man could hold in his hands, a small waist that a man's hands could span, hips that flared in a pattern that kindled a man's imagination. "You're perfect." His voice was husky and as warm as sun-heated bourbon. The look in his eyes was as potent as a straight shot of the same drink.

Jill felt her body tremble. And burn wickedly hot in places she couldn't ignore. *God, Burke, say something, do something!*

Jill, help me! I don't know how to play these stupid dating games. I've been a married man, for God's sake!

Shoving back her chair, Jill said, "Why don't you go into the living room? I'll just set these dishes in the sink." *Hold me. Take this plate out of my hands and hold me until I stop trembling.*

Burke raked back his chair and stood. "I'll help you." *I want to hold you. So bad. God, I need to feel your body against mine!*

"No, I can do it," she said, her eyes traitorously going to his lips. *Kiss me. Until I'm senseless. Until you're senseless. Until tonight has turned into tomorrow.*

His eyes had traveled to her lips. "I don't mind helping." *I want to taste you again. And again. And then make love to you. Do you want me to kiss you? Make love to you? Make love. What would it be like to make love to a woman other than Nicole?*

"No, really. I can do it. I'll only be a minute. Why don't you pour us the last of the champagne?"

Looking both reluctant and relieved, he did as she suggested.

A short time later, Jill entered the living room and found Burke staring out the window. One hand was buried in his pant pocket, the other nursed the champagne glass. His beige suit jacket lay discarded over the back of a white velvet chair, while his tie trailed across a matching white sofa. Everything else in the room was white, too, except for apricot-colored carpeting that complemented the strips in the acquamarine-apricot-white wallpaper. Jill felt as washed out as the snow-pale furniture and hastened toward her glass of champagne that sat bubbling and beckoning on the coffee table. She picked up the glass and downed a generous amount of the straw-yellow liquid.

Burke turned at her entry. Their eyes locked.

He once more had the feeling of having just stepped onto a narrow ledge of a very tall building. He also felt the blood thickening in his lower body. He briefly wondered if she could see the physical evidence of it. He decided that he didn't give a damn.

She once more felt the quickening of all her feminine senses. Dark hair taunted from the vee of his white shirt, along with a slice of tanned skin. His shirtsleeves were rolled negligently upward to reveal the same coiled, dark-brown hair. Suddenly she wanted his hair-dusted arms about her so badly that her eyes blurred with tears. She also felt her thinly held control toppling.

"What do you want from me, Burke?" she whispered, her body hot, her body cold, her body in need of his.

"What do you want from me?" he countered.

"That's a cop-out," she accused, stepping toward the alabaster mantel and presenting him her back. Her hair, gleaming a burnished gold in the room's light, flowed like a silken waterfall to her tiny waist. Burke had the strong urge to drown himself in it. "Besides," she added, taking another mouthful of champagne, "you know what I want."

"What?" The word was blunt, bold, yet braided with brittle threads of vulnerability.

Jill glanced back over her shoulder.

"Say it," he demanded roughly.

For endless seconds the only sound in the room was the fast-beating of two hearts. That and the tread of destiny.

"All right," Jill answered in a voice as subtle as the sunset that had splashed the April sky in color only hours before. She swallowed low in her throat and answered honestly. "I want you to take this glass out of my hands, tangle your fingers in my hair, kiss me silly and senseless, then carry me to the bedroom and..." She stopped. Simply because there wasn't air enough in her lungs to continue.

Time beat its trapped wings between hesitation and hope.

Slowly, his eyes never leaving hers, Burke pulled his hand from his pocket and, bending at the waist, set his glass on the coffee table. He started toward her, halting only when he stood over her. His height required her to bend her neck and look up. "And what?" he whispered in sensual challenge.

"... and make love to me." The words seemed nothing more than a mouthing of her lips. Her suddenly dry lips.

Burke watched the formation of the words, watched as her lips opened and closed, watched as her tongue moistened away the nervous dryness. Without a word, he slipped the glass from her still-curled fingers and set it on the mantel with a clunk. Turning back to her, he whispered, "Like that?"

"Yes," she sighed.

With infinite tenderness, he wove his fingers through the cascade of hair at her temples. "Like that?"

"Yes."

His thumbs at her cheeks, he tilted her chin. Slowly lowering his head, he brushed his mouth across hers. "Like that?"

"No."

His lips settled for a more committed, though still quick kiss. "Like..."

"No," she whispered, pulling his lips down onto hers.

This kiss he intended to be slow and melting. Instead, the sealing of their mouths ignited fires that neither could control. Groaning, he urgently clamped his mouth on hers. Burke's tongue rushed forward to join hers, filling her mouth the way he longed to fill her woman's body.

Standing on tiptoe, Jill wound her arms about his neck and simply hung on as white-hot heat blazed in every cell of her body.

"Jill... Jill... Jill..." he chanted as his mouth released, reclaimed and frenziedly explored hers over and over again. "I need you," he whispered against her mouth. "God, I need you so much." Tearing his lips from hers, he yanked her swiftly against the muscular length of his body. He buried his lips against the soft, fragrant column of her neck. His breath was moist and warm as it fell into the shell-like contour of her ear. "I'm afraid. Sweet God, I'm afraid." And there was fear in each honestly spoken syllable.

"Of what?" Jill asked, her breath penetrating the thin fabric of his shirt and heating his shoulder. Her heartbeat thudded a dissonant rhythm against his.

"Of needing anything this badly." His hands shook as they slid down her back and cupped her hips. He pulled her flush against his need. And rubbed the vee of her thighs back and forth against him. He groaned at this heightened torture... but didn't stop it. In truth, he couldn't stop it. "God, Jill, I hurt... so bad." The confession was ragged, rough, wrung from him in a way that tore at Jill's heart.

"I know," she said in a tattered tone as she slipped her hand between their bodies. It unerringly found its target.

"Oh, Jill!" Burke groaned as her hand spread over the thick, hard, swollen heat of his need. His hand clamped hers more tightly to him, while his body trembled under the weight of her caress.

In that moment she would have given him anything. She certainly intended to give him everything she had. And for it, she was asking nothing in return. She harbored no illusions. This was not to be a night of shared love, for they had not spoken of love. Only need. Burke had said only that he needed her. Not even that he wanted her, but that he needed her, as man needed woman. She'd be his woman. She'd give him what he needed—she would please him—because she needed him to need her, and because she needed him as badly as he needed her.

"Make love to me," she whispered, moving her hand to become the bold aggressor that no man, especially one who'd lived in abstinence for a year and a half, could resist.

Groaning, Burke lifted her into his arms.

It should have been clinical, Jill thought moments later as they stood by the side of her bed in the golden glow of the lamp. Each of them undressing in hasty preparation for going to bed and making love should have been sexually clinical. In her dreams, Burke had always meticulously undressed her, then himself. Or he'd encouraged her to undress him. But in reality, haste was in the air, bidding them to hurry, hurry. In a way that should have been clinical.

But it wasn't.

Because of the emerald heat in his eyes as he watched every move she made.

Because of the way he invited her to watch every move he made.

Because along with haste, there was something else in the air—some unnamed emotion neither wanted to consider.

Unbuttoning her blouse and rolling her shoulders from it, Jill tossed the garment to the floor. Matching her, Burke unbuttoned the shirt he wore, tugged it from his pants and slid his arms from the endlessly long sleeves. Jill watched as his chest lurched forward, wide, strong, matted in dark spirals of hair that she fiercely longed to forage her fingers through.

He waited until her skirt had been unfastened and lay, a navy-blue puddle on the carpet, before reaching for the buckle of his belt. She slid the pure-white satin straps of her slip over her shoulders and it, too, slithered to the floor at her feet. Her eyes lifting to his, she reached behind her and released the snap of her bra as he released the snap of his pants. The metal zipper rasped a sharp, sensual sound in the silent room. Both hesitated, then removed that article of clothing. Her breasts fell forward; he pulled his pants down hair-covered striated-muscled legs.

At the sight of her round, rosy-crested breasts, Burke's breathing shallowed until he felt faint. At the sight of his maleness straining against the cotton of his briefs, Jill's body flushed with a heat so profuse she felt it as bright pink color in her cheeks.

Deliberately, her actions those of consummate woman, she eased down her panty hose. The thin, lacy scrap of silk she called panties followed. When she glanced up, Burke was bare . . . naked . . . consummate man.

She saw plains of bronzed flesh, a forest of brown hair scoring chest and legs, hair that provided a triangular haven for his bold sex, his unsatisfied sex. Oh, God, she thought, she was going to die if he didn't love her soon!

As Burke stared at the ivory of her skin, the high thrust of her perfectly shaped breasts and the shadowed delta between her legs, he thought that he'd had about as much as a man could take. If he didn't love her soon, he . . .

She turned and reached for the lamp.

"No." The command was husky, as if fog had drifted into his throat.

Her hand stopped. Her eyes mated with his.

"Leave it on. I want to see you."

She inched her hand away, turned back the bed covers and lay down.

He came to her.

Instantly, bodies tangled in love.

His mouth was hot on hers, his touch fevered as his hands roamed her body. It was the kind of heated touch that belonged to a man who has long thirsted and now has his lips at a cup. But like the sun-parched man drinking cool water for the first time in a long while, there was an imposed restraint. Burke was desperately trying to love her slowly, to love her completely, to love her until she, too, was ready and satisfied. The hand moving over the curve of her hip shook from the pressure of that restraint.

"God, you're so small," he breathed, running his hand the length of her thigh. "So perfect," he whispered as his mammoth hand eased upward to cup her dainty, but womanly-full breast. "But so small. Jill, I don't want to hurt you. I won't hurt you, will I?" he mumbled, almost incoherently, unquestionably deliriously, as his lips kissed her neck, then greedily merged once more with her mouth. His tongue plunged deeply, hungrily.

She moaned, whispered a half no around the kiss, and shifted her legs beneath him. He fell into the loving vee. He lay heated, hard, moist and ready to join them. But he didn't. Instead, he gasped at the intimate contact and popped beads of sweat across his brow. His face was twisted and drawn with lines of agony. Determinedly, though, he sought to arouse her first.

"Burke," she whispered, arching against him.

"No, wait," he pleaded, "let me . . ."

"No," she argued, taking charge. She slid her hand downward. Past navel. Past whorls of crisp hair.

His hand tried to intercept hers. "Jill, wait . . . no . . . ah, God!" he moaned when she closed her hand around him. His head arched backward, just as his hips instinctively arched forward. His breath dissolved into full-throated shudders. She eased him forward and, parting the moist sweetness of her body, took him into her. Slowly. Fully. His breath ceased to be. Along with hers. Both were replaced instead by long low moans of exquisite pleasure.

Hot. She was blistering hot, he thought, painfully fighting to keep his body still until hers could grow used to him.

Hard. He was steel-hard, but smooth as satin. And she longed to feel him moving inside her.

Soft. She was softer than a new-born kitten. And wet. God, he could drown in the creamy wetness surrounding him and never care.

"Oh, Jill," he whispered near her ear as he supported himself with his hands. The muscles in his arms bulged from the strain of his weight. "So good . . . feels so good . . . nothing ever felt so good . . ."

"I know," she said, feeling the pressure of his penetration as the perfect filling of the emptiness within her. But then, her heart said, why shouldn't he be the perfect filling of the emptiness he himself had created? She moved her hands down his slide-curved back and arched against him—again and again until he had no choice but to join in.

"...so good," he whispered as his hips met hers in a steady beat, "so good...so..." Suddenly Burke felt a surge of too-keen pleasure rip through his body, followed by a feeling that was far too premature. He stilled his hips. "No, wait...too good...wait!" He tried to anchor her hips with his hand.

But it was too late. Jill knew that the instant Burke did. She felt his body tighten, felt him fight the speedy conclusion, felt him lose.

Burke felt the inexorable rush of climax. It was strong like the wind that blew in his face as he ran. It was powerful like the muscles of his legs as he ate away the miles, powerful like the sinewy muscles that presently strained and pumped against sheet and mattress.

"Damn!" he moaned, frantically increasing the rhythm of his hips. Suddenly he gasped, gasped again, then emptied himself into her in slow, hard thrusts.

Her hands slid down his back and cupped his hips as they moved against her. His buttocks were concave at the sides, his thighs rock-hard from exercise. His whole body was sweat-damp. Jill cherished the feel of his warm, wet skin and cherished also the relief he spilled into her. She hugged him to her, strangely feeling that the other times she'd made love had been but fake and false imitations. Right this moment, she felt very much like a just-awakened virgin.

At last, depleted, his eyes shuttered closed, Burke eased to her side. He drew her with him.

She watched him. For long minutes, she just watched him. He looked as much a man as a man could look, yet there was a little-boy innocence in the way his brown lashes lay crescented against his cheeks, a little-boy innocence in the part of his lips and the wayward sweep of his hair. Sweat dewed his forehead and the dimpled spot above his upper lip. His breathing was shallow, but growing stronger—so strong that his chest, woven in a furry tapestry, moved in and out. In and out in a way that begged her to touch it. She did. It, too, felt damp. And hard. And incredibly sexy.

As the latter thought was weaving a warm magic through her unfulfilled body, Jill felt her hand surrounded by one much larger. She glanced upward into Burke's eyes. He said nothing. He just stared. Softly. But thoroughly. Slowly, he raised her hand to his lips and kissed the palm. It was the most endearing, the purest, yet the most sensual, kiss she'd ever had.

"I forgot to tell you I'm a lousy lover," he said, the words shattering against her palm.

A half smile lazed about his lips—one she couldn't help but match.

"That's your opinion," she answered.

His smile suddenly faded. "I'm sorry. It had just been too long since..." He trailed off, repeating, "I'm sorry."

"It doesn't matter."

"It does to me. I wanted it to last longer."

She smiled again. "You were keeping track of time?"

"Yeah. With the second hand of my watch."

Her smile widened. So did his. His fingers inched forward and trailed across the width of her smile. His slowly disappeared again. He was remembering the way, only minutes before, her body had surrounded his. And the way he'd repeatedly, uncontrollably thrust himself deep inside her. "Did I hurt you?"

She shook her head. "I won't break, Burke. Honest." Even as she said the words, she wondered if they were the truth. Oh, it was true enough that he wouldn't break her physically, but what about emotionally? Was she getting in over her head? Or more to the point, was she getting in over her heart?

Jill might have tried to find an answer to the question, but just as she would have begun her search, Burke shifted, lowered his head, and, murmuring something about her day in court, covered the rosy nipple of her breast with his mouth. She sighed, laced her fingers in his hair and gave in to the sweet, swelling, heavy feelings that sluiced across her stomach . . . and beyond.

If she had controlled the first phase of their lovemaking, he controlled this one. The timing was all his. He kissed, suckled her breasts until they hurt with a tightness she'd never known, and when she thought she could take no more, his tongue would minister to the hurt in soft, tender licks that left her whole nipple wet and longing to be kissed and suckled again.

As honest in her passion as in all of her life, Jill held nothing back. With no inhibitions, she let him please her. She even helped him please her. When his hand slid between her legs, between petals still love-moist, she moaned and boldly drew his thumb to the heat of her passion. She eased her hand downward to cover his.

"Oh, yes, show me how," he whispered, her participation fanning the embers of his passion until he felt himself once more responding in a hard, turgid way. "Oh, Jill, you're so sexy. You make me feel so sexy."

"Oh, Burke," she groaned as her neck arched into beautiful submission.

"There?" he whispered, caressing her in a provocative, circular motion.

"Yes. Oh, yes. There. Harder!"

Under the guidance of hers, his hand became wildly creative. "Give me your mouth," he breathed, bonding their lips. His tongue dove forward in the same rhythm as his divinely ruthless fingers.

Minutes later, she cried his name in abject ecstasy as cool ripples of pleasure washed gently against the shores of her heated body. Before she could do little more than gather her breath, Burke eased his body onto hers and sank himself deep within her. Disbelieving, both once more walked on sensual shores. This time, together.

A LONG WHILE LATER, as Jill slept, Burke stood staring out into the moonlit night. He, too, had been asleep, but had wakened suddenly, restlessly. His mind was in turmoil. Nothing in his life had prepared him for this moment—this moment when his wife slept in her grave and his lover in the nearby bed.

He wasn't certain how he was supposed to be feeling. He moaned silently. Forget how you're supposed to be feeling, Rawlins, he told himself. How do you feel? He let the rhythm of his body settle into quiet contemplation. He felt...tired. It had been a long, emotionally taxing day. He also felt...unsettled. Like a fragile leaf fluttering in a wind that wasn't strong enough to blow it away, but kept it in a constant motion. But he also felt satisfied, body satisfied, the kind of satisfaction a man felt after a good and thorough loving. Jill. Thoughts of her body entwined with his shadow-danced in his mind and led to the question, Was he sorry they had become lovers?

No.

He waited for the guilt to come.

It didn't.

This gave him the courage to push the issue further, to make a comparison that no gentleman ever made, but it wasn't a crass comparison. In fact, it was a very gentle, very loving, one. He had loved his wife, he had loved making love to her—nothing could ever change that— but...but Jill's lack of inhibitions aroused him in a way— He stopped, knowing that he might be dangerously courting guilt. Say it, Rawlins, he taunted. You owe it to Jill. He sighed in acquiescence. Jill's lack of inhibitions, her raw response, aroused him in a way no woman ever hand. Not even Nicole.

He waited for the guilt to come.

Again, it didn't.

He gave another sigh, this one deep and relieved. He also realized that just thinking about Jill's lovemaking was arousing him. Once with her hadn't been enough. He had truly thought it would be. Hadn't he felt at some core level that simple, physical need had possessed him and that once that need had been met, once... But once hadn't been enough. And considering the present state of his body, neither had twice. And furthermore, he had the feeling that, if he made love to her a hundred more times, he'd still need a hundred and one. There was also the growing suspicion that he needed more than what her body offered. He needed her smile, the warmth of her personality, that special quality that made her uniquely Jill.

And how did he feel about that?

Strangely he felt both panicked and at peace. And guilty? Maybe. A little. He had grown accustomed to feeling guilty about everything since Nicole... Nicole. He frowned at the sudden realization that staggered his mind: not once, not once as Jill had lain beneath him, had he thought of Nicole. Quicker than quick, he felt guilt's powerful demons beside him.

"Are you thinking about her?" The voice was husky and came from near his elbow.

Burke turned toward the sound. Even if he hadn't been able to see Jill's silhouette in the pale moonlight, even if he hadn't recognized the voice that had so freely expressed her pleasure at his touch, he would have known it was she. No one but Jill McClain would have the guts to ask such a frank question, one that had such potential to hurt her.

"Yes," he answered. He could almost feel her stepping back under the weight of his verbal assault. He unquestionably felt her pain in his own heart. He reached out a hand to leave a solacing caress at her cheek. "But not the way you think. Actually," he said, pulling her into his arms when he realized the simple touch wasn't enough, at least not for him, "I was thinking more of you."

Jill readily went into his arms, her bare body folded close against his equally bare body. He fitted his hands at the small of her back, just beneath the wayward tumble of her hair. He rested his cheek on the top of her head. His arousal fit snugly, unselfconsciously, against her stomach.

"What about me?"

Burke's lips twitched at her expected curiosity. "I was thinking about how you arouse me."

"Do I?"

"What's wrong, lady? Can't you tell?"

He felt her smile curve into the hair on his chest. It tickled. He had the sudden urge to smother her in his arms, which tightened about her until her breasts flattened against him.

"What else were you thinking?"

He hesitated, then realized he'd been around her long enough that her honesty was rubbing off. "That you excite me," he said in a soft-rough voice, "in a way no one else ever has."

The admission was like sustenance to a starving woman. Jill hadn't even realized that she'd been hungry. She pulled back, her eyes finding his in the night. Nicole's name was never mentioned—Jill wouldn't have been that crude, nor Burke that treasonous—but her unspoken name drifted toward him in question. His answer was the gentle brush of his lips against Jill's before pulling her back into his arms. Her body hot-melted into his.

The moon had risen higher, the night had grown older, before Burke spoke again. "The answer is no."

"And the question?"

"Another one that you won't ask," he said, making it obvious that he had, indeed, known the turn of her thoughts minutes before. "I did not pretend that you were Nicole." He sighed, as if he still couldn't quite believe what he was about to say. "I never once thought of her, Jill. Never once."

Jill's heart filled with her joy and his sorrow. "And that surprises you?"

"Yes."

"And makes you feel guilty?"

"Guilty as hell."

She too sighed. "Oh, Burke, you're so determined to feel guilty, aren't you? So determined to punish yourself."

"I deserve..."

"Don't ever say that to me again," she interrupted sharply, her eyes once more finding his through the ebony thickness of the night. She deliberately softened her tone. "Don't every say that again." Her hand eased to the side of his face, where it rested against a slightly stubbly cheek. "You deserve good things. Because you're good."

Burke had the sudden liberating feeling that maybe, just maybe, if Jill said it long enough, often enough, he might believe he did deserve something good. Like her? Like a future? Like happiness?

"Are you staying the night?"

Burke heard the vulnerability in her voice and hated himself for what he was about to say. He drew the hand at his cheek to his mouth and kissed her warm, tender palm. "Jill, I don't know. I need... I need to clear some cobwebs out of my mind. Can you understand that?"

She understood. It hurt, but she did understand. "Yes." She moistened her lips and hoped her voice sounded stable. "I, uh... I'm going back to bed. If you want me to take you home, just wake..."

"I'll call a cab."

This time she didn't trust her voice. She simply nodded her head. She pulled her hand from his and stepped back. "Will you lock the door behind you if..."

"Yes."

He watched her walk away, watched her crawl back into bed, and thought that maybe it was his destiny to always be caught between. He was caught between life and death, yesterday and today, Nicole and Jill. Sighing

in frustration, he turned back to the window and hiked a
hand to his naked hip.

How much time passed he couldn't have said. Nor
could he really have labeled his thoughts into any pattern. He thought of Nicole and of a picnic they'd once
gone on. He thought of one Christmas when she'd given
him a teddy bear. Curiously, the image of Nicole was
faded, like a sepia-brown photograph from another lifetime. The only thing sharp was her voice saying over and
over that she loved him. On the heels of that came Jill's
pronouncement that love doesn't chain, it frees. For the
first time, he wondered if he were insulting Nicole by
hanging on so tenaciously to his guilt, by refusing to go
on with his life. Jill was offering him resurrection. It was
an offer he both resented and cherished.

"You deserve good things."

Burke turned toward the bed, his eyes lighting on the
small heap beneath the covers. He thought of the eager
way Jill's mouth had sought his, the unselfish way she'd
loved him, the peace he'd felt inside her. He might not
deserve anything as good as Jill, but the truth was, he
couldn't turn away from her. Not tonight. Not tonight
when his needs were so great and his thoughts so jum-
bled.

Stepping to the bed, he tugged back the covers and
eased in beside her. Neither caring whether she was awake
or asleep, he urgently pulled her into his arms. She was
awake. At his touch, her tears began.

"I thought you were . . ."

"Shh," he whispered, "I'm not leaving. I can't."

He gently, roughly, pushed her to her back and, his
mouth meeting hers, entered his male body into her feminine one. The action was as natural as night, as natural

as their heartbeats mingling, as natural as the fact that grief, if given time, heals itself. With or without the griever's permission.

CHAPTER NINE

THE BUTTER-YELLOW SUN peered cheerfully through the sheer embroidered drapes. Jill stirred as sleep lazily, reluctantly fell away. Weight. What was the delicious weight at her waist? She sent her hand on a groggy reconnaissance mission. It reported that it felt an arm. A man's arm. Burke's arm.

Burke.

Jill's eyelids fluttered to slumbery slits. At the sight that greeted her, a smile tiptoed across her lips. He was...so thoroughly male, she thought as she studied the man sleeping beside her. He lay on his stomach, his right arm flung haphazardly, yet possessively, about her waist, while his left arm arched high on the pillow above his head. Almost like a halo. The thought broadened Jill's smile. No. There was nothing even remotely angelic about Burke in bed. He was pure man. Fourteen-karat and flawless.

Because she couldn't help herself, her eyes traveled over the wide expanse of his bare, bronzed, muscle-rippled back and up to his face, where thick, dusky lashes fanned his cheeks and lips whispered slow breaths. From there, her eyes shifted to his left arm. She saw a coiled biceps, she saw hair that began about the elbow and spread like wildfire down his arm, she saw a watch at his wrist, she saw a—

—gold wedding band on his finger.

An ache, as dull and gray as an autumn morning, folded itself over her like a suffocating blanket. No, she thought, her heart denying what she saw; yes, her mind confirmed. Tears sprang to her eyes. While he'd been whispering intimacies, he'd been wearing his wedding ring. While he'd been performing those intimacies, intimacies that had never felt right with any other man, he'd been wearing his wedding ring.

On the heels of this discovery came another. This one took her breath away and flung it alongside the scattered clouds peacefully dotting the morning sky. She was in love with Burke. Nothing short of love could have felt so good last night or could hurt so badly this morning.

But what about last night? Had it meant nothing to him except the release of pent-up needs? Probably not, Jill forced herself to admit. His body had needed hers, but his heart hadn't been involved. Because his heart belonged to someone else.

But hadn't he said last night that he'd never once thought of Nicole while making love to her? Hadn't he ultimately decided to stay the night? Hadn't he then made love to her with a tender fierceness that had paled anything she had previously known about making love? Jill's heart soared, then plummeted. Wasn't he still wearing the ring that bound him to another woman?

Suddenly the thought of the thin gold band was more than Jill could bear. Slipping carefully from beneath his arm—he moaned and shifted before settling back into sleep—she eased from the bed. She headed for the bathroom, where she forced herself to be practical. Today was Friday, a workday. Therefore, she had to shower, put on makeup and dress. Shelving personal thoughts as best she could, she managed the first two tasks as well as putting in her contacts. But when it was time to dress, she slid into her yellow satin robe instead. Jill padded back into the bedroom. Burke was still sound asleep. She'd just let him sleep a few more minutes, she told herself, adding that he needed the rest. She ignored the real reason that she didn't disturb him. She wouldn't know what to say to him when he would finally awake. And how could she possibly hide what was in her heart?

Grabbing his shirt from floor, she walked to the kitchen. She leveled the ironing board from its built-in nook in the wall, set the iron to heat and measured out some dark-roasted coffee granules. Soon the room was filled with the smell of brewing coffee and heated fabric. There was also the faint smell of Burke's cologne as the hot steam released the scent from the cotton cloth. It reminded Jill of Burke's body. Moving over hers.

Somewhere between sleeve and shirttail, Burke's arm curved around her waist. In that moment when his warm touch represented cold reality, Jill asked herself if she regretted last night. No, she hastily answered. She couldn't regret their lovemaking, regardless of how the relationship turned out; but dear heaven, right this moment how it hurt! Because it hurt so badly, because self-preservation is a powerful instinct, she steeled herself not to react to Burke's nearness.

She might have succeeded had not he pulled her back against his recently showered and still-bare chest. She still had a fighting chance when his right hand cupped her chin. She was lost completely, however, when his lips nuzzled hers until they had no choice but to part and allow him good-morning liberties that seemed more appropriate in the sexually pagan night.

"You don't have to do that," he whispered against her mouth, his breath warm, his lips hot.

Like heck she didn't, she thought in lazy panic, realizing seconds later that he hadn't been referring to her reaction to his kiss, but rather to her ironing his shirt. "Yes, I do," she whispered, "if you're going to wear it to work. It looks like..." She stopped, not quite willing to say what it did look like.

"Like I'd hastily thrown it off to make love?" he asked, his lips teasing hers by hovering near but not touching.

"Yes," she breathed, praying he'd kiss her and damning herself for the prayer.

When Burke did answer it, she forgot everything but the taste of his mouth; the inviting, taunting taste of his mouth. She forgot everything except how his tongue felt stroking hers, how that same tongue could flick and curl and tease so sinfully that it should be outlawed. She forgot everything except the feel of his smooth, soapy-smelling cheek—he'd obviously used her razor—rubbing up against hers like a male feline mating.

Get hold of yourself, Jill. Remember that this isn't a perfect relationship, and you're on the verge of getting hurt. Badly hurt.

She forced her mouth from his—God, the willpower it took!—and dragged her attention back to the shirt stretched out on the board. The hand that now guided the iron trembled. "I, uh... I need to get this done or we're going to be late."

Burke didn't seem to notice the restraint she was valiantly trying to hold on to. But then, he didn't seem to notice anything but her neck, which he'd exposed by taking his finger and drawing back the long flow of her hair. He was presently delivering tiny, nibbling kisses to the ivory column that seemed determined to arch, against its owner's will, so that he could deliver those kisses all the better, and move to bite, mouth, tongue the lobe of her ear.

Hot steam billowed upward. Jill wondered if it was coming from the idle iron or her body. Fighting back the moan of pleasure she wanted to give, she forced herself to pick up the iron once more. She whisked it across the last wrinkled section of the garment.

"Thank you," Burke whispered.

"You're welcome," Jill answered, shutting off the iron.

"Not the shirt," he said, now rooting his nose against the collar of her robe and planting kisses on her shoulder, "but, thank you for that, too."

Jill's hand hesitated in pulling the shirt from the board. Her veins suddenly ran cold with ice water. Surely he wouldn't thank her for. . .

"For what, then?"

"For last night," Burke answered as innocently as a lamb going to slaughter.

Jill recognized with some rational part of her brain that she was just looking for something to get angry about, something to offset the vulnerability she was feeling, and the hurt. If it wasn't this, it would be something else, because she needed to release the pressure building around her heart. Rationality damned, she whirled around, her flashing blue eyes meeting his.

"Don't you dare thank me for last night, Burke Rawlins! Just don't you dare sashay in here this morning thanking me as if. . . as if. . ." She vacuously waved her hand in the air. "Just don't you dare!"

Yanking up the shirt, the tails of her robe flapping in the air, she slap-slapped her bare feet across the kitchen tile toward the bedroom.

Having gone from warm neck to frigid-cold words in a matter of seconds, it took Burke several heartbeats to find his voice.

"Jill!" he cried out, following her. He found her standing in front of the dresser mirror heedlessly tearing the hairbrush through her long hair.

"What in hell..." he began, his hands plumped at his waist, then changed his tack. "What do you mean, don't thank you as if...? As if what?" His own voice had undergone a thunderous change.

Jill found his eyes in the mirror. His expectant, brooding eyes. She also found his bare chest. And the unbuttoned waistband of his pants. She tried to concentrate not on what she knew lay within those pants, not on the wisp of hair swirling in the tiny vee of the waistband, but on her anger. Her self-fabricated, self-perpetuating anger. "Don't you dare come in here thanking me as if I provide a service for sexually needy men. Got a hard-on, see Jill. Need sexual relief, see..."

Burke grabbed her wrist and hurled her around. The look in his eyes effectively silenced anything else she might have said. Time stood still as chests heaved, eyes battled. Jill mentally noted that he looked madder than hell—and that she hurt way down deep inside worse than that devil-owned place.

"I didn't know you gave me anything that I needed to thank you for," he said, his words deceptively soft as they slid between a thinned mouth. "I thought what happened between us was something that we shared. I thought I gave back everything I took. I didn't know either one of us was providing a service. Is that how you viewed it, Jill?"

The look on his face was one of anger, but also hurt, such sterling hurt that her eyes misted. She longed to throw herself into his arms and apologize...and beg him to love her the way he loved his wife, the way she, Jill, loved him. "No," she said, shaking her head. "No, I...Burke, I..."

"I was going to thank you," he interrupted, "for being so understanding last night. For giving me time to sort through my thoughts without pressuring me to stay. I know that wasn't easy. It wouldn't be for any woman. Or any man. Not after what we'd just..." He paused meaningfully. "What we shared."

A plethora of emotions swamped her. She felt unworthy of the praise he'd just bestowed on her. She also felt hurt, anger, fear—fear that he'd walk out of her life, fear that he wouldn't walk out of it until she loved him so much that she couldn't survive without him. But mostly, she just felt like a woman. She knew she couldn't stop herself from saying what she was about to. She knew it had been ordained the moment she'd seen the thin gold band on his finger.

"And did you sort through your thoughts, Burke?"

"Yes. I settled some issues."

"How about the issue of your wedding ring?"

For the briefest of seconds it appeared that Burke simply had no idea what she was talking about. At last, his eyes drifted to the hand still holding her wrist...and to the ring under dark discussion. Suddenly everything came into focus like a camera that's just been adjusted. Suddenly the argument made sense. Suddenly the anger in Jill's eyes looked more like hurt than anger.

"You never even said you wanted me, just that you needed me," she said in a broken, defeated tone that somehow made her look smaller than ever.

Crush-her-in-your-arms small, Burke thought.

"All the time you were making love to me, you were wearing..." She stopped, unable to go on because of the tears beginning to pool in her eyes.

Burke slowly released her wrist. The brush fell from her hand and thudded against the floor. Neither noticed. Without a word, he walked to the window and, leaning his hand against the frame, stared out at the mockingly carefree morning. As he watched a robin search out its breakfast, he thought how easy it was to screw things up. He also thought of the distant look in Jill's eyes and the hurt that trembled in the corners of her mouth. Suddenly, he cursed. Vilely.

"Jill, I..." He straightened and turned, his eyes melding with hers. "Jill, I'm sorry. I don't know what else to say. It was grossly insensitive of me. It was unforgivable. My only excuse is that...is that I've worn it so long, it's become such a part of me, that I simply didn't think about taking it off. I didn't take my watch off either," he said, holding up his arm to show her and pleading with her to understand. In three slow steps, he stood before her. And brushed the pad of his thumb across a silently fleeing tear. "I'm sorry. I'm sorry I hurt you," he whispered.

"It's all ri..." she tried to say.

"No, it isn't. It isn't all right at all. And I'm going to try very hard to make it up to you." The fingers of his right hand went to the ring on his left. "Beginning right..."

"No!" she said, her fingers stopping his. "Don't," she whispered, her eyes burning into his. "Unless...unless last night meant more than..." She hesitated, searching for the words that were in her heart.

It was Burke who found the words. "Unless last night meant more than my body needing yours?"

"Yes."

He smiled, sadly, self-derisively, and ran a knuckle across her cheek. "I haven't given you any reason to believe anything other than that, have I? I even told you from the very beginning that maybe all I felt for you was a physical attraction. I didn't want to mislead you, Jill, and I did believe it possible that I simply needed . . ." He paused, not liking the sound of the blunt admission.

"A woman?"

"Yes. I believed it until—" he swallowed "—until last night."

Their eyes said all kinds of things that words never seem capable of expressing. Beneath her hand, Burke's moved. Slowly, never taking his eyes from hers, he slid the ring from his finger. Jill, her heart pounding, stared at the white band it left behind, symbolic that something had changed, but that time was still needed to heal all wounds. His eyes still on hers, Burke pocketed the ring.

"And now, Jill McClain, there's something that I need to make very clear to you." His hands closed around her upper arms, and he pulled her to him. "It's something I should have made clear last night. Something I would have made clear if I hadn't been such a jerk." He took both her hands in his. One he nestled in a patch of hair dusting the spot over his fast-strumming heart, the other, he boldly settled against his sex. He was hard. Impressively so, considering it was early morning following a late night of loving. "I need you." He rubbed her hand up and down, down and up, the length of him, then slowly unzipped his pants and eased her hand onto his warm bare fullness. His breath escaped in a trickle, and his heartbeat accelerated. "I've made love to you three times," he whispered, his voice strained from her touch, "but I need you again. I need to be inside you. I need to feel you wet and warm around me. I need to feel your body moving beneath mine. I need to feel your body swallowing this ache." He pressed her hand hard against him for emphasis. "Need, Jill, need. Do you feel the need?"

"Yes," she answered, her voice strained every bit as much as his.

Burke's hands abandoned hers to their gentle witchery and moved to cup her face. "Now let me tell you what you can't feel. It's what's in my heart. I want you. I want you in a way I never believed I could want a woman again. I want to need you. I want you to need me. I want you to want me...as badly as I want you. I want, Jill, want. But most of all what I want," he said, lowering and inclining his head, "is for us to stop this conversation, stop arguing and make love."

His mouth took hers roughly, reeling her senses even as her head reeled backward to accept his kiss. As his lips worked over hers, his hands left her face and deftly untied her robe. Without hesitation, yet without haste, he eased the satin fabric from her shoulders. It darted to the floor like a slice of sunshine. His tongue piercing, probing, promising, his hands smoothed across her naked back and hips and tugged her tightly against him.

"We're going...to be...late for...work," she tried to say around his ravaging mouth.

"Do you really care?" he whispered, scooping her into his arms and starting for the bed without even once fully releasing her lips.

Her arms curled around his neck just as primitive need curled deep inside her woman's body. "No," she whispered, wantonly, wantingly. She threaded her fingers through his slightly damp hair and proceeded for the next hour to do everything she could to guarantee their tardiness.

THEY WERE LATE.

It was a fact no less than three people pointed out before they'd hardly pushed through the front door.

"You're late," the receptionist said as she kicked the soft-drink machine into submission.

"What didya do? Oversleep?" Ellen said, her pink sweater clinging to her full figure the way its image clung to a man's mind.

"Well, well. Look who finally decided to come in this morning," Charles Evans teased. "Guess being the two most famous lawyers in Boston has privileges, huh? Hey listen, you guys," he said, turning serious, "congrats. You did a great job in court. I was proud to be a colleague."

Jill and Burke slowed their pace, but didn't stop. Both smiled. "Thanks," they said in tandem.

As they walked by, Charles Evans couldn't resist one last lob. "If you two hurry up, you might get ten, fifteen minutes of work in before lunch."

"Stuff it, Evans," Burke replied, feeling inordinately happy for a man who'd had only a nodding acquaintance with sleep during the past twenty-four hours. The other man laughed. Jill and Burke walked on toward their offices. "Will you wipe the guilty look off your face, McClain?" he whispered out of the corner of his mouth.

"We should have staggered our arrivals," Jill said, smiling and saying good-morning to one of the secretaries.

"They'll think we met in the lobby."

"You should have gone by your apartment and changed suits."

"They'll think I'm not clothes conscious."

"They'll think your shirt is wrinkled...which it is, Rawlins," she said out of the side of her mouth.

Both nodded another round of good-mornings.

"It wouldn't have been wrinkled if you hadn't laid it on the bed after you ironed it," he accused.

"It wouldn't have been wrinkled if you'd watched where you laid me." At the realization of what she'd said, she glanced up sharply and blushed profusely. "I mean, where you put me, placed me, arranged me..." she stuttered.

Burke smiled wickedly. "I liked what you said first."

"You would," she answered, turning embarrassment into another instant smile and a "Good morning" for someone passing by.

"Good morning," Burke echoed.

"There you two are," Ida Tumbrello said as they approached her desk. She communicated with her usual efficiency. "Andrew wants to see you first thing, and you have tons of phone messages which I put on your respective desks."

"Thanks, Ida," Jill said.

"Congratulations," the older woman offered, her fawn-brown eyes beaming from her heart-shaped face.

Both Burke and Jill smiled.

"Thanks."

"Thanks."

"Is he in?" Burke asked, motioning toward the frosted-glass door with a nod of his head.

"Yeah," Ida said.

In the few steps from desk to door, Jill whispered, "Great. He's going to fire us right off."

"He can't. I own part of the firm. Besides, he's my father."

"Is it supposed to cheer me that I'll be looking for a job alone?"

"Don't worry, McClain," Burke said, tapping on the door with one knuckle and opening it. "I'll give you a reference. An excellent reference."

At the unladylike word she whispered as they stepped into the spacious, scarlet-carpeted office, a huge smile spread across Burke's face.

It was his son's smile that Andrew Rawlins saw first. He reacted like any father. With a silent prayer of gratitude for whatever—or whoever?—had put it there. His wise eyes roved to the woman beside his son.

"Good morning," Andrew Rawlins said with a smile of his own.

As always when confronting the senior member of the firm, the word distinguished came to Jill's mind. "Good morning, sir."

"Good morning, Dad. Sorry we're late. We had something we needed, wanted," Burke added, his eye catching Jill's, "to do."

Despite the inappropriateness of their surroundings, despite the numerous times they'd made love, Jill felt a tremor of renewed excitement course through her. She also felt unqualified love for this man. She was certain he saw her desire. Did he also see her love?

"No problem," Andrew Rawlins said, motioning for them to be seated. "You two earned a slow morning. By the way, I'm not sure I ever congratulated you yesterday, what with all the circuslike atmosphere toward the end. You did a fine job."

Burke and Jill nodded their appreciation.

"I was a little disappointed, though," Jill said, "that the verdict rested so much on outside intervention rather than on our legal cleverness."

"I have to confess to a little disappointment too," Burke said.

"I certainly understand what you're saying," Andrew Rawlins agreed, "but when you've been at this game as long as I have, you learn to gratefully accept help from any quarter. And I totally disagree," he said around a pair of steepled hands, "that your legal cleverness was lacking. You couldn't possibly have known what secret Paula Keszler was living with. The only thing you could do was present the case and create an atmosphere in which the woman wanted to come forward to help your client. You two did that. Obviously." The silver-haired man shifted in his chair and reached for a note. "All of which brings me to what I wanted to speak to you about. Mrs. Stroker called for you earlier and, when she couldn't get you, I talked with her. It seems she wants to make some fair settlement with regard to Ms Keszler and her daughter."

"Classy lady," Burke commented.

"I agree," his father replied, handing over the slip of paper.

Burke reached for it . . . with his left hand. There was only a brief hesitation, only a fraction of a second in which Andrew Rawlins's eyes fell to the pale circle of skin that indicated the absence of a ring. A long-worn ring. His eyes jumped to his son's and held for a meaningful moment. Gentleman that he was, he never glanced at Jill—she knew this was deliberate—and never missed a beat in the conversation. "This is where Mrs. Stroker said you could reach her."

"Thanks," Burke said, rising and picking up his briefcase.

Jill, too, stood and collected her case. She felt very much as if she were naked on a stage. Seconds later, as she and Burke were once more walking down the hall toward their offices, she said, "He knows."

"He approves. And even if he didn't . . ." Burke said, stopping in front of her office. The sentence was never finished because the two stood staring at each other like starry-eyed, high-school lovers walking each other to class and trying hard to get up the courage to say good-bye. "How in hell am I going to work, with you across the hall?" Burke asked, his voice husky and deep.

"The same way I am, Rawlins. With exemplary self-discipline."

"I don't seem to be real high on that commodity of late," he said, reminding her with the darkening of his eyes just how little self-discipline he'd had the past few hours.

Slowly those dark eyes lowered from her heaven-blue eyes to her moist, pink lips. It was a natural journey for what was on his mind.

Jill felt her whole stomach cave in. "Don't," she whispered.

"God, I want to," he whispered, his eyes brazenly meandering about her mouth before trailing upward. Blue and green eyes burned in a rainbow fire. "Shall I call Mrs. Stroker in lieu of a cold shower?" he asked finally.

She smiled. "Good idea, counselor."

"Right. Good idea." Burke took a step backward, then another, then turned and walked toward his office. Jill turned to enter hers.

"Jill?" he called out.

She turned back.

His face wore a haunted, vulnerable expression that bespoke long months spent alone. "I just wanted to see if it was true. That someone would be there if I called."

It was the hardest thing Jill ever did, but she somehow managed not to take him in her arms.

CONTRARY TO EXPECTATIONS, Jill did get some work done, primarily because the recent trial had knocked everything else into second place, a second place that now demanded attention. The list of that morning's return calls alone was staggering. Included in the list was a message for Jill to call Rob Sheffield. At first seeing the note, a frown had claimed her lips. Rob had never called her at work before. Was something wrong? Jill immediately thought of Mary, but told herself not to worry when she remembered the wonderful mood she'd found her sister in Sunday afternoon. Curiosity replacing concern, Jill had dialed Rob's number...only to be told that he was out and would call her back.

When lunchtime came, Burke and Jill found themselves committed to separate engagements. Both loathed the idea, though both agreed it was probably for the best. When Burke stuck his head in her door for a quick "See you later," the farewell turned out to be less than quick. Seeing the same need in her eyes that he felt, he had closed the door behind him and took her in his arms. The kiss ended only when it became necessary to end it or carry it to the natural conclusion. Both had endured frustrating lunches that in no way appeased the real hunger gnawing at their bodies. When Jill returned from lunch, she found another note saying Rob had called. She immediately phoned him back. He was once more out of the office.

If possible, the afternoon was busier than the morning. Jill heard Burke in the hall a couple of times, but he didn't stop in. She was and wasn't glad. When a light tap sounded on her door at a quarter to four, however, she half expected and wholly hoped it would be Burke.

It wasn't.

"Rob!" she said in surprise.

"Am I interrupting anything?"

"No, no. C'mon in." She stood and rounded the desk as her future brother-in-law closed the door behind him. "I tried to call you..."

"I know. I've been working in the field off and on today. I, uh...I was near here and thought I'd just stop in."

As he walked toward her, Jill's worry was reborn. Never had she seen his coffee-brown eyes without a smiling twinkle, never had she seen his face gaunt and haggard. He suddenly looked far older than his fifty-one years. He also looked scared.

"What is it?" she asked, indicating a chair and taking the one across from it. "What's wrong?"

"When did you last talk to Mary?"

Jill's heart accelerated. She had intuitively known what the topic would be. "Sunday. She seemed fine, though. Better than she has in a long while."

"What time, Sunday?"

"Afternoon. I probably left about six or seven. I left her in the attic packing. Why?"

"I called Sunday night about ten and got no answer. By eleven I still had no answer. I was frantic, so I went over, used my key and let myself in. I found her in a fetal position on the sofa." Here, his hand raked through his sun-bleached blond hair. "Jill, she was almost catatonic. She was in a world all her own. For a minute I don't think she even knew who I was." He paused, then added, "When she finally came around enough to be coherent, she said she was sick."

"Maybe she was," Jill said, grasping for straws.

"No," he said with finality. "She was lying. I know it. I could feel it." Restlessly, he stood and paced about the room. "She's been... I don't know, jittery, nervous, all week. The kicker came this morning." He sat back down as if he didn't realize he'd just gotten up from the same chair. "She called me about seven o'clock. She wanted to borrow two thousand dollars. Said it was for school, but I don't believe it. She was lying again."

The idea of Mary borrowing money was so foreign to Jill's thinking that it took a moment for Rob's words to register. "Mary borrow money?"

"Yeah. That's how it struck me, too." He was suddenly angry, the kind of anger that came from fear. "I don't care about the damned money, or what she's going to use it for—hell, she can have every dime I've got and burn it to cinders—but something's wrong. Badly wrong. And she won't tell me what it is... She won't trust me." The last remark revealed clearly that he wasn't only worried, he was also hurt.

"Rob, she loves you more than..."

"Will you talk to her?" he interrupted. "Maybe she'll tell you." His eyes turned glassy, and he fought to hold in check the strong emotions swamping him. "I'm losing her, Jill. To something. I don't even know what it is."

"Losing her....losing her... I'm losing her..."

The thought wormed its way in and out of Jill's mind a thousand times after Rob left the office, and she started trying to reach Mary by phone. She tried every ten minutes until it was way beyond the hour Mary should have returned home from school. With each continued ring of the phone, Jill's own anxiety increased. Was something going on? And if so, what? And where the devil, Jill thought as she sat listening to yet another unanswered ring, was Mary?

MARY McCLAIN STOOD in the Boston Public Garden. She was as close to panicking as she'd ever been in her life. She was supposed to have made the drop by four o'clock. It was now five-thirty, and the wooden bench under the crooked elm tree still held the sprawled figures of some of Boston's misfit youth. Punk hairstyles in flaming shades of purple and orange stood out against black leather worn so tight it was a miracle that it didn't restrict circulation. A safety pin pierced the ear of one young woman, while one young man wore a tattoo on his muscle-bulging arm that did more than suggest doing some obscenity to the world. What passed for music blared from a radio at such an obnoxious level that the pansies and tulips seemed to droop beneath its silence-shattering beat.

Two things were obvious: the punkers weren't leaving and she couldn't leave the money until they did. And furthermore, though she'd tried to be discreet, they were beginning to eye her suspiciously. Perhaps even maliciously.

Was he around? Could he see her dilemma? Or would he only think she hadn't complied?

"Hey, you!" the kid with the tattoo yelled.

"Hey, Momma, wanna party?" another hollered out and started toward her with an outstretched joint. The others laughed and jeered.

Fear, ugly and serpentine, slithered an acid streak through her stomach, causing adrenaline to spurt in her limbs. She started to run. Clutching the tapestry bag to her chest, she ran and ran, never once stopping, never once catching her breath. She ran from the ugliness in the park, she ran from the ugliness in the world, she ran with a prayer on her wind-chafed lips. *Please, please, let him call again! Please, please give me the chance to tell him it wasn't my fault!*

CHAPTER TEN

"WHY DON'T YOU try her again?"

Burke asked the question that Friday evening as he stood in the middle of Jill's kitchen. When he'd stopped by her office at five o'clock—the first time he'd seen her all afternoon—he'd been surprised to find her upset. He had immediately demanded to know what the problem was. She had immediately told him of Rob's visit and of the on-again, off-again worrying she herself had done over Mary the past few weeks. In a way neither thought to question, it was taken for granted that Burke would share her problem, just as it was taken for granted that they would share dinner.

"What time is it?" she asked. Glasses had replaced her contacts, jeans the dress she'd worn to work. Nothing had replaced the anxious look in her eyes.

"A quarter till seven."

"Where in hell could she be?" Jill said, her concern crossing over that thin line into anger as she snatched the phone from its hook and dialed. She leaned back against the wall. Even with her mind preoccupied, she couldn't help but notice, and react to, the truly fine way Burke's jeans fit across his derrière, stomach and thighs. After work, they had made a mad dash to his apartment so he could change clothes. They had then gone by a Chinese restaurant for take-out food. Burke had suggested the latter in lieu of dining out because it would keep Jill close to the phone. His sensitivity made her fall in love with him just a little more. She told herself she was possibly just that little bit more a fool.

"Do you want any more of this?" Burke asked, starting to clear the white cardboard cartons of egg rolls and shrimp-fried rice from the table.

Jill shook her head as the phone began to ring. She was already preparing herself for a long series of unanswered peals when Mary's voice came on the line before the first ring had even been fully completed.

"Hello?" There was a frenetic anticipation in the one word.

Followed by overwhelming relief in Jill's reply. "Mary?"

There was a pause. Then a deflated "Jill."

At that moment, Mary's disappointment eluded Jill. "Where have you been?" she asked in a lovingly fussy way. "I've been trying to get you for hours."

"I, uh... I had an errand to run after school."

Jill waited for an elaboration of said errand. When it was obvious that none was forthcoming, she asked point-blank, "Are you okay?"

"Of course I'm okay," Mary answered quickly—too quickly. "Why would you think I'm not?"

It crossed Jill's mind that she conservatively could give a score of replies to that single question. She settled on the response that first came to mind. It was also straightforward enough to be in tune with her personality. "Rob stopped by the office today. He's worried about you."

If the cold vibrations of surprise could carry through the phone lines, Jill's ear would have been frostbitten. "He did what?"

"He stopped by the office. Mary, he's half out of his mind with worry. He thinks something's bothering you." She didn't think it necessary to add that she herself shared the same concern.

"I . . . I . . ." Mary laughed nervously. "That's absurd. There's nothing bothering me. The last weeks of school are always hectic, you know that, and I'm trying to plan a wedding, for heaven's sake. I just wish the two of you would stop . . ." An uncharacteristic irritability had crept into Mary's voice. She deliberately deleted it when she added, "Nothing's wrong. What more do you want me to say?"

I want you to tell me about the two thousand dollars you borrowed from Rob, Jill thought, but decided to wait until she was face to face to broach that subject. She consoled herself that she'd only have to wait overnight. Forcing lightness, she said, "What I want you to say is what time you want me to pick you up in the morning."

"Pick me up?"

"Yes. As in going shopping for a wedding dress. Remember?"

No, Mary hadn't remembered. Obviously. As the mile-thick silence attested to.

Jill's stomach retied itself in worry knots. "You are going, aren't you?"

"Ah . . . actually, Jill, I can't. Not tomorrow."

The knots tightened. "Why not?"

Silence stretched to the furthermost shores of frustration, where it crashed into bits of awkward flotsam. "Ah . . . Rob and I are going to the Berkshires for the weekend," she blurted out. "He thinks I ought to get away. In fact, we're leaving in a little while."

Jill first thought the answer was too fast, too pat, and too tidy, but then she remembered Rob's concern. It seemed well within the realm of probability to believe that with his protective personality he had persuaded Mary to go away for the weekend. But why hadn't he mentioned it that afternoon in her office? Maybe it had been spur of the moment. Yeah, that made sense. It also sounded like a good way to get Mary to open up to him. Which is probably what he had in mind.

"That sounds like fun."

"Yeah. I guess I have been working too hard."

"You'll be back Sunday?"

"Yeah. Most likely late."

"Then I'll talk to you Monday, huh?"

"Right." Silence. And more silence. "Look, I gotta run," Mary added, trying to keep her haste to get off the phone hidden.

"Sure." More silence, followed by Jill's sudden and strong need for reassurance. "Mary, everything is all right?"

"Everything is . . . great."

"Swear?"

Without the slightest hesitation, Mary answered, "I swear."

Even after both women had hung up, their hands reposed in contemplative stillness on the receivers. The phrase "I swear" echoed and reechoed in two minds.

SLOWLY, LIKE THE FIRST TREMORS of an earthquake, Mary's fingers began to tremble. Putting down the phone, she pressed them against her lips. Her lying lips. She'd never before lied to Jill. Never openly, never deliberately. The other had been a lie of omission; this was a blunt, purposeful distortion of the truth. And it had been so easy. Her mouth had so easily sworn to a falsehood; her mind had so easily conceived the lie about spending the weekend in the Berkshires with Rob.

Mary laughed—thin, tattered notes of a shallow hysteria that wove themselves in and out of shaking fingers. And what was worse, she was going to lie again. Now that the idea had occurred to her—the idea of making Jill and Rob believe she was spending the weekend with the other—she'd lie to Rob, too. Her future husband would call soon and, when he did, she'd lie. Easily. And necessarily. Because she had to have time and solitude. She had to wait right here by the phone until the blackmailer called. She had to make him understand that she had tried to deliver the money. She had to keep her secret safe from Jill.

Jill. Mary's eyes stung with salty tears. She had become the one thing Jill detested most. Or, perhaps, she'd been thus all along. Deceiver. Perjurer. Liar *extraordinaire*.

"WHAT'D SHE SAY?"

Jill slowly released the receiver and focused her eyes on the inquiring green of Burke's.

"That she'd run an errand after school. She said everything was all right. Even swore it."

"Do you believe her?"

Jill considered, brushed back a wisp of hair that had fallen to her forehead, and said, "She's never lied to me before."

"Then maybe that's reason to believe her now?" The comment was more question than statement.

Jill shrugged...and eventually smiled. "There is some logic to that." The smile faded. "I don't know, Burke. It's been like riding a roller coaster for weeks. One minute I think everything's all right, the next..." She sighed in frustration. "And then there's the question of the money. Why did she borrow the two thousand?"

"Maybe, just maybe," Burke said, "there's a logical explanation for the money. Maybe it does have something to do with school."

"But she never borrows. Anything. Certainly nothing that big."

"It's not like she went to a stranger for it. She's going to marry the man in a matter of weeks. Which brings me to another point," Burke said, stepping forward and raking back the same reddish-blond swath of hair that had once more stubbornly tumbled forward. "Maybe the vibes the two of you are picking up on are nothing more than the fact that she's just a little jittery about the wedding. How old is she?"

His touch was warm and created feather-fluttery feelings that scrambled over her body. "Fifty," she said on the breathless cloud of air his caress inspired.

His eyes dropped to her sweet-sighing mouth, while his voice just dropped. "You don't reach the age of fifty, without ever having been married, and enter lightly into the institution. Maybe she's just a little spooked."

"Yeah. Maybe. The idea had sorta crossed my mind, too," Jill agreed, adding, "She and Rob are going to the Berkshires for the weekend." She watched Burke's mouth as if it had become the most fascinating thing in the world. Her lips unconsciously parted.

Burke's eyes darkened at the unspoken invitation. "Good move. They can discuss whatever's wrong intimately."

"Intimately," Jill repeated.

To both the word suddenly sounded very... very intimate. And the kiss they'd shared at lunch suddenly seemed like a very long time ago.

"There's probably nothing wrong that Rob can't fix with a few reassuring words," Burke said, his voice growing shallow, his body needy and hard.

"You may be right," Jill agreed, feeling that he might be right . . . and also feeling very soft and tingly in some very feminine places.

"A few caresses . . ." His hand moved from the stray hair to her cheek.

"A few caresses . . ." she repeated, her cheek nuzzling into his palm. Greedily nuzzling.

". . . A few kisses . . ." His thumb slid across her lower lip.

". . . A few kisses . . ."

". . . And he can probably get to the bottom of this," he whispered, his voice no longer substantial.

"And he can probably get to the bottom of this," she echoed, as though she had just enough breath to repeat this.

"There's no need to worry until you know you have something to worry about."

"No . . . no need to worry . . . until . . ."

Jill's eyes closed. She sighed and swayed into the welcoming warmth of him, her fingers hooking into his belt loops for support. She felt weak from the ravages of worry and anxiety, weak from a day's worth, a lifetime's worth, of needing and wanting.

Burke's massive, comforting arms closed around her. As if he wanted to protect her from all troublesome things. As if he, too, were weak from needing the feel of her body against his.

"Don't leave me," she whispered in desperation. Tonight, tomorrow night, or a thousand nights from now, she pleaded silently.

"No," he whispered back.

Jill had no idea what he was promising temporally. And didn't really care. Right that moment she was in his arms. Right that moment his nearness overshadowed any lingering anxiety over Mary. Right that moment her love for him was greater than anything she'd ever known.

"...OH, BURKE..."

"Does that feel as good to you as..."

"Yes! Yes!"

"I'm so deep inside...are you sure I'm not hurting you?"

"You're not hurting me."

"But I'm so deep."

"You're not hurting me."

"I've wanted to be inside you all...oh, God, yes, do that..."

"Like that?"

"Yes! Oh, yes...ohh...ohh...oh, Jill!"

"Burke!"

"YOU HAVE THE SEXIEST BACK."

"Do I?"

"Yes. Remind me to tell you sometime how it once almost drove me crazy."

"Speaking of driving someone crazy, what are you doing?"

"Will you just lie still?"

"What are you doing?"

"I'm kissing this patch of freckles...and every, every, every vertebra of your spine...and..."

"That's not my spine. That's not even my back."

"Did you know you have a dimple on your tush?"

"Not until your tongue... What are you doing?"

"Rolling you over...and kissing your tummy... Did you know you had a dimple on your tummy?"

"That's my navel, idiot...and your tongue tickles...it.... Oh!"

"Oh, God, Jill, you taste so sweet. Like flowers and honey and Milky Way starlight."

"Burke!"

"Easy, love, easy. Just open up to me."

"Ah...ah...oh, yes..."

"I ALWAYS HATED BEING SMALL."

"Why?"

"Small isn't sexy."

"Wanna bet?"

"Will you keep you hand still? You're diverting me, and I'm trying to pour my soul out to you."

"Can I help it if your breast begs to be touched?"

"I don't hear it begging."

"You're too busy talking. Trust me, it's begging. So pour out your soul."

"Well, I always had these freckles..."

"I love freckles."

"...and I've worn glasses since I was five."

"I love glasses. They remind me of Sandi Turner."

"Who's Sandi Turner?"

"She was champion of the sixth-grade spelling bee. She had braids and braces and a pair of inch-thick glasses. That was when I first realized I was turned on by brains. By the way, McClain, you have a great pair of IQs."

"You're crazy."

"About your IQs. Incidentally, my IQ is not at zero, which is fortunate for you since it enables me to see the real gist of this conversation. You're asking me—in a roundabout way, of course—if I think you're pretty."

"I am not!"

"Yes, you are."

"I am not that insecure a person. I am not that desperate for approval. I am not ... So do you think I'm pretty? Don't laugh at me."

"That's not a laugh. That's an indulgent smile. And no, I do not think you're pretty."

"No?"

"No. I think you're absolutely beautiful. Here and here and here and ..."

"Mmm ... You kiss good."

"Pusillanimity."

"What?"

"The word Sandi won my heart with."

"Bet you can't spell it."

"H-o-r-n-y?"

"Close enough."

"Did you always want to be a lawyer?"

"Yeah, Even when I was a little girl. It was sorta like it was programmed into me. I was hooked the moment I saw a *Perry Mason* episode. How about you? Did you always want to be a lawyer?"

"Nope. At five, I wanted to be a fireman. At ten, I wanted to be a policeman. At fifteen, I wanted to be a rock singer and have all the girls at my feet. At sixteen, as I recall, I wanted only two things: for my complexion to clear up and to get cheerleader Chrissie Newcomb in bed."

"Well?"

"Yeah, the complexion finally cleared up. Ouch! The hair on my chest is attached, McClain!"

"Not necessarily an unalterable fact, Rawlins. Give. What about Chrissie Newcomb?"

"By the time my complexion cleared up, she was going with Mean Tom Henderson. Tackle on the football team. There weren't no way I was messin' with him."

"So when did you decide on law?"

"My junior year of college. When Dad threatened to stop the money if I didn't major in something other than good times. But I loved law the moment I settled in with it."

"You're a good lawyer."

"I want to be better."

"Yeah. Me too."

"Why haven't you ever married?"

"That was an abrupt change of subjects, counselor."

"Not really. It's been on my mind for a long time."

"I don't know why I never married. I never wanted to be alone. I always saw myself with a house in suburbia, a station wagon, a dog with floppy ears and 2.5 kids, but it just never worked out. Oh, there were a few times it looked promising, but...I guess I was just too busy with my law studies. Sometimes lately, though..."

"Sometimes lately what?"

"I don't know, Burke. It's just that sometimes my life seems so empty. And at night. God, the night's are so long and...and..."

"And it seems that there's this big crack that you're falling through?"

"Yes. That's it exactly. And you're falling all alone...with nobody to give a damn that you're falling. Burke?"

"Hmm?"

"Do you still miss her so terribly?"

"That's funny. A week ago, I would have unequivocally said yes, but now..."

"But now?"

"Now I feel a hand pulling me out of the crack in the night."

"Burke?"

"Uh-huh?"

"You have hair on your chest..."

"Oh, my God, when did that happen?"

"...and I can find but one word to accurately describe it."

"Dare I ask what..."

"You dare. The word is yummy."

"Yummy?"

"Ellen was right all along. You are yummy...all over yummy...you're..."

"You're obviously giddy from no sleep."

"I told you my brain shuts off at 4:00 a.m."

"Do you want to go to sleep?"

"No. Do you?"

"No."

"So what do you want to do? Raid the refrigerator? Watch the late, late, late show? Hey, what are you doing?"

"Showing you what I want to do. Damn, McClain, you don't weight ten good pounds. Here, put your leg on this side...that one there...now, straddle me just like that...and let me look at you. Ah, Jill, you're so beautiful."

"Am I?"

"Yes, you am."

"Then why are you frowning?"

"I've kissed you too much. You're lips are swollen. Don't do that. Don't part your mouth that way or..."

"Or what?"

"Or I'm just going to have to kiss you again. Dammit, Jill, you did that on purpose."

"You're right. I ...mmm..."

"Mmm yourself."

"Your lips are soft."

"So are your breasts. They feel so soft and full."

"Kiss them."

"Come here."

"Oh...oh, Burke...I love it when your tongue..."

"God, all I have to do is touch you and your nipple hardens. Look. See?"

"Yes...umm...oh, Burke, they hurt..."

"Funny, so do I. Slide your hips down."

"You're hard."

"You're dewy."

"You're hot."

"So are you."

"Oh, Burke, I..."

"Put me inside you. Ohh... God, Jill, what you do to me is criminal!"

"So try me in court, counselor."

"I'd rather try you right here in bed!"

JILL AND BURKE AWOKE in the middle of the day just as the sun was climbing to its highest, hottest point. They toyed with the idea of feeling guilty about still being in bed at such a decadent hour, but both decided that guilt could go take a flying leap. So fainéant and indulgent did they become, that they breakfasted in bed, read the morning paper in bed, then crawled into the shower— together—for a sinfully slow soaping and nothing even resembling a rapid rinse. That completed, they once more found themselves in bed—toweling each other off amid giggles and tumbling play.

They forced themselves to reenter the world of responsibilities at three-thirty. But even then they fudged. Though they made the most valiant of efforts to keep their minds on the task before them and their hands off one another as they negotiated the grocery basket, their efforts met with failure. Somewhere between floor wax and furniture polish, Burke pulled her into his arms and kissed her as soundly as both products promised to perform. Later, as he carried their sacks to the car, he realized it was the first time in months that buying groceries hadn't depressed him. In fact, he felt downright happy.

After shopping, Jill dropped Burke off at his apartment. Their plans were simple. She would pick him up again at seven o'clock, they would go to dinner and she'd spend the night at his apartment. What wasn't simple was how each would manage until seven o'clock. The prospect of a few hours apart seemed unbearable.

Jill spent the time doing the laundry and her nails and fighting niggling thoughts of Mary. She consoled herself with the fact that Mary was with Rob. Which was exactly where her sister needed to be, right? And hadn't he probably by now righted whatever the wrong had been? The truth was, she thought, as she stroked the frosted white enamel the length of her nail, there wasn't anything she could do about the real or imagined problem until Monday. That being the case, she considered a happier topic: Burke.

In regard to him, she allowed herself to feel a cautious optimism. She knew that she made him happy in a way he hadn't been in a long, lonely while. She knew that slowly she was tearing down self-imposed walls, walls erected with the concrete substance of regret and bitterness and held together with the mortar of guilt. She knew also that she needed desperately to tell him of her love—

it was a heavy, smothering burden on her heart—but she was afraid to. Would it draw him nearer? Or distance him? It was a question for which she had no answer.

No more than Burke had an answer to his question. How had his life taken such a drastic turn in less than forty-eight hours? He didn't know. He knew only that it had. He knew only that he felt a soul-trembling jubilation—that kind of euphoric exultation that comes only from finding yourself alive after having already given yourself up for dead. It was the kind of rescue that heightened one's senses. As he dressed for the evening, the shower stung his skin with greater force, the cologne he splashed over his chest smelled richer, more fragrant, the cloth he wore felt stimulating to every newly awakened skin cell. Life suddenly seemed real, not merely pretended. And furthermore, it suddenly felt good—good, do you hear it, world?—to be alive.

Adjusting the silk tie, Burke turned and reached for his jacket. In midstretch, his eyes connected with the photo that stood a silent vigil at his bedside. He stopped, straightened and stepped toward the picture. He lifted it. And stared down into the face of the woman who'd been wife and lover to him. She smiled back in an eternal pose of joy. And understanding?

Burke made no attempt to classify his feelings, nor censor them, nor punish himself for them. He simply let them be, like mountains and night and silvery moonlight. Love. He had loved Nicole; he still loved her in a way that would always be real. In that way, he would be ever-faithful to her. But she was now a misty shadow-siren moving over the landscape of his sweet memories. She was yesterday. And things he could not change. Because mortal man had not the power. She was part of him, soul of him, heart of him; yet dead to him. She could never again call his name, never hold his hand, never dream life-dreams with him. She could not save him from the crack in the night. Only Jill could do that. Jill, who was becoming part of him, soul of him, heart of him. Jill, who was today and tomorrow and, in her own way, things he could not change, for he could not change what was growing in his heart.

Raising his hand, Burke brushed his fingertips across the zenith of a flawless cheek. He felt the dead-coldness of the glass, the live-warmth of his memories. He felt free. Free at last. Sighing her name in loving farewell, he stood, walked to the dresser and stored the picture of Nicole Lynch Rawlins in an empty drawer. Next to an abandoned circle of gold. Never looking back, Burke grabbed his jacket, turned out the light and walked from the room . . . and yesterday.

THE CHARLES RESTAURANT on Chestnut Street in historic Beacon Hill was a cozy little Italian hideaway. Nestled among town houses, it had a bay-windowed front and a brown-and-white canopy that umbrellaed over the entrance like a giant, benevolent caterpillar. Inside were chocolate-brown walls accented by white latticework and candelabras that gleamed with golden light.

At a back table, a sumptuous meal of chicken with fontina cheese and mushroom sauce behind them, Burke sat unabashedly adoring the woman before him.

"The breast of chicken was wonderful," Jill said, her chin resting on her steepled hands.

"Yes," he replied, his eyes drinking in the way curls dipped and plunged in wayward, drunken fashion from the silken knot secured atop her head. Though the strawberry-blond mass of hair looked beautiful in the severe style, Burke longed to free the pins from their imprisoning duties and let the hair flow through his fingers. He longed to feel it wrapped around his body with its fragrance tempting and teasing his senses.

"The wine was exquisite," Jill added.

"Yes," Burke agreed as his eyes delved into and sensuously swam in the deep, ocean blue of hers.

"The spumoni was great."

"Yes," Burke answered, his eyes roving from her soft, bronze tinted lips to the dusky peach of her skin. She wore an ivory knit sweater with a turquoise-and-gold snake choker coiled around her neck. Matching turquoise and gold studded her ears.

"There's a three-headed green monster sitting on your shoulder."

"Yes," he said, his eyes roaming over the gentle swell of her breasts, then roving upward to join once more with hers.

Jill's lips twitched. "You're not listening to me."

Burke's lips sliced into a slow grin. "Yes, I am. I have a three-headed green monster sitting on my shoulder." Without missing a beat, he added, "Have I mentioned to you tonight how beautiful you are?"

"Twice in the car, once as we were walking into the restaurant and once—or was that twice?—as we ate. But I have no objections to hearing it again."

"Greedy."

"Insatiably so."

"You're—" His hand stretched forward and his fingertips grazed her cheek "—gloriously beautiful. So very beautiful."

Unsteepling her hands, she placed her palm atop the warm hand at her cheek. For seemingly endless, for outrageously sensuous seconds, they simply stared at each other. Fiery vibrations flashed across the short distance separating them.

"Do you have any idea the restraint I'm exercising?" he whispered as he turned his hand over and meshed his fingers with hers. Drawing her hand to the table, he held it tightly, possessively, in a way that left no doubt as to the restraint he spoke of.

"You don't need to on my account," she taunted in a soft, seductive, steal-away-your-control voice.

Burke's eyes darkened in response. "Oh, but I do. I couldn't possibly do to you here what I want to. Not and stay out of jail tonight."

"What do you want to do to me?" They were playing games, lovers' games.

"You're playing with fire, McClain," he warned.

"A little heat never hurt."

"How about a lot of heat?"

"How about burning together?"

Leaning forward, speaking low, with his eyes and his lips, Burke answered her question of what he'd like to do to her—boldly, frankly and in minute and sensual detail. The intimacy was somehow made all that much greater by the crowd of people around them.

Jill felt her body go all steamy and smoldery. Burke felt his grow impossibly tight.

"You're right," she said with a sudden breathlessness, "you'd most definitely spend a couple of hours in jail over that."

"Would you bail me out?"

"Maybe," she said. Her free hand made daring little circles on the hand that held hers. "If you'd promise to do what you suggested to me again."

Slowly, suddenly, surely, the world receded. There were only two people in the room, two people with bodies aflame, two people with the need simply to be alone. Burke swallowed low; Jill sang a small sigh between provocatively parted lips.

"Let's go," he whispered roughly.

Settling the bill was torture, waiting for the valet to bring around the car a punishment that neither Jill nor Burke wanted to endure. A gentle rain had begun to fall, making a pattering, peppery noise on the overhead canopy. Somehow the tapping sound of the rain, its fresh, cool, earthy smell, only added to the sensuality of the moment.

Burke's hand rested at the small of Jill's back, where it burned . . . burned . . . burned. As did their eyes, each melting into the other's. The night had grown thick with longing.

Thighs brushed. Bodies begged. Breath halted.

"Burke . . ." she whispered, having no idea what words were to follow, knowing only that she had to say his name.

He groaned, circled his arm about her waist and blatantly hauled her to him. Before the night, before all of Boston, his mouth took hers. His lips had but sealed with hers, his tongue had but pierced the sweetness of her mouth, when the moment was shattered by—

"Burke?"

Their mouths fell apart. Burke's head jerked upward and around. His eyes met the fog-gray eyes of the man who'd called his name. His eyes then went to the brown eyes of the woman beside the man. Familiar brown eyes.

"Frank . . . Marlene . . ." Burke said in a tone that underscored his surprise.

The woman's brown eyes shifted, slowly, subtly, to the woman still partially in Burke's embrace. The gray eyes followed. Both pairs of eyes glazed with hurt; the gray filled with censure. In an instinctual move, Burke's hand slid from Jill's waist, leaving her with the sudden feeling of dread. No one spoke. For an embarrassingly long time.

At last coming to himself, Burke said, "I'm sorry. I'd like you to meet Jill McClain. Jill, Marlene and Frank Lynch." There was a hesitation, as if Burke were pulling the next words from deep within himself. He then added, with lips that still tasted of Jill, "Nicole's parents."

CHAPTER ELEVEN

SHE HAD KNOWN.

In an inexplicable way, Jill had known the couple were Burke's parents-in-law. Maybe it was because the brown eyes staring softly, sadly, at her were an exact replica of those in the picture in Burke's apartment. Maybe it was the disapproval imprisoned in the gray eyes. Maybe it was the way Burke's arm had slipped from her waist as if he'd been caught in some compromising situation. Whatever—she had known.

Just as she knew she had to respond in some way. "How do you do?" she answered, nodding and praying that the words hadn't sounded as stiff to them as they had to her. She also longed to wipe the incriminating wetness of Burke's mouth from her own. Contrarily, she longed to step back into his protective arms.

To her greeting, Frank and Marlene Lynch mumbled socially correct responses. Marlene even managed an awkward, insincere smile.

"Jill and I . . . we work together," Burke said.

And do a whole lot more together, the following silence accused.

Burke looked at his parents-in-law, the Lynches looked at their son-in-law and the woman who'd usurped their daughter, while Jill glanced up at Burke. His jaw was rigidly squared, with just a hint of a muscle twitching at the corner of his mouth. He didn't look at her. Whether it was deliberate or not, she didn't know.

Finally, and curiously, it was Marlene Lynch who tried to save the moment. "I saw your picture in the paper," she said to Jill. "You and Burke worked together on that trial."

"Yes," Jill answered, feeling that the woman was hurting desperately, but trying, just as desperately, to be fair. That attempt at fairness stabbed at Jill's heart and made it bleed with empathy. It also made her feel a guilt she knew that logically she didn't deserve to feel. Her reaction went a step further in making her realize the irrational guilt that had paralyzed Burke all these many months.

"Congratulations," Marlene Lynch said.

Jill tried to concentrate on the conversation, caught the word, and realized that the woman was speaking once more of the trial. "Thank you," she answered.

Another silence descended. The two men eyed each other and, though there was keen disapproval in the gray gaze of Frank Lynch, he eventually did say, almost resentfully, Jill thought, "You're looking well."

"I'm feeling well," Burke replied. "How have you been?"

"Not worth a damn."

"Don't you think we ought to go in?" Marlene Lynch interrupted, looping her arm through her husband's. "Our reservation is for nine o'clock." The look she gave the man beside her was pleading.

Another crisp, tart silence ensued. The moment, the people, seemed poised on an emotional precipice.

"Yeah," Frank Lynch said at last, adding in curt dismissal, "Burke."

Though Frank Lynch never once glanced back at Jill, Marlene gave a small, embarrassed smile that seemed to encompass both her and Burke. The woman had taken only a few steps when she stopped and briefly, so briefly, laid her hand on Burke's arm. "Keep in touch," she whispered. The couple then disappeared inside the restaurant.

The night grew darker. The rain pummeled harder. The car awaited them at the curb. Burke and Jill stood in place as if too war-weary to move. At last Burke gave a heavy, emotion-laden sigh. Jill turned toward him, wanting from him—as she wanted to give to him—some solace and comfort, some assurance that everything was all right even though the world at present seemed crazily tilted off its axis. Seeking, wanting, needing, her eyes climbed to his. Her heart stopped cold at the emotion she saw clouding the green irises. Anger. In all its chilling presence.

"Burke..." she whispered, confused and suddenly feeling as though she had washed ashore on a lone, deserted island. She reached out her hand to touch him. He rebuffed it by turning away.

"Let's get the hell out of here," he growled, and started for the car.

Jill's heart fell at her feet.

The drive back to his apartment was bleakly quiet except for the rhythm of windshield wipers. Jill negotiated the streets of Boston, while Burke seemed to negotiate those of hell. Staring straight ahead, never once looking at her, he seemed lost. Which was exactly how she would have described herself.

Why? she wanted to scream. Why had they had to run into Nicole's parents now? Why did they have to open wounds that had begun to heal? Why did they have to

awaken a guilt that had begun to sleep? She understood
with the clarity of a lover's paranoia that Burke's anger
was directed at her, probably even at himself. It was the
kind of anger that accompanied resentment and regret.
Regret. Oh, God, she thought, as she remembered the
way his arm had slid from her waist, the way his eyes had
not met hers, the way he'd deliberately avoided her touch:
he regretted their relationship!

Not a word was spoken as she parked the car in the lot
behind Burke's apartment building, not a word was spoken as they took the elevator to the fifth floor, not a word
was spoken as Burke unlocked the door and threw it open
wide. He walked directly to the bar in the kitchen and
poured himself a stiff bourbon on the rocks.

"Help yourself," he said gruffly, throwing off his
jacket, wrestling loose the knot of his tie and whipping
open a couple of buttons of his shirt. He headed for the
glass door of the balcony, slid it to the left and stepped
out into the rainy night. An overhang protected all except the balcony's wrought-iron rail from the free-falling
rain. It was to this rail that Burke walked and stood staring out into the moist darkness. He drew the drink to his
lips.

From the light of a lone living-room lamp, Jill watched
him. In shadow, his shoulders were mountain broad. And
isolating? Yes, isolating. They had become a wall of flesh
that he was, even as she watched, erecting between them.
He was shutting her out. He was pulling once more into
himself. He was running away from her.

Jill's stomach emptied, then filled with a fuliginous
panic. On the heels of that came a fiery-eyed anger. How
dare he discard so lightly what they'd shared together!

Burke turned at the sound of Jill's advancing footsteps as she came outside. Silhouette met silhouette. Each

sought the other's eyes, but could not find them in the night blackness. Instead, both settled for the other's presence.

Jill felt her heart pumping a pace that threatened survival. Burke felt his heart swelling with an emotion so powerfully tender that it practically knocked him back against the rail.

"Jill, I'm sor..." he began in a choked voice.

"No," she interrupted sharply. "I won't let you say it."

Burke's eyes narrowed.

"I won't let you tell me it's over. I won't let you tell me you're sorry about what's happened between us." Unknowingly, she took a step forward. Just as unknowingly, her bottom lip began to tremble. "I told you once I wouldn't fight Nicole for you. Well, I've changed my mind. I'll fight her, I'll fight her parents, I'll fight you..." Jill's voice cracked. "I'll fight the devil himself, but I won't..." Plump tears plunged from her eyes and rolled down her cheeks. "I won't... let you walk away."

She stood in dewy-eyed defiance; Burke stood in speechless surprise

Finally, he bent, set his unfinished drink on the glass table flanking the chaise lounge and closed the short distance to Jill. He roughly pulled her into his arms. The actions knocked her topknot askew and sent hair spilling over an ear. "Where in sweet hell," he said, smothering her with his nearness, "did you get the idea that I'm walking away?"

"You're angry with me," she whispered, her arms clinging in tight desperation. Her warm breath penetrated his shirt and heated his chest, just as her tears seeped through and dampened it.

Burke was again speechless. What she'd just said made no sense. It made no sense at all unless... Pushing her just that distance from him that allowed his eyes to peer down into her tear-ravaged face, he said, "Angry, yes. At you, no. Ah, Jill," he added, his voice sandpaper scratchy, "I'm angry with myself."

"For getting involved with me?"

"No. God, no! Is that what you think?" She didn't have to answer. It was written in the moistness of her dark eyes. It was written in the mascara smudges on her cheeks. It was written in the quivering silence that followed the question. He pulled her back into a fierce embrace that cascaded another section of her partially upswept hair. "For a smart lady, lady, you sure can arrive at some dumb conclusions."

Her arms folded about his muscle-corrugated back. "I thought... I thought... you pulled away from me," she added in a lover's accusation.

"I didn't deserve your touch."

"You're not angry with me?"

"No! No!"

Tears again filled her eyes. These tears, however, were tears of relief and release. They were the kind of tears a woman didn't have to explain because they were granted to her simply by being a woman.

Burke asked for no explanation as he scooped her small body into his arms and carried her to the chaise lounge. Carefully, he lowered her to its padded depths, then stretched out beside her. Once more, his body swallowed hers in an embrace.

He was warm and safe and hers in this dark night.

She was warm and woman-sweet and his in this dark night.

"Oh, Jill," he whispered as his lips spoke near the curve of her ear. "I'm sorry about this evening. I'm sorry you had to go through that with Nicole's parents." His voice lowered to the sound of regret dragged through jagged gravel. "I'm sorry I betrayed you."

She turned her head until her face was full with his. Their noses brushed, their lips almost touched, their breaths twined and laced. "Betrayed me? I don't under—"

"What else can you call what I did?" he interrupted irritably. "I sacrificed you at the altar of Nicole's parents." His jaws clenched, along with every muscle in his body. "Why didn't I tell Frank to take his rude censure and go straight to hell?"

"Because you're a caring, sensitive man and you knew that he was hurting." Jill eased her hand to Burke's neck and rubbed. The muscles there felt like gnarled knots in a tree trunk.

"But I should have defended you, our relationship. I should have told them you're the only good thing that's happened to me in so long... Oh, Lord," he said with a haunted sigh, "why do we never say what we later wished we had?"

"Because we're human."

He sighed again, this time resting his forehead against hers. "It was so stupid, Jill, but I felt this instant guilt at being caught with a woman in my arms." His voice roughened. "I hated myself for it, but even as I was hating myself, I felt my arms pulling away from you." As if to somehow make up for that fact, his arms now tightened about her.

"I know, Burke. I felt the guilt, too."

He looked down into her face. "You did?"

"Yeah," she said with a soft smile. "Guess I've been hanging around you too long."

"I hope not," he said, his expression dead serious. Her expression sobered to match his. "Oh, Jill, I'm sorry if they hurt you. I'm sorry if I hurt you."

"The only way you can hurt me is if you regret . . ."

"No," he said, the pad of his thumb drying the last of the tears from her face. "Never. And you don't have to fight anyone for me."

With a sensual slowness, his thumb caressed the softness of her cheek. Jill closed her eyes and gloried in the feel of him, gloried in the feeling of belonging to him. And she did belong to him. In a way that she didn't even belong to herself. For nothing in her incomplete being could satisfy her need to be possessed by him.

"Oh, Jill," he whispered, his lips roaming over her ear, her temple, the cheek his thumb was lovingly tormenting. Guiding her head with the deft pressure of that thumb, his mouth dropped to hers.

Sweet. His lips were candy sweet and fire hot. Just the movement of them on her mouth made her breasts grow firm, her body soft with dewy want. Like a lover who knew her body as well as his own, he sensed her instant response and brought his hand to her breast. He cupped the fullness, kneading and stroking until her nipple peaked and her breath trickled between his lips. Smoothing his hand down her skirt, he molded the cleft between her legs. He could feel the passion-heat seeping through the layers of fabric. His thumb made intimate swirls on the outside of the cloth. She melted, moaned, arched closer to what he temptingly offered.

Around them the night sang. Of blackness. Of rain. Of man and woman engaged in the oldest of rituals.

Jill's senses were swollen with the moment—the woodsy smell of Burke's cologne, the flowery smell of spring, the musky smell of desire, the feel of occasional raindrops splattering on the rail and wetting her stockinged legs.

Burke, too, was lost to his senses—the porcelain-fragile feel of the woman in his arms, the honeyed taste of her lips, the shadowy sight of her as she lay beneath him . . . responding honestly to every move of his body.

"Burke . . ." her lips pleaded against his.

He slid his hand beneath her skirt and slowly, maddeningly, trailed it up her thigh. With agile movements, he found and unfastened the garters she wore. He peeled away the scrap of cloth masquerading as panties. Then, with slight, subtle, actually quite discreet adjustments of their clothing, he shifted his weight and entered her.

Jill's body opened to receive his, just as her heart opened wide and full.

"I love you," she whispered, her hands easing into the loosened waistband of his pants and splaying across hot bare flesh.

"I know," he whispered. "I know. It's all that saves me!"

He didn't say he loved her—which she desperately wanted him to do. She felt his love, though. She felt it in his touch. She felt it in the way his body made love to hers. She heard it in the sweet-calling of her name in the dark, damp night.

As Jill and Burke exercised the sacred rites of love, Lenny Larimer exercised the profane rites of hate. His unconsecrated mementos before him—the letter he'd read a thousand times, the obituary he'd read a thousand times a thousand—he sat by the phone. His fingers stroked the receiver's smooth black surface in an unholy caress. A smile misshaped his slender lips.

He was making Mary McClain wait. He was making her sweat. He had seen what had happened in the park Friday and knew that she would be frantic to hear from him. He'd call her... oh, yeah, he'd call her... but he'd call her in his own time. For once, Leonard Larimer was calling the shots. For once...

He jerked his head upward at the sound of his name. His eyes scrambled about the room for the source of his mother's voice.

"Leonard Larimer, have you no conscience?"

"No," he whispered in protest to the noises invading his head. The way they always did of late, they made his heart throb... throb... throb... until his chest felt as if a heavy weight were crushing his ribs from front to back. His breath grew thin and slack. His hand clutched, frenziedly, at the shirt collar of his security-guard uniform, trying to rearrange it so he could breathe better.

"Have you no human decency?"

"Stop it!"

"Aren't you even the slightest bit ashamed?"

"No! Go away!" he roared, drawing the gun from its holster.

The noises stopped. Instantly. As though they'd never been.

He waited, brandishing the gun in warning.

Slowly he reholstered it. All remained quiet. Except for the throbbing thrum of his heart. This time there had been a pain in his chest, but it was going now, easing, dissolving into the flesh of his body.

"No," he whispered one last time, chasing away the last of his she-demon mother. The hand on the receiver once more stroked back and forth in an unholy caress.

MARY McCLAIN'S HAND slowly, limply fell from the phone that was tucked at her side. She slept. At last. Finally. And for the first time in days. Shifting her weight on the sofa, she dreamed—of Rob and weddings, of a tiny baby she'd named Jill and of a man named Tommy, a first love, an innocent love, a love of so very long ago.

SUNDAY MORNING at four-thirty, Jill and Burke made the prudent decision to spend Sunday night in their respective homes since it was apparent they weren't sleeping while together and since it was also apparent that they had jobs to hold down. That decision made, they sealed it by again making love. Exhausted, sated, entwined in each other's arms, they fell asleep a little after five o'clock. They slept all day and parted that afternoon at four. By the following morning, both were suffering from withdrawal symptoms and were desperately in need of just a glimpse of the other. Jill arrived at the office first. She'd hoped to find Burke already there. She found Rob Sheffield's phone message instead.

She immediately called him. "Rob?" A horrible feeling of déjà vu swept over her. Rob sounded as if a storm had swept over him, leaving him tossed and twisted inside out. "What's wrong?" In some hazy quadrant of her mind, she realized she had asked what was wrong, not if something was.

"I wish I knew. I called Mary last night when I thought she'd be home." The words didn't sound appropriate for a man who'd spent the weekend with Mary, but under the duress of the moment, Jill let this pass. "I couldn't get her. I couldn't get her early this morning, either. I called the school at eight—she's always there by then—and they said she'd called in sick. So I called the house again. She still didn't answer. Jill, what's going on?" he said, his voice suddenly sounding wind wild. "Where in hell is Mary?"

Jill's pulse rate had increased the second Rob had begun to speak. It now ticked with a rampant rhythm. She told herself to just stay calm and rational. In honor of both, she said, "If she's sick, maybe she's gone to a doctor."

"I thought of that. But why not call me to take her? Or you?"

The same thought occurred to Jill even as she was making the comment. She was searching for another calm and rational explanation when Rob asked, "Did she give any indication this weekend of what's been bothering her?"

The question bit at Jill's composure like a sharp-toothed serpent. "What?" she asked breathlessly.

"Did she say anything this weekend? I thought maybe just the two of you together, she'd tell..."

"You didn't go to the Berkshires." It wasn't even a question. In her heart Jill already knew the hideous answer.

"What?"

"She told me...she told me the two of you were going to the Berkshires."

The silence was complete as the implications settled.

When Rob finally spoke, his voice was disturbingly calm. "She told me you and she...that you were going to finalize the wedding plans...look for dresses and all that. She made it sound like it was a girl-stuff weekend at your place."

Jill turned an unlikely mixture of searing hot and freezing cold. In all of her life, she had never felt so scared or so helpless. She would have given anything for the shelter of Burke's arms.

"Ji-ll . . ."

She heard the voice of a strong man crack and knew that at the other end of the phone Rob Sheffield was coming apart. For his sake only, she forced herself to be strong. "Rob, listen to me. There's got to be an explanation for all of this, and we'll find out what it is. You're at work, aren't you?"

"Yes. I, uh . . . I have a couple of things I have to do around here." He had entered the numb, nonfeeling world of shock, and his words had a spaced-out quality. "A report on an experiment . . ."

"Rob, I'll start calling her the minute I hang up. If I get her, I'll call you. In the meantime you finish up there, and can you go by the house and wait there for her?"

"Yeah," he said. "I'll . . . I'll take the rest of the day off."

"Everything's going to be okay," she said, praying to God she was right.

"Yeah . . . yeah."

"I'll talk to you later, then."

"Right." As Jill was lowering the phone from her ear, she heard, in a tone that cut at her heart, "Jill? Where is she?"

"I don't know, Rob," she replied, her own voice breaking. "I don't know."

MARY MCCLAIN SAT huddled on her sofa, the tapestry bag of money clutched tightly to her chest. Beside her, the phone rang. She had lost count of how many times it had rung. A dozen? Two dozen? She didn't know, and it didn't matter. She wasn't going to answer it. He had called the night before and had told her to bring the money at noon today. That had been the only phone call she'd wanted to take. She didn't want to talk to Rob or

Jill. Talking to them only made her feel guilty. She had lied to them. The only two people in the whole world she really loved and she'd lied to them. And she felt sick, sick at her heart, that she had.

The phone stopped.

She relaxed her hold on the bag.

And checked her watch.

Three hours and it would be over. Or would it? Was this only the beginning? Would this nightmare go on and on and on until money and truth had been bled from her? Was it destined that she be exposed for what she was?

The phone began another sharp peal.

Mary jumped.

And fought back the clawing fear that her world was about to shatter.

IT WAS PRECISELY 9:09 a.m. when Burke tapped on and pushed open the door of Jill's office. A smile was already traveling to his lips, and that light-headed feeling he always got when he saw her was already thinning his thoughts.

At the sound of the door opening, Jill turned from where she was standing at the window. The incessant ringing of an unanswered phone still echoed in her ears.

When his eyes found hers, Burke frowned, slowed, then stopped altogether. "What's wrong?" he asked, knowing immediately that she wasn't crying, but close to it.

Jill swallowed back the clotted knot in her throat. "Mary didn't spend the weekend in the Berkshires with Rob."

"What?" he asked, stepping forward and placing his briefcase on the edge of her desk. Hers, too, lay there, unopened. "I thought..."

"She told Rob she was spending the weekend with me." Jill inclined her head to meet the eyes of the man now standing before her. "Rob called earlier and said that she called in sick today. But there's no answer when we call the house. Oh, Burke," she whispered, allowing her composure to slip now that he was near enough to catch it, "she's disappeared again."

The despairing look on her face, the blue eyes glassy with crystalline tears, tore at his heart. He did the only thing he could to comfort her: he pulled her into his arms.

Hers wrapped about his waist fiercely, as if she were trying to push her body into his. "Hold me," she pleaded. "Please hold me!"

"I've got you," he said, fitting her so tightly to him that body angles and planes blended and melded. "I've got you." His hand moved to cup the back of her head, burrowing her face deep into his shoulder.

"I don't understand," she whispered. "I just don't understand what's happening." His suit jacket had come unfastened, and she stood with her cheek flush against his shirt. Her words were fluttery vapor that drifted to his ears. "She lied, Burke. She's never lied to me before." Hurt was profoundly present in her voice.

"Maybe..." he began, but didn't finish. There was no ready reassurance on the tip of his tongue. "Have you tried to call her?"

Jill glanced up into his concerned face. "Conservatively, a hundred times."

"What's the number?" he asked, slowly disengaging their bodies and picking up the phone. She told him. He dialed it. Spreading his hand inside his jacket and at his waist, he waited for the phone to ring. Which it did. Again and again.

Jill watched, hoping, praying this was the moment Mary would finally answer. Her eyes locked with Burke's, she waited. Waited. Waited.

"I hate that damned phone!" she said when it was obvious Mary wasn't going to answer. "That stupid wrong number was the beginning of Mary's strange behavior."

"The call she got the night you had dinner with her and Rob?" Burke asked, remembering Jill's mention of the call Friday evening, when she'd first worried about a vanishing Mary.

Jill nodded, raking back her hair with a hand that looked none too steady.

"I will admit," he said, "that she acted a little peculiar the evening I ate there. When the phone rang while we were playing ball . . ." He stopped at the sudden look that flashed across Jill's face. "What is it?"

"I just remembered another phone call," she said, her eyes going hazy blank with her effort to uncover details that were buried deep within her mind.

"When?"

"A week ago Sunday when I dropped by the house, I left Mary in the attic packing. As I was leaving, the phone rang. I answered it, but thought it was a wrong number."

"What did the caller say?"

"It was a man, and he said . . ."

"What?"

"I can't remember exactly. Something about . . . something about needing to talk about your daughter again." She shrugged. "I don't really know why I thought of it now, except it's just one more phone incident. You don't

think it could have anything to do with ... What is it?"
she asked, concerned by the look on his face.

"Nothing," he said, but in his heart he wasn't so sure
the thought that had just crossed his mind was nothing.
In fact, he thought it might be a very decided something. He had just made a murky association between
Mary McClain's frantic need for money and a strange
caller who'd talked about a daughter. The thought was
wild, the thought was crazy, but, dammit, the thought
made sense! Most particularly in view of everything that
was happening.

"No, it is something," Jill accurately assessed, moving toward him. "What?"

His hands gripped her shoulders. "Let me do some
checking ..."

"What?"

"I may be wrong."

"Tell me!"

He didn't want to. God, he didn't want to! What if he
was wrong? But, worse, what if he was right?

"Please," she whispered, her eyes, her touch, begging
in a way he couldn't resist.

"Jill, think about it. The scenario is perfect for ... for
blackmail."

The word hung in the air. Blackmail. It was that sinister crime that happened occasionally in real life, but
mostly in dramatic mystery movies or TV soap operas.

"That's absurd," she said. "What would Mary have
in her life to be blackmailed about?"

"Let me check on something," Burke repeated, reluctant to add anything more without proof.

"If you know something, if you only suspect something, I want to know what it is."

Her voice had a steel edge. It was the same steel that ran down the back of her diminutive frame. She might be physically pint-size, but she was emotionally pounds-strong. *In many ways, she is stronger than me,* Burke thought.

"I think it's possible... What if Mary has a daughter? What if someone found out and is blackmailing her?" His words were blunt. But it was the truth the way he knew Jill would want it.

He watched as denial registered on Jill's face. He then saw her struggle to at least accept the possibility. That acceptance was not without a price, however. He felt her knees weaken. At the slackness, he eased her into the nearby chair and, pulling at his pant legs, hunched down before her. His palm splayed across her cheek. It felt chilled.

"I could be wrong, you know. Dead wrong."

"How... how can you verify it?"

"Do you want me to try?"

She swallowed, making her mouth form the hateful words. "You know I do."

Yes, he did know it. And in that moment he prayed harder than he'd ever prayed for anything that he was wrong. "Let me go to my office and make a few phone calls..."

"No!" she said, grabbing his hand in hers. "Make them here."

His eyes bore deeply into hers. Slowly, he brought her hand to his lips and tenderly kissed her knuckles. He then pulled his hand from hers and stood. Walking to her desk, he sat down in her chair and picked up the phone. The receptionist came on the line.

"Would you get Harriet Cummings for me?" he said, his eyes on Jill. At the mention of the corporate lawyer who had bureaucratic connections, Jill's blue irises glazed with a thin sheet of surprise. She said nothing, however. Seconds later, Burke spoke again, "Harriet, Burke Rawlins here. Fine, thanks. Listen, I want you to do something for me. Can you give me the name of someone in statistical records who can rush something through for me?" He listened. "Yes. Very important. Thanks. I owe you."

He hung up the phone and looked over at Jill. The usual color in her cheeks had faded to a white comparable to the shade of the ivory suit she wore. It took all of Burke's willpower not to get up and go to her.

"Is someone going to call you back?" she asked, wondering if the calm voice was really hers.

He nodded. They waited. For two long minutes. At last the phone rang. "Rawlins here. Yes, yes, I appreciate your calling, Susan. Listen, I, uh . . . I need to confirm a birth. I know the mother's name, that the child was a girl, and I guesstimate it occurred about—" he remembered Jill's saying that Mary was fifty years old "—let's say thirty, thirty-five years ago." He frowned. "No way at all without the child's name?" He waited, listened. "That's great. Then let's try hospitals. Yes, I know they're a lot of hospitals in Massachusetts," he said semi-irritably. "For that matter, it could have been anywhere in the country. No, no, I know you can't check every hospital in the United States. Look, try the hospitals in Shawsheen under the name of Mary McClain. That's correct. M-c-C-l-a-i-n. Yes, I'll hold."

He looked up at Jill, who seemed even paler than before. The shock was receding and pain settling in.

"I'm waiting while she uses another line...something about a computer terminal." A seemingly endless period of time passed before he once more said into the phone, "Nothing?" He gave a disgruntled sigh.

"Try Massachusetts General," Jill said.

Burke glanced up. "I was born in Massachusetts General. Maybe Mother would have taken Mary...maybe Mary would have gone there to..." She stopped. "A large hospital away from home would have been more discreet for an...unwed mother."

Approving the logic, admiring the lady, he said, "Check Massachusetts General."

Time dragged. The clock ticked mockingly. Burke willed part of his strength to the woman who sat quietly waiting. Finally, "Yeah? Okay, give me that information," he added, picking up a pen and scribbling the notations on a pad. "Yeah. Yeah. When? Right. 1952." Abruptly, his hand stopped in midmotion. Along with his heart. He jerked his head toward Jill. "What did you say?" His voice was only a filmy pretense of speech. "Are you sure about the child's name? Well, dammit, be sure! I'm sorry. Please check again." His eyes darkened. "I see. Yes. Yes. I appreciate your help."

With nerveless fingers, Burke hung up the phone. A sick feeling snake-crawled through his stomach. Everything in him was screaming no! No, he couldn't be the one to tell her this. But, dear God, how could he trust this to anyone else?

Jill sensed Burke's sudden reticence. Her heart accelerated. "What is it? What did she say?" Her eyes pinned his, demanding an answer, an honest answer.

"Jill..."

"Just say it. Whatever it is."

But he couldn't. He couldn't!

"Dammit, Burke, what is it?" Jill asked, jumping from the chair and leaning across the desk to turn the notepad toward her. Burke's hand stopped hers. Her eyes warred with his. They also begged him to answer... and to somehow protect her from the ugly revelation she knew was coming.

"A Mary Elaine McClain gave birth to a daughter." He swallowed. "On January 12, 1952."

The fact that Mary McClain had, indeed, given birth to a daughter took precedence for a full cycle of wild heartbeats. When the date finally registered, Jill frowned. "But that's... that's my birthday." Still, the full implication of Burke's words had not dawned. Like a withering bolt out of the blue, it suddenly did. Her face blanched; her heart stopped. "What... what are you saying?" she asked, her string-thin voice a stranger to her own ears.

Slowly Burke stood, walked around the desk and took both of her hands in his. He felt them trembling even as he heard his own voice tremble. "She named the child... Jill Elizabeth."

CHAPTER TWELVE

"NO. IT'S NOT TRUE."

Jill heard the obligatory denial slip through her lips and thought how contradictory it was to what she was feeling in her heart. For there, in an intuitive way she couldn't explain, she believed totally, unequivocally, what Burke had just told her. She felt its truth. That truth, however, distorted her life as if she'd unexpectedly been shoved before a fun-house mirror.

No, Jill thought wildly, this newly revealed life was not the distortion. The old life, the old belief, the belief that Mary was her sister, that was unreal.

She realized vaguely that someone—Burke? Yes, Burke—was saying something to her. She tried to concentrate on what that something was.

"...right?"

"What?"

"Are you all right?"

She focused on his face and saw eyes that were bright with worry. She also noted that, while one of his hands still held one of hers, the other had slipped about her waist to offer a greater measure of support. She swayed into him and let his arm tighten. "Yes," she said, nodding. "I'm fine."

"Why don't you sit down?" Burke said, urging her toward a chair.

"I don't want..."

"Sit down," he said softly, but firmly. He exerted just enough pressure to force her onto the chair. "Stay right there," he ordered, trying to pull his hand from hers. Unconsciously, she held onto him, resisting abandonment. "Jill, turn loose," he commanded, prying at her fingers. "I'll be right back." She let go of him,...or maybe he was just stronger than she. "Don't move. Do you hear me?"

Jill nodded again, her hair gently swaying about her shoulders.

With rapid steps, Burke crossed the room, opened the door and disappeared into the hall. Jill leaned back in the chair and closed her eyes. Her heart was hammering a swift rhythm that left a residue of smothered sound in her ears. Beyond it, she could hear the mocking repetition of her name: *Jill Elizabeth...Jill Elizabeth...Jill Elizabeth...*

She thought back to the day in the attic when she'd felt such a sharp sense of separation at the thought of Mary marrying Rob. It was an almost too-keen feeling for a sibling relationship, but not for a child-parent one. Had some intuitive force been at work even then?

"Here." She opened her eyes—a shock-hazy fluttering of reddish-hued lashes. Burke was squatting before her and holding out a paper cup of water. She reached for it, took it, and they both watched as her hand trembled so badly the water almost sloshed over the edge.

"I'm shaking," she said in disbelief.

Burke placed his strong, steadying hand over hers. "Drink," he ordered in a tone that could only be described as a loving whisper.

The water tasted cool and moistened the stress-parched dryness of her mouth. With Burke's help, she took another sip, followed by another. She lowered the cup to her lap. Her eyes went to his. Subliminally, she realized he was worried about her. A warm feeling seeped through her. It was the kind of feeling people hold on to when the world is coming apart at the seams.

"Why?" she whispered. "Why let me believe all these years that Mary... I don't understand. Why, Burke?"

His fingers tucked a truant wisp of hair back behind her ear. "I don't know, baby. I just don't know."

"What am I going to do?"

Her eyes shone wide, blue and with more vulnerability than Burke had ever seen in them. He longed to take her to bed, pull her next to him and shelter her with his body. And he would at some point because he needed to protect her the way she needed his protection. But right now, he said, "You're going to ask Mary the question you just asked me."

"Will you go with me?"

"Do you want me to?"

She reached for the hand at her cheek and threaded her fingers with his, a desperate lacing. "Yes. Please go with me."

He stood, drawing her up with him. "Let's wait for her at her house. Wherever she is, she'll go home eventually."

Within minutes, Burke had ordered all their appointments cancelled and was escorting Jill to her car. His arm at her waist was her only reality. There was a moment's silent apology as he held the door while she seated herself in front of the wheel. His look eloquently said that he should be driving and not she.

"I'm all right," she said. "Really I am."

And she did feel better. At least in some respects. There was something wonderfully comforting, something wonderfully normal, about stepping out into the sun-dappled spring morning. The world was still as it should be.

A thousand feelings—some she could catalog, some she couldn't—wandered in and out of her being as she drove the twenty-plus miles to the little yellow house that now had a poignant familiarity that was soul-painful. Shock, nature's kind, benevolent anesthetic, still numbed the outer edges of her consciousness, but deep within were churning the feelings of hurt and anger. How could *they*—she could not yet nominally distinguish between her mother and grandmother—betray her so? And why would they choose to?

"Do you have a birth certificate?" Burke asked, breaking into her musings.

She turned her eyes to him. "Yes." She knew what he was asking. "My parents are listed as Margaret and Edward McClain." Somehow that planned deception, even from the moment of her birth, deepened the hurt.

Burke saw the pain. "Jill, give her a chance to explain. There may even be a chance we've misinterpreted..."

"Do you believe that?" she interrupted. When he didn't, couldn't, answer, she added, "Neither do I."

Slowly, she turned the car into Mary's driveway. The shades were pulled like lids over sleeping eyes, and the house looked lonely and vacant. Suddenly, Jill's heart filled with anxiety. Where was Mary? Was she in danger? Just as suddenly, her heart filled with a thick, loving emotion. It didn't matter what her biological tie was to the woman, it didn't matter about lies and deceptions and betrayals, she cared about her. She always had, she always would. It was the unbending, unending nature of love.

IT WOULD HAVE BEEN HARD to say who was the more surprised—Jill at unlocking the door and finding a missing Mary sitting on the sofa, or Mary, at finding an unexpected Jill standing before her.

"Mary!" Jill said, relief flash-dancing through her body.

"Jill!" The hands holding the tapestry bag tightened until the knuckles were bleached of color. Normally docile eyes were suddenly streaked in panic. "W-what are you doing here?"

"I've, we've, been trying to reach you all morning," Jill said, thinking that Mary looked awful, a sleepless and sallow-skin kind of awful.

"I . . . I was just on my way out." Her response was in no way an appropriate explanation of why she had been unreachable all morning, and all three people in the room knew it.

"Where are you going?" Jill asked, her eyes, along with Burke's, lowering to the bag being throttled to death in Mary's lap. Mary's eyes followed theirs. She forced herself to relax her grip. "I, uh . . . just out . . . an errand . . ."

"Out to meet a blackmailer?" Jill suggested, posing the question in her typically blunt fashion.

The room grew silent. Suck-in-a-breath silent. Mary McClain's face drained to a color so sheet-white that the freckles dotting her oval face seemed to turn pitch-black. The bag in her suddenly lifeless hands slid in slow motion, then fell from her lap and to the floor. In the stillness, the fall sounded like a deafening thunk, just as the fluttering of twenty-dollar bills escaping the bag sounded a great deal like the end of the world. Three pairs of eyes lowered to the incriminating green-and-white currency.

Burke sighed, momentarily closed his eyes and wished to God that he'd been wrong.

Mary prayed—foolishly, she knew—that Jill didn't know why she was being blackmailed.

Jill felt a wave of nausea. In spite of everything, she realized that she was still holding out hope that she and Burke had been wrong. But they hadn't been. Dear God, they hadn't been! And if they were right about the blackmail, they were right about . . .

Jill raised her eyes to meet those of the woman before her. What was to play out now was nothing more than a verbal ritual. Jill would ask the question, just as each knew she would, just as each knew she must. Mary would answer, in exactly the same way, for exactly the same reason. And the answer, both women already knew.

"Are you my mother?" Jill asked softly.

In an unconscious gesture of protection, Burke stepped closer to Jill. His hand touched the small of her back.

Mary McClain swallowed, deeply, and opened her mouth. No words emerged from her pallid lips. Ultimately, she pushed herself from the sofa and stood. Shaky, unsteady, she swayed. Instinctively, Burke grasped her upper arm to balance her. She glanced up at him and smiled. "Thank you," she whispered, then woodenly moved off toward the window. She stared out into the sun-drenched morning and thought about her first-graders who were probably at recess—playing ball and jumping rope and squealing in tag, doing all those innocent things that children do. Innocent. The opposite of guilty.

"Mary?" Jill pleaded in an I-need-to-hear-you-say-it tone.

Mary McClain turned, her autumn-brown eyes glistening with the tears of thirty-four years' worth of sorrow. She also felt a keen sense of resignation. She supposed she had always known this moment would come. It briefly crossed her mind to wonder how Jill had discovered the truth, but admitted that the how didn't really matter. Nothing mattered except the cleansing of guilt, the begging of forgiveness.

Mary again swallowed; this time she spoke. "Please believe me, Jill. I never intended for you not to know. I promised that to myself, and to you, the first time I ever held you in my arms."

Fine tremors had begun a wavy surge over Jill's body. "Then why?" Her voice was barely audible.

"I was waiting for the day when you were old enough to understand. I . . . I guess I didn't know how to judge that day." She smiled again, this time sadly and in accompaniment to a lone tear that slid down her cheek. "I kept thinking that tomorrow would be a better day to tell you. And then it was too late. Too many tomorrows had passed." She wiped at the tear with the heel of her hand. "And in a strange way I guess I had begun to believe the lie I had lived so long. Lies are like that. They deceive the liar as well as those lied to."

"But why lie at all?" Jill asked, not even attempting to hide her lack of understanding. "Why not from the beginning . . . ?"

"Don't you think I wanted to?" Mary asked, slicing through Jill's question with a voice harsh and rough and totally atypical. Fresh tears flooded her eyes, robbing her words of their stability. "Don't you think I wanted to claim you as my daughter?"

"Then why?" There was an equal roughness in Jill's voice, an impatience, a make-me-understand.

"Your grandparents!" Mary shouted before deliberately forcing her voice to a lower pitch. "Your grandparents wouldn't let me." Bitterness clung like cloying hands to each word as she added, "I don't think I've ever forgiven them for that. Or ever will."

The couple she'd always thought of as parents being referred to as her grandparents further disoriented Jill. She had the sudden urge to pinch herself awake from a bad dream. She also had the sudden need to be in Burke's arms. She settled for stepping closer into the hand still at her back. It splayed wide in a way that was comforting.

"I don't know," Mary said, "maybe I should have stood my ground. But I was only sixteen, Jill. Sixteen. And scared. And we'd already had a battle royal. When I told them I was pregnant, they insisted I give the baby up for adoption. I told them I'd never do that. Never. And I meant it. I also accused Mother of being more concerned about her social standing in Shawsheen than she was about me." Mary's face clouded with painful memories that the years had not been able to whitewash. "It was the only time Mother ever struck me. But it was true. God help me, it was true. She was more concerned about what her friends and neighbors would think than she was about what happened to me."

For the first time Mary's prejudice against small-town thinking made sense. What didn't make sense was the fact that never once had Jill suspected Mary's antagonism toward Margaret and Ed McClain. Perhaps it was to Mary's credit that she'd tried not to taint Jill's opinion of the couple.

"So they told you you could keep the baby, but that they'd raise it as their own," Jill offered, unable now, though, to keep a sense of bitterness at bay.

"Yes," Mary concurred quietly. "Oh, and they concoted an elaborate plan," she said with a mirthless laugh. She wiped futilely at the wetness on her cheek and sniffed. "Suddenly, and very conveniently, Mother had an aunt dying in Boston. Mind you, the aunt had already been dead three years when Mother moved to Boston to take care of her." An unaccustomed sarcasm laced Mary's words. "I went with her, of course. She told everyone I was transferring to a school there. Which wasn't true. I studied on my own. Anyway, Mother planted all kinds of clues before she left, like the fact she couldn't keep anything on her stomach in the mornings, so that when she wrote back that she was pregnant, everyone bought it—hook, line and sinker." The sarcasm was back when she added, "And everyone thought it so wonderful that Margaret and Ed were having another child because they'd wanted another one for so long." Mary's eyes filled once more, and she turned back to the window. Her shoulders heaved in silent tears.

Jill longed to comfort her, but couldn't. Everything was so new, so changed, and she herself was hurting. So badly. "So I became . . . your sister."

Mary nodded and spoke in an uneven, moist voice. "Yes. You were born in Massachusetts General, and somehow or other, Dad persuaded the records people to just list M. McClain as the mother."

Jill frowned. "But the birth certificate says Margaret."

"You assumed it said Margaret. Just as the records people assumed the *M* stood for Mary. Oh, it was well planned," Mary said, "down to the last detail and with the stipulation that . . . that the deception was never to be mentioned. Not even among ourselves. And that you were never to be called my daughter, nor I your mother. And I was never to care for you as a mother. I was never to do motherly things for you." Her voice broke again. "We were all to play the game. And we did. I swear, I think that Mother actually grew to believe you were hers.'' Her shoulders heaved again, this time expelling great tears of great hurt. ''I never—'' her voice sounded blubbery, quavery ''—I never found it that easy to play the game.''

Heartache. It filled the room like a tangible entity. Jill felt it undulating in cresting and ebbing waves, felt it welling and swelling in herself. Tears rushed to her own eyes.

Burke's arm slid about her waist. He simply held her to him as tightly as he could. He let her cry, knowing it was useless to try to stop her, knowing, too, that the release was therapeutic.

''Mary,'' Burke called softly when he thought the moment appropriate, ''who's blackmailing you?''

She turned, assessed the intimate posture of Jill and Burke—on some faraway level she approved—and shook her head. ''I don't know. Some man. He just started calling. He first asked for five thousand...''

''Did you pay it?'' Burke asked.

She nodded. ''I had to. I...'' She broke off in deference to another scalding wash of tears.

''And he asked for more?'' Burke rightly assumed.

''Yes. Two thousand more.''

''You have no idea...''

She shook her head again. ''No. Only the three of us knew—Mother, Dad and me.''

''What about...the father?'' Burke asked...and felt Jill's muscles stiffen.

Mary's eyes lowered from Burke's to her daughter's. ''No,'' she whispered, ''he never even knew I was going to have his baby.'' A tremendous sadness shaded Mary's eyes, leaving them the somber color of regret.

"Who is my father?" As she asked the question, Jill realized that she had been so caught up in the discovery that Mary was her mother that she had given only the most marginal consideration to her father. She now found herself waiting with bated breath.

"He's dead, Jill. He died in Korea.

"Oh."

Mary took a tentative step forward. "It was not...a tawdry affair. We were in love." She smiled again, plaintively. "Mother assured me it was only puppy love, that you couldn't experience the real thing at sixteen, but I knew better. I knew what I felt. I knew what he felt." She sniffed. And stepped closer. "He was a neighbor and two years older than me. We had known each other for a long time, then suddenly—" the look in her eyes became youthful as she relived happy memories "—suddenly everything clicked. We fell in love. We were going to be married." The happiness of yesteryear faded slightly though not fully. "He had just graduated from high school, with honors, and wanted to go to law school..."

Jill's eyes questioned.

Mary smiled, genuinely. "Yeah. I could hardly believe it when you told me you wanted to be a lawyer. It was like a little part of him lived...that and your eyes. You have his eyes. His eyes were always so..." She again seemed lost in some bittersweet past that had draped a gauzy curtain about her. "Anyway," she said, continuing after a long pause, "he wanted to go to law school, but Korea broke out and..." She sighed, stepping closer. "He died a hero. They said that he saved five men's lives. He's buried in Arlington. They gave him...the Medal of Honor." Silent tears had begun again—both Mary's and Jill's. "He died before...he never even knew that I...

Oh, God," she said, crazily raking her fingers through her shorter-than-short hair, "he never even knew."

"The man in the picture," Jill said lowly.

"What?"

"The man in the picture was my father." *Don't ask me how I know,* she thought, *I just know.* It was the way she had felt the truth of Mary's relationship to her. Somehow, the hidden truth exposed, everything seemed right.

"Yes," Mary answered. "Tommy Wilson."

For a reason that made absolutely no sense, knowing that the man in the picture was her father increased Jill's sense of loss, personalized it in a way it hadn't been before. Jill's own heart ached at the callous unfairness of life. And, curiously, she felt an irreplaceable loss. She would never know the man who helped give her life. Suddenly that was very important. And supremely tragic.

Mary stood only inches from Jill. Tentatively, uncertainly, she reached out a hand. She hesitated, as if unsure she had the right, then brushed a strand of hair back from Jill's face. Her hand trembled. Jill felt the shaky motion at her temple. "Don't cry," Mary begged. "Please don't cry." It was a strange request, coming as it did from a woman who herself was crying.

Until that moment, Jill hadn't realized that she was crying. She sniffed and swiped at tears and ran a hand beneath a runny nose.

"He would have been so proud of you," Mary whispered, still stroking Jill's hair as if she couldn't stand the thought of drawing her hand away. "And he would have loved you—" her voice cracked into a million irreparable shards "—as much as I've always... They couldn't order me not to love you."

Burke had stepped away, leaving the two women to the private moment. He found his own eyes misty and his throat painfully constricted.

"Mary..." Jill began, to say heaven only knew what.

"Don't hate me," Mary interrupted. "Please don't hate me." Tears swelled and streamed. "I've already paid a price you can't possibly imagine. I paid it every time you called her mother, I paid it every time you ran to her with a scraped knee, I paid it every time you reached for her hand when you were scared."

Selfish. The word danced across Jill's conscience. She had been so concerned with her own feelings—her own feelings of confusion and betrayal—that she had quite forgotten she wasn't the only one suffering, that Mary had already done so, and would continue to do so, in ways that Jill could never equal. Mary had lost the man she'd loved and been denied her child. All in one fell swoop and at such a vulnerable age.

"I could never hate you," Jill said, now touching Mary's hair in a way that echoed Mary's last gesture. "I love you."

The declaration brought a fresh batch of tears from both women. Like intimate strangers, they just stood staring at each other, trying desperately to make the pieces of the world, the pieces of their lives, fit together.

"Sometimes at night when you were a baby," Mary said, her voice nothing but a wisp of sound, "I'd sneak into your room and...just hold you...just...just..." As if she had no will, she pulled Jill into her arms and cupped her hand at the back of her head. "I'd hold you." The words trailed into a mother's infinity. "Shh," she crooned as she gently stroked Jill's head, "it's all right. Everything's all right, baby...my sweet, sweet baby... everything's..."

Mary's eyes connected with those of the man standing only feet away. The abrupt, scissors-clipped silence drew both Jill's and Burke's immediate attention. Jill turned . . . and slowly stepped from Mary's embrace.

Rob Sheffield looked like a man shot and left for dead. That he'd been standing there long enough to piece a whole lot of facts together was more than obvious. It was also obvious that he was hurting.

"Why?" he asked gruffly, yet softly. "Why didn't you trust me?"

There seemed little emotion left in Mary, certainly no fight, no defense of herself. She answered honestly, tonelessly, as if she were speaking for and of someone else. "Second chances in life are hard to come by. I didn't want to do anything to jeopardize mine."

"But surely I had a right . . ."

"I had loved Tommy very much," she interrupted. "So much that I spent years of my life mourning him. And then you came along. I couldn't believe I was falling in love again—and in a way that was much stronger than I'd ever loved before. I didn't deserve you—I knew that—but, God forgive me, I couldn't do anything that might drive you away. I reasoned that if Jill didn't know, why should anyone else?"

Rob worked his hand through his already finger-tangled hair. "Dammit, Mary, marriage is based on trust!"

A last light dimmed, then died in Mary's eyes. She smiled dejectedly, but with acceptance. "Yes, it is, isn't it?" she said, her eyes walking through the endless boundaries of his before dropping to the diamond on her left hand. It sparkled beautifully, but mockingly. She had slipped the ring to her knuckle when Rob abruptly stopped her by shoving it back into place.

Her eyes flew upward.

"Don't you ever take that off," he barked tenderly, seconds before yanking her into his arms.

She went. Tears that she had believed to be cried out resurfaced. "I'm sorry," she sobbed into his shoulder. "Oh, Rob, I'm so sorry. I never meant to hurt... anyone."

"Shh, everything's all right...everything's all right..." he whispered over and over in the same litany that she, only minutes before, had chanted to Jill.

Jill's eyes filled again, and she glanced over at Burke.

His eyes sent her a heated, caring message before he stooped to pick up the money and stuff it back into the bag. That accomplished, he stood. "Mary?" She was still buried in Rob's embrace. "Mary?"

It was Rob's attention that he finally ensnared. Rob nudged the woman in his arms. She looked over at Burke

"When and where were you to deliver this?"

She told him.

The two men's eyes met and spoke. "Call the police," Burke said, "and tell them to meet me there."

He started for the door. Jill fell into step beside him.

"Where do you think you're going?" Burke asked, scowling.

"With you," she replied, stubbornly.

"Oh, no, you're not."

"Oh, yes, I am."

"Jill, this could be dangerous."

"I'm well aware of that."

"No."

"Yes."

"No! I won't..."

She grabbed his arm. "Burke, let me do this. Let me do it for Mary and...a man I'll never know." Time

plodded by, an ceaseless patter of seconds. "Besides,"
she added, a slight smile curving her mouth, "who's
gonna drive?"

The last question carried less weight than Burke would
have thought possible days, weeks, months before. Jill's
first statement, however, was another matter. It was
something he simply did not have the right to deny her.

"Okay," he relented, "but you're going to stay in the
car when we get there. You hear me?" They pushed
through the front door—neither heard it slam—and out
into the yard. Their steps briskly cut through grass and
gravel. "Do you hear me, McClain?" he repeated, jerk-
ing open the car door and ducking his head inside.
"Jill?"

"I hear, I hear!" she said, giving a final swipe to her
nose and starting the engine.

It was high noon, and the hour of delivery, when Jill
parked the car and silenced the motor. She immediately
unlatched the door and swung it wide.

"Jill," Burke said, the one word a reminder of their
agreement.

She got out and rounded the hood of the car.

"Jill!" he barked, throwing open his door.

Ignoring him, she headed off in the direction of the
Boston Public Garden.

He grabbed her by the wrist, twirled her around, and
pinned her against the car. "You promised me..."

"I said I heard you," she cut in, looking up into eyes
that were caringly harsh. "I never said I'd stay in the
car."

"We had a verbal contract based on a tacit implication."

Despite everything, maybe because of the pressure of
everything, Jill smiled. "You sound like a lawyer."

Burke's lips curved into a slow smile. "Don't change the subject." His smile trailed away, and a fistful of knuckles grazed her chin. "If anything should happen to you, I . . ." He quite literally couldn't finish the sentence for the iceberg-cold feeling invading his heart. It threatened to frost the breath in his chest.

"Nothing's going to happen to me," she said in a sweet, silver-laced voice. "But that's why I have to go with you. I have to see that nothing happens to you. I'm not through loving you yet, Rawlins."

Her love words, the nearness of her body, thawed the glacial fingers choking his heart. That and the brilliant sun beating down on them. Nothing too tragic could happen on such a fair day to such a fair lady who did such unfair things to his heart. "Don't ever," he whispered, adding, "get through with loving me."

"No," she whispered with a shake of her head.

His eyes scanned her face. It bore the ravages of stress. Crying had puffed and reddened her eyes and had stripped mascara from lashes and left it in sooty lines on her lower lids. Her makeup had been streaked, her blusher eliminated entirely. It looked as though the color had been stolen from her lips and deposited at the end of her nose. In short, she should have looked awful. Burke thought she'd never looked more beautiful.

"You've had a bitch of a morning, haven't you?" he asked, his admiration growing with each moment he knew her.

"Yes. Why don't you kiss it and make it better?"

The set of knuckles beneath her chin exerted the pressure necessary to tilt her face up to his. His mouth lowered. His lips touched hers. At sublime contact the boundary between his and hers was obliterated. There was only the gentle working of mouths, each against the other. Slow and sure, familiar and intimate. In clingy reluctance, they parted.

"Please understand that I have to go with you," she whispered.

"All right," he agreed, "but will you stay out of sight and let me deliver the money?"

"No, let me drop it."

"Jill..."

"Burke, listen, he's expecting a woman. Seeing you might spook him."

"He's expecting Mary. And you don't look a thing like..."

"And you do look like her? Besides, he may not know what Mary looks like."

Burke hung his head in defeat, sighed and glanced back up. "Why don't we just wait for the police..."

"For the same reason you didn't want to wait just a second ago. It's time for the delivery now, and you know darned well we can't risk losing him. We have to at least give him the bait. And I'm the logical one to do that."

Burke hated himself for the admission, but there was a reasonableness to what she was suggesting. Surely there was safety in a public park in broad daylight. Surely the police were only seconds from arrival. Surely he must be half out of his mind to be agreeing. "Okay. But you put the bag on the bench and then walk away. Back toward me. Do you hear me, Jill? And I mean it this time. So help me, God, I'll come in after you." The look in his eyes left no doubt that he would.

"Okay."

"Promise."

"I will, I will. I promise. We have an explicit verbal contract."

"We better have," he said, a loving threat threading his words together. "This is one time, lady, I'll beat your fanny for breach."

"You have an intriguing concept of punishment, counselor," she said, taking the tapestry bag from him and moving off toward the garden.

Burke watched her go, allowing her to gain the distance necessary to make it appear that they weren't together. With each step that she took, she grew smaller and his fear greater. He told himself that the knot in his stomach was foolish. He told himself that nothing was going to happen. He told himself that it would all be over soon.

But stubbornly the fear persisted.

LENNY LARIMER KNEW the moment he saw the woman that she was Jill McClain. He knew also that something had gone wrong. His first reaction was to panic, to run. His second, was to conclude that everything might be all right after all. So Jill now knew about her birth? So what? Little Miss Hoity-toity Lawyer was obviously eager to keep her illegitimacy a secret. Otherwise, she wouldn't be delivering the money, would she?

He smiled and smeared nervous-damp hands along the length of his pants. He liked the idea of punishing Tommy's daughter personally. He liked the idea of her hurting, too. He liked the idea of her being under his control. Yeah, he liked it a whole lot. He also might like all that lawyer money she had.

She moved closer.

He stepped back into the shady shadows of the mammoth green-leafed oak. And waited. And watched. And willed his heart to stop its crazy, excited beat.

In the far distance the famed Swan Boats gently glided along the silver surface of the pond, giving visitors a scenic tour of the garden. Lenny's eyes darted to them, then to the man moving along the walkway. To the tall man in the business suit. For the briefest of moments, the man looked familiar, but the recognition fled under the pressure of the moment.

And he did feel stress, Lenny thought. Was that why his chest felt so heavy? Was that why his breath was short? Yeah, yeah. Maybe, though, he'd take some of the money and see a doctor. Maybe...

He watched as Jill looked about her—was she looking for him?—then she deposited the bag on the deserted bench. She hesitated, and looked about again, before starting back the way she had come. She glanced up at the man coming down the walkway. Even as far away as he stood, Lenny saw relief scoring the man's face. They knew each other! The fact slammed his heart into a rapid rhythm. It was a setup! He remembered now. The man was the lawyer he'd seen in court with her! It was a setup! It was...

Two uniformed police officers came into view.

Lenny Larimer's heart skipped a whole series of beats...

Right before the world went crazily out of control.

Jill saw the officers, Jill saw Burke pointing, Jill whirled. In the shadows of the tree, she felt the man. Then saw him. He was wearing a stricken look and a gray plaid shirt. Across the distance of yards and years, their eyes met. His were haunted, dull, the color of unrealized wants. They were also winter cold.

Her eyes, Lenny thought wildly, were exactly like Tommy's. Or were they like his mother's? Perfect...

censuring...perfectly censuring...censuringly perfect...

"It's your own fault you've been found out." his mother's voice began to accuse in his head.

"No," he whimpered in protest.

"You always force people to hurt you."

"No!" he cried, the voice growing louder, more deafening. His heartbeat accelerated, pelting inside his chest at a thunderous speed. His heart felt as if it were a separate entity and threatened to split skin and sinew and spring forth in its own birth.

"I tried to love you, but you're sick, Lenny... sick...sick..."

"No!" he cried, covering his ears. The sound only increased. Now it was laughter. His mother's laughter. Tommy's laughter. The world's laughter.

Noises screeched in his head.

His chest hurt. Pain. Pain. Bad pain. Bad.

"You've been a bad boy... bad boy... bad boy..."

Lenny Larimer reached for the gun that he carried to work each night. He had tucked it into the waist of his jeans, beneath a sleeveless denim jacket. He aimed it at the woman, the woman with Tommy's eyes, the woman with his mother's laugh, the woman who represented everything that Lenny had always been denied.

And then, without the slightest bit of guilt, he pulled the trigger.

CHAPTER THIRTEEN

"Nooo!" BURKE'S VOICE rang out.

Helplessly, he listened as a shot pierced the park's peacefulness. Helplessly, he watched as Jill crumpled, without a sound and like a wireless puppet, to the ground.

An ice-death seized Burke, freezing him to the spot. Conversely, startled birds fast-fluttered a frenzied ascent. A millisecond and a thousand eternities passed. Suddenly, though his brain was still chilled, his legs began to thaw. He began to run. Instinctively. Desperately. In one mere stride, he outdistanced the policemen who were now in pursuit of the man running from the darkness of the oak tree. Another shot rang out—sharp, clear, sinister—this one discharged from a policeman's gun. Burke marginally noted that the blackmailer grabbed his leg and tumbled earthward. He heard the man muttering cries of pain.

Jill, on the other hand, was silent. Sickeningly silent. Frighteningly silent. Wearing her ivory suit and slumped on her stomach, she lay—a small white heap on the spring-green grass. She reminded Burke of a beautiful, peaceful dove shot from the sky by a callous hunter.

"Jill?" he whispered, dropping to his knees beside her. Deep inside him, the prayer had begun. *Please, God, please, don't let her be...* Even in the silence of his heart, he couldn't say the word.

His hand at her waist, he gently rolled her to her back within the framework of his arms. She was limp and pale and her eyelashes splashed thick and spiky against her colorless cheeks. A bright crimson stained her blouse in a visibly increasing circle.

Burke's heart stopped. "Jesus," he breathed, his fingertips trailing across the sticky wetness of the scarlet puddle. "No...please...no..." It crossed his mind that he was diabolically caught in some eternal punishment of loving and always losing whomever he loved to the remorseless arms of death. His own arms tightened in resistance to the idea.

Jill's eyelashes fluttered and slowly rose.

Burke's heart began to beat again. "Jill?"

Shock had widened the irises of her eyes until they appeared bottomless pools of cool blue water. She attempted to smile, but it came across a pathetic, one-cornered affair. "Are you ... going ..."

"Shh, save your energy."

"...to beat my fanny...for breach?"

Burke's eyes stung. "You're damned right I am," he said in an unsteady voice.

"I ... only stopped ..."

"Shh, be quiet, Jill."

"...because you pointed..."

"Shh," he commanded again, running his hand into a back pocket of his pants for a handkerchief. Once produced, he laid it across the spot where he determined the bullet had entered her body. Somewhere near her breast, her incredibly beautiful breast. Somewhere near her life-necessary lungs and heart. Panic again cruised down the length of his spine.

"Burke?"

"What, honey?"

"I shouldn't . . . have stopped. He . . ."

She coughed and Burke heard a hateful gurgling sound. He heard voices to his left.

"Momma," came the less-than-lucid call of Lenny Larimer. "Momma . . . Momma . . ."

"His heartbeat's erratic," one of the policeman said.

The other answered, "I only clipped him in the leg."

"He's cold and clammy. Could be a heart attack."

"I'll call for an ambulance."

"Check on the woman."

"How is she?" an officer said, immediately appearing at Burke's side.

"She's shot." Burke swallowed. "A chest wound."

"I'll call for an ambulance."

"No, I can get her to the hospital faster." More than careful with the treasure he had, he gingerly lifted Jill into his arms. She moaned and cut out his heart with the sound. "Hang on, honey."

It seemed to Burke like a thousand years, but it could have been no more than three minutes before he was settling her in the front seat of the car. He knew she'd have been more comfortable in the back seat, but couldn't stand the thought of her being that far away from him. Stripping off his suit jacket, he bunched it into a pillow for her head. He then closed the door and ran around to the driver's side.

The inside of the car was stifling hot, and Burke plunged his hand into her purse for the key to start engine and air conditioning. When his fingers didn't readily find the keys, he cursed and emptied the purse's contents onto the car seat. The keys jingled out. Throwing everything back into the purse, he tossed it to the back and slipped behind the wheel. Never once did it cross his mind that he hadn't driven in eighteen months.

All he knew was that he had to get Jill to the hospital...before she bled to death on the front seat of her car.

Turning the wheel sharply, he pulled out behind the police car now acting as escort. The car's siren began to wail, a menacing sound that parted the traffic like Moses parting the Red Sea.

"Am I...am I going to die?" Jill whispered halfway to Massachusetts General Hospital.

Burke's head jerked toward her. She was semipropped against the door. Her eyes were hazy, her skin pallid. "No!" he said gruffly. "Don't even think that!"

"If I do," she said, ignoring his command, "I want you to know..."

"Don't, Jill! You'll be all right!"

She swallowed and sought for a proper breath. "...that I love you more..."

"Jill, please!" he pleaded in a ragged whisper.

"...than I ever loved anything...or anybody." She smiled faintly, but strangely contentedly. "You made me happy."

It was the past tense of the verb that totally destroyed him. Burke fought to continue breathing and to keep the moisture from his eyes. *You can't drive if you can't see!* he screamed to himself. Break down later. Not now! Dammit, not now!

"You're going to be all right," he repeated, for his sake far more than for hers.

When she spoke again, her voice was thick, her words rambling toward incoherence. Her eyes were glazing over. "I thought it hurt...to be shot. But I don't—" she licked her lips "—feel...anything."

"You're in shock," Burke said, refraining from pointing out that once the shock receded, she'd be screaming for something, anything, to ease the pain.

"I don't feel...anything...bleeding...mmm..." she moaned.

Burke threw her another glance. "Hang in, honey. Only a couple more blocks."

"Burke...feel anything...mmm." She moaned again and a grimace split wide her face.

"We're almost..."

"Oh, God!" she groaned as a burning shaft tore through her body.

Burke drew the car to a screeching halt beside the entryway. Killing the engine, he threw the door open and practically jumped the hood of the car. A stretcher, manned by two competent men in white, bolted through the hospital door just as Burke lifted Jill into his arms. She was crying, soft tears falling on gasps and moans.

"Burke...it hurts. It... Oh, God!" she cried, grasping his hand just as he laid her upon the sterile linen of the stretcher sheet. Her strength, even under the circumstances, threatened to stop the flow of blood in his fingers.

"Jill..." he began, running alongside the stretcher that had just entered the hospital. A horde of people in white descended.

"Sir, you're in the way. Sir..."

Someone, some well-meaning someone, wrenched apart the lovers' hands.

"Burke!" Jill cried in agonized desperation.

"Jill!" he answered, the word screaming from his very soul.

And then there was silence as the stretcher was rolled beyond swinging doors that read Emergency. Staff Only.

As he stood in the middle of the suddenly quiet room, a horrible feeling of déjà vu closed in around Burke. He remembered standing once before in almost exactly this same spot. He remembered the deafening silence. He remembered the overwhelming feeling of helplessness. He remembered the sickening feeling of fear.

EVERYTHING WAS THE SAME, Burke thought hours later as he impatiently waited for news from the operating room. The hospital reeked of the same sharp, antiseptic smells, and the same muted, muffled voices crawled down the hallways. Hope and hopelessness eternally sat side by side in waiting rooms, and everywhere there was the familiar surreal feeling that time had been suspended.

Restlessly, and for the thousandth time, Burke stood and walked to the window. He stared out at a late afternoon that seemed to have come from nowhere. Sunset had already brushed the sky in rainbow colors—bold indigo and shy lavender, bright tangerine and traces of vermilion red.

Red.

Like the dried blood on his white shirt. Like the rusty-red stains on his fingertips.

No, Burke suddenly thought, everything was not the same. Nicole had died with him at her side. If Jill died, she would die with strangers. And one other thing was different. She would die without ever hearing him say he loved her. Why had he never said he loved her? he asked himself desperately. Why had he just assumed that he'd had all the time in the world to come to terms with what he was feeling for her?

"Burke?" came a soft voice at his side.

He glanced around and into the face of Mary McClain. She was red-eyed and pale. That she was suffering was etched in every line and crease of her face and, yet, as she had been all afternoon she was sensitively aware of his pain.

"Why don't you go get some coffee?"

"No, I—"

"Why don't I go get you both some?" Rob said, laying a comforting hand on Mary's shoulder. His fingers tightened in reassurance before he stepped away and from the room. Mary watched him go with a look of total adoration.

It was a look that increased Burke's pain. Would he ever again see that look of love and devotion on Jill's face? He glanced back out the window and did what he once said he'd never do again. He prayed.

"How long has it been?" Mary asked.

Burke angled his wrist to look at his watch. "Four hours and almost ten minutes." A lifetime, he thought miserably. A damned lifetime! Or was that a deathtime? Were they all just marking time until Jill... He made himself stop and concentrate on what the nurse had said two hours before. Updating them on the in-progress surgery, she'd said that Jill was alive. He was going to hold on to that. With every ounce of strength he had. He had to, because if he didn't, he'd go absolutely mad.

"It's all my fault," he heard Mary say in a faltering voice. "If I hadn't agreed to the blackmail, if I had just told the truth from the beginning, if..."

"Don't," Burke demanded in a tone that instantly brought her red eyes to his. "Don't do it to yourself. Take it from someone who knows every subtlety of the word guilt." He smiled faintly. "None of it was your fault, Mary. None of it."

The way none of what happened to Nicole was my fault, he silently added to himself. Neither her death, nor my survival. How perfectly clear it all seemed now. And how useless all the guilt, when everything that had happened had been nothing more than the fickle, accidental nature of life. And yet, maybe it was the capacity to feel guilt that indelibly marked one as a normal, and caring, human being.

"You're in love with her, aren't you?"

Burke's attention shifted back to Mary. "Yes," he answered, adding hoarsely, "but I've never told her."

"You will," Mary said.

It was a hope they both clung to.

Seconds later, at the sound of footsteps, Burke whirled around.

"Sorry," Rob said at the obvious expectation scoring Burke's face.

Burke sighed in disappointment and reached for a Styrofoam cup of steaming coffee. "Thanks," he said, drawing the cup to his lips and drinking. The coffee was scalding hot, and he relished the mini-diversion of his attention.

"One of the officers just told me that the blackmailer was DOA," Rob said. "They think he died of a coronary."

"Do they have any idea who he is...was?" Burke asked.

Rob shook his head. "They found in address in his wallet, but that was all. They're checking it out."

"I was hoping he'd live," Burke said.

"Yeah," Rob agreed.

The three also agreed that if they didn't hear something soon, they were all going to scream. But hear they didn't. At least not soon. Four-fifteen faded into four-thirty, which in turn gave way to four-forty-five and five o'clock, then six o'clock and beyond. Burke paced, sat, paced again. He sighed. He prayed. He rummaged fingers through his hair. He finally lost his patience.

"How the hell long can one surgery last?" he barked, jumping up and starting in on another pacing routine. "It's been almost—"

"Ms McClain?"

Burke's head, accompanied by two others, jerked toward the doorway. At the sight of the man still dressed in surgical-green attire—he carried a mask, and sweat stained the front of his shirt—Burke's heart slammed against his ribs.

"Yes," Mary whispered, rising. Rob instinctively moved to her side.

The doctor smiled wearily, reassuringly. "Your daughter's going to be all right."

Relief, more powerful than the adrenaline of concern, swept through Burke's body, leaving him weaker than had hours of anxiety.

"How...what kind of damage..." Burke stammered.

The doctor turned his attention to the man asking the fractured questions and obviously felt that the pallor of his skin entitled him to an answer. "The bullet entered the fleshy part of the right breast, angled downward, and lodged itself in her left side. Fortunately, it missed her lungs entirely. Unfortunately, it nicked the right ventricle of her heart."

The last words caused Burke's own heart to jump into an erratic rhythm. "But...that sounds serious," he managed to say.

"Not really. There was a lot of bleeding, which was one reason the surgery took so long, and then it also required some delicate suturing. Actually," the doctor said, still talking primarily to Burke, "she was lucky. If the bullet had been just an inch higher..." He left the remark unfinished.

Burke, however, silently filled in the missing words.

"Are you all right?" the doctor asked suddenly as Burke's complexion dimmed from pale to snow-white.

"Yes," he answered in a contradictory tone that barely rose above a whisper.

"I could get you some water—"

Burke cleared his throat, trying to clear his head of the hateful inch-higher theory. "No," he said gruffly, "I'm fine."

"She'll be all right," the physician repeated. "Barring complications, and given a proper period of convalescence."

"May I sec her?" Mary asked.

The doctor was sympathetic but firm. "She'll be in recovery a while longer, then in intensive care for the rest of the night." He smiled. "Why don't the three of you get some sleep and come back tomorrow? I promise I'll let you see her then."

While none of the trio seemed inordinately pleased with the decision, all bowed to the doctor's superior judgment. Within minutes, they were stepping from the hospital and out into the April evening. Sunset had given way to a gloaming twilight that seemed to cover the city like a gray, gauzy canopy. First-stars friskily glimmered their arrival.

"Would you take her car home with you, Burke?" Mary asked, then remembered his aversion to driving. "Unless, of course..."

"I'll take it," he answered.

"Well, I...I guess I'll see you tomorrow."

"Right," Burke said. "Try to get some rest. Both of you." The two men exchanged a tired but friendly handshake. Burke then dropped a kiss on Mary's cheek. "Good night."

The farewell was echoed.

All the way home, Burke felt it building. Exactly what "it" was, he wasn't altogether sure, but by the time he'd pulled the car into a slot at his apartment complex and shut off the engine, he felt the acute symptoms of emotional distress.

He had almost lost her!

And in almost losing her had come the cold, stark reality that he was once again vulnerable. Love and the unpredictability of life had once more placed him on a high wire without a net.

"If the bullet had been just an inch higher..."

"...She would be dead," Burke whispered into the car's quiet listening interior. "Sweet Jesus, she would be..." He couldn't repeat the all-too-sobering word.

A fine, delayed trembling started in his hands, and he reached for his suit jacket that still lay crumpled on the far side of the car. He drew it close and inhaled the subtle, sweet smell emanating from where Jill's head had lain. He also saw the once-crimson, dark stain blotching fabric and memory.

"If the bullet had been just an inch higher..."

He closed his eyes and swallowed back the knot of fear that jumped into his throat and heart. It was the most all-consuming, all-debilitating feeling he'd ever known. It threatened his well-being. It threatened his very sanity. Suddenly it was crystal clear what he had to do.

He'd make her understand, he thought. Somehow he'd make her understand that he loved her and that, because he did, he had to banish her from his life.

CONSCIOUSNESS SLIPPED BACK in snatches of light and sound and pain. And in snippets of awareness that Burke sat at her bedside. Continuously, it seemed, for each time Jill rallied in the following days, a hazy though familiar figure was always only a smile away, a touch away. Sometimes she even imagined that Burke spoke to her, but it was of things she didn't understand, things about an inch higher, things about a high wire and no net, things about fear and cowardice and forgiveness.

On the fourth day after surgery, on a Friday afternoon that sang with a sprinkling rain, Jill opened her eyes. Really opened her eyes. She saw a white room. Heard the gentle patter of rain. Knew the smell of...roses? She inclined her head to the garnet-red blossoms spreading their petals in a fragrant fullness. The motion produced a silent grimace, and she eased her hand to her chest, her securely bandaged chest. She was on the verge of wondering where she was and what had happened when the past came flooding back. A shot. The park. Burke carrying her. Burke. Where was...? Her eyes shifted toward the miniscule sound of a magazine page turning.

He looked tired, she thought, as if he'd lost sleep and spent hours worrying. He also looked thin, gaunt even, and there were shadows lurking deep in the hollows of his cheeks. Even so, he had never looked better.

"Hi," she whispered, the word cutting her throat with its sharp edges.

Burke's gaze flew upward. The magazine slid to the floor. "Jill?"

"You got nothing better to do—" she stopped to corral her wispy breath "—than hang around...hospitals?"

He didn't answer. Instead, his concern evident, he stood and stepped to her side. "How do you feel?"

Jill smiled weakly. "I don't . . . know." She passed the tip of her tongue over her cracked lips. "Could I . . . have a drink?"

Burke poured water from the carafe and into a glass. Adding a straw, he brought it to her lips. She sipped. Good. It tasted good. And cool. And deliciously wet to a medicine-dry mouth.

"You want some more?"

She shook her head and, tired from the overexertion of drinking, snuggled back into the pillow. Burke returned the glass to the stand.

His eyes sank deeply into hers. "Do you hurt?"

She considered his question. "No," she said finally, shaking her head again. "Burke . . ."

"What, honey?"

". . . am I all right?"

"Yes, you're all right. The bullet nicked your heart . . ." At the sudden distraught look on her face, he hastened to add, "It sounds worse than it is. The doctor swears you're all right." Her face still wore a troubled expression. "I wouldn't lie to you."

The worry lines disappeared. "No," she said with a relieved smile, "you wouldn't."

"You want me to get you anything? Something to drink? Something to eat? Something . . ."

"No," she cut in, asking, "Did they get the man?" Before he could answer, she said, "He was the man I saw in court."

"He was DOA, Jill. He died of a coronary."

"Who was he?"

"His name was Leonard Larimer. He was a cousin of your father's." The relationship never ceased to surprise Burke, nor did his blinding hatred for the madman.

"A cousin? I don't understand. Why . . ."

"The police are still trying to figure out why. Don't worry about it now. Wait until you're stronger." His hand brushed back a lock of her hair as his eyes hungrily scanned her face, looking for every subtlety, every nuance, of her well-being.

"Don't look at me," she said, turning her face into the pillow. "I must look awful."

"No," he contradicted roughly as he gently brought her face back to his. "You've never looked more... beautiful." The word sailed between them on gossamer wings of feeling.

With his fingertips at her chin, with his eyes warm and soft, Jill would gladly have given part of her soul for Burke's kiss. That Burke was feeling the same need to kiss her she would have bet her life on. Yet, he didn't. She told herself it was out of deference to her condition.

"Who gave me the flowers?" she asked, noticing that the red roses were only the proverbial floral tip of an iceberg.

"The daisies are from the gang at work, the yellow roses are from Dad, the whatever-that-is," he said, pointing to a orange-blooming plant—

"Kalanchoe," she said with a half smile.

The other half of the smile slowly appeared on Burke's face. "The kalanchoe is from Mary and Rob."

"How is she?" Jill asked, suddenly serious.

"She's all right. She's been worried about you. She'll be back later this evening."

A strange blend of emotions bathed Jill's heart. On the one hand, she still thought of Mary as her sister—and always would. On the other hand, there was already growing a different kind of feeling: the feeling a child knows for her mother.

"What about the red roses?" she asked, letting the confusing subject of Mary rest until another time. "Who sent those?" Her eyes merged with Burke's as she awaited his answer.

"Just some guy who's been half out of his mind," he said unsteadily.

It suddenly seemed like a lifetime since she'd touched him. Which she had to to or simply die on the spot. Slowly, she inched her hand forward—it felt so heavy she could hardly lift it—and cupped the side of his face in her palm.

His jaw began a slow quiver beneath her touch, and his eyes burned with deep emotion. He covered her hand with his and drew her palm to his mouth, where he kissed the tender flesh. "I almost lost you," he whispered, burying his face in her hand as if she were silk and satin and all things sweet and soft. "I almost lost you. Oh, God, I almost lost you."

Jill stretched out her other hand and rested it on the crown of his bowed head. Neither spoke. She had the sudden and curious feeling that, despite what she'd been through, she was in far better shape than Burke.

It was the next evening, though, that she first suspected something was wrong. Burke had spent much of the day with her and, although everything appeared normal on the surface, there was an undercurrent that she couldn't quite interpret. He seemed to be...distancing her. Without question, he went out of his way not to touch her. And still he had not kissed her, although she had found his eyes on her lips more than once.

At eight o'clock sharp, the stout and stern night nurse ordered Burke from the room.

"I think she's hinting that I leave," he said, smiling as he stood by the side of the bed.

"Ms Subtlety," Jill teased back, though her crooked smile said she was tired.

Burke saw her fatigue and felt guilty. "You're exhausted. I should have gone earlier."

"No!"

Something in the passionate delivery of the one word created an instant intimacy. It was there between them, thick and vibrant and undeniable. Burke's eyes traitorously slid from her eyes to her lips. He swallowed. And fought against the urgent need to kiss her, to hold her.

"Well, good night," he said in a strangled voice.

"Burke?"

He hesitated, caught in the silken, silvery web she spun so effortlessly.

"Kiss me good-night."

Time stopped. Jill waited. Burke suffered. Finally, his head lowered and his lips swept across hers. It was an impersonal kiss, full of self-restraint that fairly shuddered through his suddenly taut body. It reminded her of the first time she'd kissed him. Then, however, she'd understood the restraint. Now, she didn't.

"Burke?" she whispered, her lips trembling beneath his as she pleaded for an explanation. Of necessity, the plea parted her lips and her breath flowed against Burke's mouth in a warm, moist wave. Their tongues met.

Burke was lost. Moaning, he widened his mouth over hers in a way that was very personal, most intimate, and totally without restraint. He kissed her deeply, hungrily. Slipping his arms beneath her shoulders, he smothered her body with the enormousness of his. In his touch was a gentle savagery, a wild desperation. In his touch was . . . fear. A fear that clearly transmitted itself to Jill's heart.

An indelicate cough at the doorway brought the kiss to an abrupt end. Burke left, shaken. Jill was confused.

THE NEXT MORNING, the first day of May, she asked the question. "What's wrong?"

Burke turned from where he'd been silently staring out the window. "What do you mean?"

"Something's wrong," she said from her position against newly fluffed pillows. "What is it?"

Burke's heart surged toward a scampering pulse. "Nothing's wr—"

"You don't lie to me, remember?" Jill interrupted.

She had been freshly bathed and wore a lacy pink gown that Mary had brought her the day before. Her hair was piled haphazardly but attractively atop her head and tied with a matching ribbon. Burke thought she looked like a child-woman, a child-woman who needed protection not hurt.

"I deserve to know the truth," she prompted.

The truth. What was that elusive substance? Burke thought. Was it the fact that he didn't have the courage to love her? Was it the fact that he was going to have to hurt her to save himself? Was it the fact that he was really doing her a favor because she deserved so much more than he could offer? He turned back to the window, shutting out the beauty of her face, the challenge in her sea-blue eyes.

"Burke?" she said, refusing to shelve the issue.

He didn't answer. He wanted to wait to tackle the subject of his leaving until she was stronger. Stronger. Maybe the elusive truth was that Jill, even flat on her back healing from a bullet wound, was stronger than he. For after all, he was nothing more than a coward.

"I'm taking another leave of absence from the firm," he heard himself saying.

The blood in Jill's veins chilled by degrees. In the long, long night, when she'd pondered over and over Burke's desperate, fear-laden kiss, an idea had occurred to her, but she had rejected it simply because it was too painful to even consider.

"Why?" she now whispered.

"I'm ... I'm going back to the Cape."

The idea was back, swarming around Jill in all its hideous glory. "You're running away," she said flatly.

He whirled. "Yes!" he admitted bluntly, roughly, raking fingers through his neatly combed hair. "Yes, I'm running away." He stood a room away, a world away. Suddenly, he sighed. The sound was laced with self-hate. "Jill, I don't expect you to understand. I won't even ask you to."

"Make me understand," she said in a voice that both begged and demanded. "If you're walking out of my life, I have to understand why."

"Because I'm a coward," he said with no hesitation.

"I don't believe that."

"Believe it. It's true." Unknowingly, craving her nearness, he stepped closer. "When I..." He stopped, as if what he must say was so painful he could find neither breath nor words. "When I lost Nicole, I didn't think I was going to survive. For a long time I didn't want to. I never expected to ... to love again. And then, you came into my life. You made me feel ... alive. You made me feel ..." His eyes glazed over with a film of moisture. "Oh, God, Jill, I love you so much," he whispered.

Jill's eyes, too, teared under the bittersweet irony of the moment. The words were what she had waited a "forever'' length of time to hear. It was the timing that was wrong. All wrong!

"Then why leave me?" she asked, knowing the answer even before she heard it.

"Because I almost lost you," he said, the words refusing to slip easily through his tightened lips.

"If you leave, you lose me anyway."

"It's not the same thing."

"Isn't it?"

"No!" he hollered, then lowered his voice. "No," he repeated, "it's not the same. Jill," he pleaded, now desperate to make her understand, "I can't live through losing someone else. I can't bury..." These words would not pass through his lips. "I'm afraid," he confessed. He smiled self-derisively. "It's not very heroic, but it's the truth."

"So what are you going to do? Run away and conveniently forget you love me?"

"I'm going to try. I have to."

Green eyes and blue sparred in a silent, loving battle.

He looked so vulnerable, she thought, standing there with his heart on his sleeve and his past in his hand.

She looked so vulnerable, he thought, lying there pale and beautiful and bleeding from the barbs of his words.

"Don't ask me to stay," he begged in a whisper. "I would. I'd do anything you ask me to. But this time, it would only make us both miserable."

Miserable. Jill didn't see how she could be more miserable than she already was. Yet her love for Burke would not allow her to be the cause of his misery. If leaving her meant he'd be happier, she must set him free. Mustn't she? Why, then, did she want more than anything to beg him to stay? Slowly, faintly, tears held at bay, she smiled.

"Love doesn't chain, Burke." Her voice cracked. "It frees."

The room was silent, a silence punctuated only by the sound of heartache. His heartache. Her heartache. Their heartache.

Walking to the bed, he entwined his fingers with hers and gently drew her knuckles to his mouth. He didn't kiss them. He just held them against the warmth of his lips. His trembling lips. His eyes closed in a savoring attitude, as if he were storing memories for lonely, black nights.

"You can't run away from love," Jill whispered at last. "You can run over every inch of the Cape, you can run through heaven and hell, but you can't run away from love."

He didn't argue the point. He looked long past arguing any point. He merely lowered her hand to the bed and slowly, and finally—oh, God, so finally she thought she would die!—unthreaded his fingers from hers. His tear-sheened eyes met hers briefly. Then, without a backward glance, he walked from the room . . . and from her life.

CHAPTER FOURTEEN

JILL DIDN'T CRY. She couldn't. She was too numb. She simply, and silently, succumbed to the pain in her heart that had nothing to do with the bullet's nick.

A single red rose was delivered that afternoon, along with a note that read: *Forgive me.* It was then she cried, tears that fell from her eyes and onto the velvet petals of the rose like giant drops of dew. She could take no comfort whatsoever in the fact that, had Burke loved her less, she would not now be alone.

Nor did the fact lend comfort in the endless days that followed. In truth, nothing lent comfort. Jill felt as if a hole had been carved in her heart, in her life, and that nothing would ever again fill it. At first she believed— possibly because she had to to survive—that Burke would eventually come to his senses, but when day followed day, and lonely night succeeded lonely night, she had to face the fact that he might never reconsider his decision. Oh, he might return to Boston—of that she had no doubt— but it grew daily more and more unlikely that he would return to her.

How could she live without him? she asked herself over and over.

By keeping busy, the survivor in her always replied.

To which she would respond, with a growing, surly impatience: How do you keep busy lying flat on your back in a hospital?

It was a toss-up who was the happier—Jill or the hospital staff—when she was discharged exactly three weeks to the day of the shooting. From the beginning, she abused her doctor's orders. She did not take things easy. She did concede to staying in bed, possibly, probably, because Mary took an early summer leave from school, moved into Jill's apartment and threatened to tie her down. Of necessity, Mary and Rob's wedding plans were postponed. Since it was just one more thing for Jill to regret, she worked harder and harder on the briefs that she had smuggled in from the office.

By the first of June, Jill had lost twelve pounds, had lost enough sleep to qualify her as a bona fide insomniac, and had lost her patience so many times that it was doubtful that she'd ever find it again. And through it all, there was not one minute of one hour of one day—or night—that she did not wonder what Burke was doing. It was certainly the question that kept her company that hot, sleepless, June-first night.

FIFTY-SEVEN MILES south of Boston, in a small white beach cottage, Burke stared at the glass of untouched bourbon and water that temptingly sat on the kitchen table. Through the open window, a warm summer breeze drifted in, swaying the ruffled curtains and infusing the room with pine and salty-sea scents. In also came the sound of the Atlantic tumbling in rhythmic, and eternal, play. Burke, however, heard nothing except the siren call of the bourbon and water... and the haunting words of Mary McClain. The latter had been responsible for his pouring the former. The question now was: Who was stronger? Him or the liquor?

On returning to the Cape, he had vowed not to drown his problems in a bottle. He would not make the mistake

he'd made once before. Until tonight, it had been a fairly
easy vow to keep. Until tonight, talking weekly with his
father had left the impression that Jill was coping. After
all, she was slowly integrating herself back into work by
insisting material be sent to the house. Tonight, however, for a reason he couldn't explain, he'd needed more
reassurance. He'd called Jill's house, hoping Mary would
answer. She had.

"What do you want me to say, Burke?" Mary had
asked kindly, but with no punches pulled. *"That she's all
right? Well, she's not. Oh, she's getting over the gunshot
wound, but she's miserable. She won't eat, she's working herself to death despite the doctor's orders to the
contrary, she's not sleeping, and though she tries hard
not to cry in front of me, her eyes are always red."* There
had been a pause in the long-winded recital. *"Oh,
Burke,"* she had said, her voice suddenly contrite, *"I'm
sorry. I have no right . . ."*

"To remind me that I'm a son of a bitch?" Burke
whispered into the room's stillness. His eyes were still
pinned to the glass. Inside the amber liquid, the ice cubes
were beginning to melt.

The truth of the matter was, he mused, that he was in
no better shape than Jill. Possibly he was in even worse
shape. He was more miserable than he ever remembered
being in his life. As for sleep and food, he'd had far too
little of each. The only area in which she might be better
off than he was was in the area of work. She at least had
something to occupy her time. And she could at least cry.
God, how he envied her that!

Yet, in all his pain, in all his guilt over her pain, he
knew he'd done the right thing in leaving. In time, she
would forget him. In time, he would forget her. And to
help him forget tonight, and what he was doing to Jill,

why didn't he just drink the ready solace that stood on the table?

His fingers slid up and down the cool, moist-growing glass, caressing it as if it were a cherished lover. His fingers closed around it. He lifted it. He brought it to his lips. But he didn't drink. Instead, he returned it to the table, roughly scraped back his chair, and headed for the door. He hit the beach at a run and didn't stop until beads of sweat bathed his body in exactly the same way that beads of condensate bathed the warming, untouched glass of bourbon.

For tonight, Burke had been stronger than temptation.

The only thing stronger was his memory of Jill.

IN THE SECOND WEEK of June, on a summer-warm Thursday afternoon, a double-chinned, jovial-eyed police officer brought a cardboard box to Jill. Inside were the effects of the late Leonard Larimer, who left behind no relatives, except the obscure, and ironic, one of Jill McClain.

With imagination, it was possible to piece together what had happened. The letter from Margaret McClain to Maude Larimer set the stage, and, though it would never be known with certainty how Maude Larimer had discovered the truth of Mary's pregnancy—had Margaret told her? Had Maude astutely guessed?—it was obvious that the woman had asked to be informed of the birth of her nephew's child. There was also a between-the-lines hint that the woman never meant to interfere in the mother's or child's life, which, of course, she never had. Not so, however, Leonard Larimer. While the motivation behind the blackmail was murky, it was still visible. Disjointed notes written in the margins of the letter and on a newspaper obituary column spoke powerfully of Leonard Larimer's love-hate relationship with his mother. And of his obsession with Tommy Wilson's perfection. It was a logical surmise that Mary and Jill, simply because of their relationship to Tommy, had been chosen to receive the brunt of that hate and obsession. Through them, Leonard Larimer would avenge himself. Regrettably, but perhaps just as importantly, Jill didn't know every nuance of the demented man's motivation and knew that she never would.

One thing she did know was that almost the entire sum of blackmail money had been recovered. She knew one other thing as well. She got a warm, goose-bumpy feeling when she held the Medal of Honor that had been found in a worn case in the bottom of the box. It was the only link she had with her father. It was the only link she would ever have. And yet, it was enough. It spoke to her of love, devotion, courage.

Courage.

Cowardice.

Burke believed himself a coward. She knew better than that, but there was no way that she could convince him of it. She also knew with a clarity that belied any contradiction that he should be there with her, sharing the night, sharing life. A familiar ache settled in her chest, and equally familiar tears filled her eyes. Would the pain ever end? Would she ever feel whole again?

At the sound of Mary at the bedroom door, Jill quickly sniffed and plastered a too-bright smile at her lips. "Hi," she said, laying the medal on the bedside table.

Mary hesitated, then crossed the room and sat by the side of the bed. Her eyes automatically went to the medal. She said what she always did when reminded of what Jill had endured . . . all at the hands of a distant relation. The fact that it had been a relative who had tried to take her life not only angered Mary, but also made her feel a sense of guilt she couldn't explain even to herself. "I'm so sorry that Leonard..."

"It isn't your fault. You're not to blame for Leonard Larimer's actions."

"I know, but..."

Jill reached out and took Mary's hand. "But what? If you hadn't fallen in love at sixteen? If the man you'd loved hadn't had a cousin?" She tightened her hands around Mary's. "It isn't your fault." She gave a small laugh. "And I guess in a way it wasn't even his. No court would have considered him sane enough to stand trial."

"I'm glad he's dead," Mary said simply. "Is that an awful thing to say?"

"It's an understandable thing." Jill didn't know how she felt about the man who'd tried to take her life. Whatever the emotion it wasn't hate. It was closer to pity. And in a strange way she was grateful for a lesson the stranger had taught her at a time in her life when she'd needed to understand the lesson most. She had learned how precious it was that she had first come to know her mother through friendship and love. Even though the sands of their relationship had shifted, demanding readjustments in thinking and attitude, there would never be hate such as Leonard Larimer had felt for his mother. She wanted to tell Mary all this, to share all that was in her heart, but the time didn't seem quite right yet, though Jill knew without a doubt that it was very near. "Mary," she said, glancing once more at the medal on the table, "if you'd like to have the medal..."

"No," Mary said quickly. "I want you to have it. Your father would want you to have it." The moment grew heavy with emotion, the way it always did when Jill's parentage was mentioned. To ease that heaviness, Mary changed the subject. "You're sure you're going to be all right if I go home tomorrow?"

"I'm positive. Didn't the doctor say I could resume my activities?"

"He said you could resume some of them," Mary corrected.

"Go home," Jill said, a real smile working at the corners of her mouth.

"Trying to get rid of me, huh?" Mary teased.

"Yeah."

Mary's smile faded. "You've been crying."

"You're not supposed to notice."

"But I do." She didn't add that it was something mothers automatically did with their children, because it was still hard to talk about their new relationship. But the time would come when they could, and would, talk. Mary knew that.

"I'm fine, Mary," she said. "Really, I—" the tears started as if responding to some perverse cue "—am." Long weeks of heartache, and restraint, had reached their end. Long weeks of loving Burke without him at her side, and the hurtful, unchangeable knowledge that he never would be there, had taken their toll.

Mary pulled her daughter close. Jill went willingly, needing to feel a pair of comforting arms about her. "Shh," Mary whispered as she rocked Jill back and forth.

"It hurts. It hurts so bad."

"I know."

"I . . . I love him so much."

"He loves you."

"But not enough. Not enough."

Jill cried, Mary consoled, and over and over Jill babbled about love and hurt.

Hurt.

Burke's whole body hurt from the exhaustion of running. His chest hurt, his legs hurt, even the rugged beard bristling his face seemed to hurt. But he ran on. To the murmuring ocean, he pleaded for help in forgetting Jill's smile. To the ebony night, he prayed to forget the taste of Jill's lips. To the moon, round and full and burning the sky in platinum, he begged to forget the feel of Jill in his arms.

But forgetfulness eluded him, just as pain consumed him.

What was she doing?

What was she thinking?

Had she forgotten him?

"You can't run away from love..."

Yes. Yes, he could. He had to!

Digging his feet into the moist beach, he sprinted forward, driving, pushing his body to the limit of endurance. Just as he was driving, pushing his heartache to its limit.

An image of Jill all soft eyed and dewy mouthed from loving him rushed through his mind. It was followed by an image of her laughing, an image of her combing her hair in sultry strokes, an image of her crying. He saw her standing in the shower, he saw her standing at the kitchen cabinet, he saw her ready to stand by his side forever. His heart ached, unbearably and in full measure, for the mere sight of her.

"Jill!" he cried, stumbling, then falling to his knees like the broken man he was. His heart pounded an absent lover's rhythm, and he searched deep in his lungs for another lonely breath. Briny tears stung his eyes before spilling over and heedlessly streaming down his hair-roughened cheeks.

Damp gritty sand beneath him, the moon shining over him, he wept. From his heart. From his soul. For the first time since he'd left her. In the cool, salt wind whispering against his face, he heard the mocking refrain of Jill's song: "You can't run from love, you can't run from love..."

When the tears and the darkest of the night were over, when his soul lay gutted at his feet, when he cared not for that day's sunset nor the morrow's dawn, Burke made a startling revelation. He had survived. Again.

LATE SATURDAY AFTERNOON, in a church filled with friends and flowers, Mary and Rob were married.

Wearing the palest of pale-blue chiffon, carrying a bouquet of pink-throated white orchids, Mary walked half of the church's long aisle alone, where she was met by Rob, who was symbolically pledging that he would always meet her halfway. Then, his love so obvious it warmed the hearts of all there, he escorted his bride to the hand-carved mahogany railing of the two-hundred-year-old church. Mary slid in beside a smiling Jill; Rob, in beside a nervous best man—his nineteen-year-old son.

After an appropriate preamble of welcome, the minister's deep baritone voice echoed the vows throughout the cavernous church.

"Do you, Robert Donald Sheffield, take Mary Elaine McClain to be your lawfully wedded wife..."

Rob's eyes plunged deeply, lovingly, into those of the woman beside him...and Jill's heart turned over in bittersweet remembrance. How many times had Burke looked at her in just that way? How many times had his body told hers what he had not verbally been able to say until the very last—the very last when it had been too late? What was he doing at this very minute? What was he thinking? Was he all right? Please, God, let him be all right . . .

"Do you, Mary Elaine McClain, take Robert Donald Sheffield to be your lawfully wedded husband . . ."

Jill studied the rapt expression captured in the love-softened features of the older woman's face and thought how perfectly deserved her happiness was. It was a happiness reflected in Mary's tear-glittery brown eyes. Jill felt her own eyes clouding beneath her contact lenses. She shed tears of both happiness and unhappiness. She was happy for Mary's sake, undeniably so, but unhappy for her own. She knew that she would never be sharing these sacred vows with the man she loved.

"May I have the ring?"

Jill shifted her divided attention back to the ceremony . . . just in time to take the bridal bouquet Mary handed her. For a brief moment, Mary's eyes scanned her daughter's face, looking for signs of fatigue. Jill smiled reassuringly.

At the same time a wave of semisuppressed but infectious titters spread through the guests as the best man dealt with that mandatory moment of panic when he couldn't find the ring. Instinctively, Jill glanced toward the laughter and added her broadened smile to it. Far at the back of the sanctuary, well beyond the scattering of people seated on the front pews, Jill saw a man enter the church and take a seat in the last row. She made the mental notation that he was probably a late guest. Seconds later, the ring being produced from the pant pocket of a red-faced best man restored solemnity once more and drew Jill's attention back to the front of the church.

"The ring is the outward symbol of an inner commitment..."

But her wayward attention wouldn't be tamed so easily. She would never wear Burke's ring, Jill couldn't help but think. She would never again sleep beside him. She would never have his children. She would never... Stop it! she silently shouted. Why keep punishing yourself?

"By the power vested in me, I now pronounce you husband and wife. What God has joined together, let no man put asunder. You may kiss your bride."

Jill watched as an almost-disbelieving Rob lowered his head to kiss his wife. She watched as their lips connected. Sweet feelings burst to life in her own body as she remembered the feel of Burke's lips on hers. It was a magic she could never forget.

Rob eased his mouth from Mary's, leaving her breathless and blushing. In one fluid motion, Mary turned toward Jill, and Jill handed back the bouquet. Stretching, she placed a kiss on Mary's cheek.

"Be happy," Jill whispered.

"We will," Mary answered, giving her daughter a quick hug before taking her husband's arm and starting back down the long aisle.

Transferring her bouquet of white carnations and yellow rosebuds to her right hand, Jill took the arm the best man was offering her, and the two slowly moved into step behind the bride and groom. Suddenly Jill was grateful for the support of a strong arm. She had grown tired. Beneath the champagne-hued dress she wore, the scars were healing, but her stamina was still not back to normal. She wondered how much of that fact had to do with her emotional unrest.

As she passed by the third pew, she saw Andrew Rawlins sitting beside Ida Tumbrello. There was a sadness in the moss-green eyes that looked so like Burke's. She knew that he, too, was hurting, for his son and for her. They smiled, each offering the other what comfort they could. Jill noted that Ida patted his hand reassuringly, affectionately, and hoped that the rumor that the two were at last dating was true.

Passing down the length of the aisle, Jill pondered again her decision to resign from Rawlins, Rawlins, Nugent and Carson. Her mind was already made up, her resignation was already typed, and come Monday morning she was mailing it to Andrew Rawlins. The resignation was equally for her and Burke's sake. She couldn't work alongside him—not after what they'd shared—nor was he likely to return without the same misgivings.

She had accepted the fact—not gracefully, but necessarily—that she would never see Burke again. Except perhaps in a courtroom. Except perhaps at some legal social function. Except perhaps...

Suddenly the newly married couple slowed their pace as they neared the back of the church. Then they stopped, necessitating that Jill and the best man do so as well. Slowly Mary and Rob parted. Jill instinctively peered through at the object of their interest.

Her heart immediately erupted into a fast, discordant rhythm. Was she hallucinating? No, Rob and Mary saw him too. Why else were they exchanging knowing looks and stepping around her and back up the aisle, Rob dragging his confused son behind him? Why else were they meeting the guests and herding them out a side door? Why else were they leaving the figure on the back pew and her alone?

Slowly, uncertainly, Burke stood.

Jill watched as his body unfolded to its tall, lean height. He was all silver-gray suit, striped shirt and yellow tie. He was all longer-than-usual hair and recently shaved cheeks. He was all beautifully bronzed skin, all beautifully seductive male.

Burke's smoke-green eyes roamed from the froth of yellow flowers and lace in her free-flowing hair to the satin shoes on her small feet. In between, he drank in the sight of champagne-colored brocade and ivory skin, of shiny taupe-glossed lips and empyrean-blue eyes.

"You were right," he whispered in a husky voice that seemed swallowed alive by the large, hollow-sounding chamber.

"About what?" Her voice was delicate, as fragile as the rosebuds and carnations she was crushing to her.

"You can't run away from love." He smiled—a mocking, sarcastic slant of his mouth. "Though, God knows, I tried."

Jill's heartbeat accelerated, pumping blood at a pace that spun her head.

"I, uh...I ran over all three hundred miles of the Cape. Maybe twice over. But no matter how far I ran, you were always there. No matter where I tried to hide, you were always there. No matter..." His voice broke into fractured decibels; his eyes glazed. He visibly fought to keep from falling apart. He wanted to say that he'd heard her voice in the wind. He wanted to say that he'd heard her laughter in the ocean, seen her hair in the silver moonlight, felt the heat of her body in the golden sun, but he couldn't find the words. All he could find were simple words that came from the heart. "I...I love you, Jill," he whispered in a shredded voice. "I can't live without y—"

The sentence was never finished. The words were caught somewhere between two hungry mouths. The words were caught somewhere between two desperate bodies. The words were caught somewhere between two loving hearts.

CHAPTER FIFTEEN

"THAT'S FAR ENOUGH," Burke gasped, slacking his pace from jogging to a dead halt. Exactly two weeks and three days had passed since Mary and Rob had become husband and wife.

Jill sailed on past Burke, hollering something about the boulder in the near distance. As she spoke, a wave crashed against said boulder, causing a fine curtainy mist to arc toward the end-of-the-day sky. In the west a majestic sunset gathered around a dying ball of sun-fire, while overhead a whitish-gray sea gull shrilled an evensong.

"Jill!" Burke cried in reprimand. "The doctor said to ease into exercise. Ease, as in take it slowly." His voice rose an octave as Jill drew farther and farther away.

Dragging his hands to his hips, he watched in exasperation as his wife defied him and the doctor. He also watched the sway of lean hips—her too-lean hips, in white running shorts—and the rhythmic undulation of shoulders beneath a red T-shirt that read Rawlins, Rawlins, Nugent, Carson and Rawlins, across the back. The promotion had been his dad's wedding present to her, while Ida Tumbrello's had been a word of caution: Never let Burke make the coffee, because the inability to do so might run in the family. Burke couldn't keep a smile from his lips when he remembered Ida's revelation that it was Andrew who'd always been responsible for the horrible office coffee, and that she'd agreed to go out with him only if he'd turn the job over to her. The smile on Burke's lips slowly disappeared as Jill reached the boulder, then jogged right by it.

"Okay, lady, that does it," he said, his bare feet coming alive as he started in after her. With his long legs pumping powerfully beneath the blue nylon running shorts, he reached her in seconds and snatched her up into his arms in midrun.

Startled, Jill gasped and giggled and tried to feign irritation. "How am I ever going to get my 'tamina back..."

"Your what?" Burke teased, hugging her close to his chest with one arm at her waist, the other under her knees. He started back toward the spread beach blanket at a sedate walk. He carried her as if she were feather light and precious.

"Stamina, stamina, and if you'll...let me catch my breath...I'll say the darned word. How am I ever going to get my stamina back if you don't let me exercise?"

"I can think of far more rewarding exercise," he said, a salacious grin on his lips.

The twin of the grin danced on her mouth. "I'll just bet you can, counselor."

It was uncertain whose lips made the aggressive move. All that was important was that they were kissing—again. That, and other refined ways of making love, seemed to be the only thing they'd done the three days they'd been married and honeymooning at Cape Cod. Burke said that the two weeks she'd made him wait to marry her was all the restraint he ever intended to display. As if remembering that pledge, his lips now sealed hers more fervently. She tightened her arms about his neck and snuggled more deeply against his bare chest. She made a tiny little sound of complete contentment.

The next thing she knew she was slowly, gingerly, being laid flat on her back on the beach towel. With reluctance their lips parted. She stared up into the face only inches from her own. It was a face she knew every line and crease of. She knew also that she loved it more than any face in the world. At that very moment, Burke was thinking similar thoughts about the oval, freckle-dusted face before him.

"I love y—"

"I love y—" they both said together, and laughed at the timing. Legs and bodies, more nude than clothed, automatically entwined, and he dropped a light kiss on the end of her nose.

Sobering, he said, "You're still too thin."

"I'm gaining," she said defensively.

"You still have circles under your eyes."

"They're not near as dark as they were."

"You're still too pale."

Jill's lips twitched. "Is there anything you like about me?"

"Yeah," he said with a fat grin. "I like your name, Mrs. Rawlins."

"What a coincidence," she said. "So do I."

Grinning, Burke eased beside her and rolled to his back. He tugged her across his bare, sweaty, hair-sprigged chest. Her strawberry-blond hair fanned out from the confinement of the scarlet-red sweatband encircling her head. Perspiration dotted her upper lip and moisture-glazed her cheeks.

"How do you feel about children?" she asked suddenly, as her fingers played in the damp hair on his chest.

"Children in general or ours in particular?" he asked, tugging her T-shirt upward and spanning her waist with his hands. Beneath his palms, he could feel her skin moist and warm from running.

"Ours in particular."

"Talk it up."

"Well," she said, tracing the pad of her thumb across his nipple—it hardened and his breathing nosedived—"they're cute and cuddly when they're young."

"And?"

"And they're a comfort when you're old."

"And?"

"And—" she grinned "—they're a lot of fun to make."

The smile that stole across his lips was so devastating that Jill felt her heart beat an entirely different rhythm. "How much fun?" he asked, slowly sliding his hands up her sweat-slick back.

"Lots," she purred, sprawling across his chest like a cat curling atop its master.

Their lips were mere inches apart.

Burke's lips lost their tease. "When you health's better, we'll talk about it seriously."

"We could name a boy Andrew Thomas, after his grandfathers, and we could name a girl Mary?" The sentence was more question than statement.

"We can name them anything you like ... as long as you're healthy when you have them...and as long as you let me be their father." The hands at her back exerted the pressure necessary to meld her mouth with his.

"I promise you can be their father," she whispered as her mouth settled against his.

His kiss was instant seduction. Drugging her with promises she knew his body could fulfill, his lips worked gently, provocatively, against hers. His tongue teased—just the tip piercing the gates of her open mouth—then plunged inside deeply, erotically. Her mouth was smooth, his tongue deliciously rough and well-practiced.

"Oh, Burke," she moaned.

She angled her head so his nibbling mouth could nip and bite her ear and rousingly travel the column of her neck. Gently, lost in the feel of her, he rolled her to her back. His hands fit just beneath the slopes of her breasts, and his fingers swished back and forth, swelling and hardening her nipples.

"God, you feel so good," he whispered. "You feel so..." He stopped, his fingers grazing the inches-long scar on her chest. As always, the experience sobered. As always, there was a shudder that ran through his body before he could stop it. As always, Jill noticed. And worried. It was the only thing that marred the perfection of their marriage.

"Burke..."

His eyes found hers. They were hazy with the remembrance of the color red staining the color ivory. They were hazy with the remembrance of fear, a fear that had once driven him from her.

"...I have no guarantees, no warranties, no indemnities, concerning life and death. As much as I would like to, I can't promise you..."

"I know," he interrupted. "And I can't offer you guarantees, warranties, or indemnities. I can't promise you that I won't die before you. If I do, you'll survive. If you...die before me, I'll survive. It's what human beings do best."

Jill looked deeply into his eyes, searching for sincerity. She found it. Though it was mingled with fear, it was there. She thought back to the moment she first saw him when he'd returned to work following Nicole's death. She had seen pain in his eyes, she had seen the hell he'd walked through, but she'd also seen a strength. She had thought then that it may be a strength he didn't yet know he possessed. The man before her now knew. Somewhere on the beach of the Atlantic shore, somewhere in the eastern wind, somewhere in the solar sun, he'd learned a universal truth.

"Yes," she whispered, her hand cupping the side of his face, "human beings survive."

"I know. I learned it here on this beach . . . one night when I had nothing more to lose."

The dying sun splashed the seaside in gray and silver shadows. In the distance the ocean rumbled and rolled toward shore.

Burke's mouth eased once more to hers. It was a gentle kiss that moved her as profoundly as any they'd ever shared.

"Let's die together," she whispered.

"Let's live together," he whispered back.

"Agreed."

A slow grin once more claimed Burke's mouth. "How do you feel about making love on a beach?"

"It's illegal, Rawlins."

His smile widened. "Not if you don't get caught."

Instinctively, Jill glanced around her. The isolated beach was as deserted as it had been the entire three days they'd been there.

"Burke Rawlins, you're so bad," she said, unable to keep her body from responding to the thought of making love there by the ocean in the twilight.

Easing her T-shirt upward, his nose nuzzled the swollen softness of her breast before his lips kissed the rosy crest. His fingers worked their impatient way inside the leg of her shorts. Boldly, he touched her in a way that was familiar and intimate and loving.

"Umm. You're so bad, you're good," she amended on a half cry, half sigh as her hips arched into his talented fingers. She felt his lips smile around the tip of her breast. She heard him mumble that she tasted salty. And sexy. And that he wanted her more than any man had ever wanted any woman.

Minutes later, they lay naked. Hands entwined—his ring exactly matching hers—he slowly, greedily slipped inside her waiting, willing, woman's body.

"Oh, Burke," she whispered at the glorious feel of the deep masculine pressure. Tightening the mesh of their fingers, she brought her hips up and against his.

"I love you," he whispered, his lips blanketing hers.

"I love you," she answered.

There on a secluded, sparkling-white beach, vows were silently repeated, repeated in caresses, kisses and the sacred joining of bodies and souls. There on a beach washed clean by the ocean, two lovers vowed to love until parted by death.

IT'S NEVER TOO LATE FOR LOVE....

A SEASON FOR ROSES

A VERY SPECIAL SUPERROMANCE
BY A VERY SPECIAL AUTHOR

Ashley Harte is an elegant fifty-year-old widow whose
fondest desire is someday to have grandchildren. But
from the moment the handsome and distinguished Ryan
McKay sets eyes on Ashley, he courts her with the fervor
and determination of a man half his age. Ashley had always thought that romantic love was for her children's
generation. Ryan McKay is about to prove her wrong....

A SEASON FOR ROSES is a heartwarming story, filled
with the intensity that well-loved Superromance author
Barbara Kaye always brings to romance.

Coming in April 1987

Harlequin
Superromance

COMING NEXT MONTH

#254 DRIVE THE NIGHT AWAY • Jocelyn Haley
Sara Deane thinks she's found love at last in the
arms of Cal Mathieson. But she's a teacher, he's a
woodworker, and Cal is adamant their relationship
won't work. Sensing that Cal's hiding the real
reason for his reluctance, Sara devises a plan to
uncover the truth....

#255 TANGLED DREAMS • Lynn Erickson
When financial consultant Margery Lundstrom
meets Dr. Warren Yeager, a brilliant scientist, she
finds her emotions soaring. But she soon decides
he's beyond help in matters of romance. It's up to
him to prove her wrong....

#256 CHANCES • Janice Kaiser
Blaine Kidwell is a professional poker player.
Caleb Rutledge is a man of the cloth. They've got
as much in common as a church and a gambling hall.
So why are they falling in love?

#257 A SEASON FOR ROSES • Barbara Kaye
Fifty-year-old widow Ashley Harte thinks romantic
love is for her children's generation. But the
handsome and distinguished Ryan McKay sets out
to change her mind.

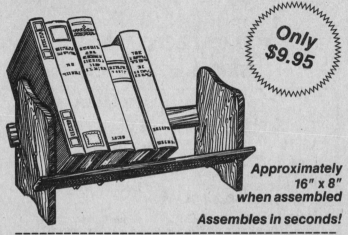

Can you keep a secret?

You can keep this one plus 4 free novels